THESE MONSTROUS TIES
K.V. ROSE

For everyone with a monstrous secret

PLAYLIST

16 - Highly Suspect
Psycho - Brooke
Ghost - Badflower
what you need - Bring Me the Horizon
Hear Me Now - Bad Wolves ft. DIAMANTE
Through Ash - Moon Tooth
Upperdrugs - Highly Suspect
The Old Me - Memphis May Fire
Every Time You Leave - I Prevail
Starlight - Repair to Ruin
Your Mother Was Cheaper - Two Feet
My Name is Human - Highly Suspect

PROCEED WITH CAUTION

This book contains adult content, including language, violence, and sexual scenes. Only suitable for those 18+. It is a **dark** romance.

There will be content that is upsetting to some readers. It doesn't get lighter. I recommend staying away from this book if you're apprehensive reading this.

It is not your typical romance.

CHAPTER ONE

Present

I DON'T THINK this is fun anymore.

Jeremiah spins me round and around and I'm going to be sick, but I can't tell him to stop. He doesn't listen. He never has.

The night blurs around me, my stomach churns. The crisp fall air doesn't help. It hurts. Because it reminds me of Lucifer. Of the Unsaints. It reminds me of hell, of his demons in the woods.

It reminds me of living.

Nearly one year ago, I planned to die. Halloween night I was ready to do it. Then Lucifer showed up, kept me alive long enough to ruin me, and then he left.

It was Jeremiah that had found me.

I start to heave.

Jeremiah's deep laugh rumbles in the night but finally,

mercifully, he stops. Slowly, the miniature merry-go-round comes to a halt, too. I close my eyes, swallowing past the bile in my throat. My pulse starts to slow a little. But I know better.

Jeremiah isn't merciful.

Strong hands haul me off the pink pony and throw me to the ground. I land in the wood chips of Raven Park and scramble to my feet. I'm unsteady, dizzy. Nauseous. But Jeremiah won't stop until I fight back.

He's grinning at me as I try to hold my gaze on him. I want to puke.

"That's all you got?" he taunts me, hands in his pockets. He's tall, broad shouldered. I swear to God, even in the night, his pale green eyes glow.

We're only three years apart. He's 23 to my 20. But in moments like these, I feel we're lifetimes away from each other. I don't want this. I never would've asked for it.

"Fuck you," I spit at him, the world slowing around me. I can see clearly again. I'm not going to fall. Not yet. It's two weeks until Halloween and I know Jeremiah is going to make every single one of these two weeks hell until the grand finale. It's his way of punishing me. For what he saw.

He whistles, then runs a hand over his short brown hair. His jaw is lean, his body muscular. I know he boxes. I know he trains. I do too, but I still know he could take me anytime, any day, whether he'd just spun me around in circles or not. I know it and I hate it.

"That's all you got, Sid? 'Fuck you'?" he mimics my voice. He shakes his head. As if he's disappointed.

I steel myself. Straighten my spine. I know what's coming next.

But he waits. He waits a second longer than I think he will, and in that second, I start to relax. I start to lower my hands, clenched into fists in front of me. I start to breathe again. Maybe tonight he will be merciful.

Maybe he'll give in. Maybe we'll go home. And just when I think that, because I'm nothing if not optimistic about my brother, he tackles me.

My head hits the ground with a thud, and I gag, my stomach convulsing. He wraps his arms around my head, almost as if he's cradling me. I feel every inch of his body pressing into mine. The world spins again.

I don't move. Now it's too late to fight back. Now it's better to give in.

"Shh, baby," he says. "I've got you." He holds me tighter. My stomach heaves underneath him again. "It's okay, baby."

But it's not okay. It'll probably never be okay.

Then he whispers in my ear, "Why do you make me do this to you, Sis? Why do you want to hurt?"

CHAPTER TWO

Halloween, One Year Ago

IT'S GOING to be tonight.

Halloween has always been my favorite holiday. I like wearing masks. I like being in disguise. Baring my body for a living for the past year, since I left my latest foster family after a disappointing string of them, it felt good putting on something different. Something strange.

It seems fitting, for what I plan to do.

I don't bother locking the door to my shithole apartment when I leave. I won't miss this place.

Instead, I stand at the railing of the stairwell, looking out at the darkening sky over Alexandria. The lingering scent of cigarette smoke and the promise of a wild night is on the air. Alexandria is a college town. I know all about the wild parties, the crowded bars, the rich pricks that are abundant in this place.

But I know nothing about the college.

I dropped out of high school.

Being an escort has paid the bills, and a college degree was never really in the cards for someone like me.

I run my hand over the gun strapped on my thigh over my fishnet stockings before I take the steps down two at a time.

People will think it's fake. No one really wants to look behind the mask tonight, anyway.

Mine is only heavy white makeup, white textured horns attached to the headband over my brown, chin-length hair. It's disguise enough.

When morning comes, it might be hard to recognize me anyhow.

I take a breath, steady my nerves as I walk along the sidewalk leading out of the apartment complex. I taste the rum on my tongue from the two shots I downed before I left; I didn't think I'd be scared of this.

I've been afraid of a lot in my life. From foster families, strangers, my mother when I was a child. My brother when I was a child. A brother I haven't seen since we got pulled from Mom's after she caught the house on fire when she fell asleep with the stove on. Fell into a drug-induced coma is more like it. I was five when Jamie and I split up. He was eight.

Fourteen years have passed since then, and I think of Jamie every day. I don't miss him, exactly. He'd been a terror in my life, from what I could recall of my earliest memories. Pinching me, kicking me, dragging me into his room during the night, locking the door. I thought, looking back, he might have done some of it to protect me. But he was as loving as my mother had been. Which is to say, not at all.

I shiver against a gust of wind and glance up at the full moon as I make my way down the sidewalk on the main road. Alexandria—halfway between the beach and the mountains in North Carolina—is a big city, but my little pocket of it is like a small town in itself. There isn't much traffic, although I smell a bonfire on the breeze, hear someone howling like a wolf somewhere down the street.

I wait at an intersection past my apartment, watching two cars roll off almost lazily down the road. I could cross now. No one is coming.

But I like the waiting.

It's the last bit of it I'll do in my life.

Someone's shoulder brushes against me, startling me out of my revelry. The light hasn't changed.

I jerk my head around, frowning.

And some asshole blows smoke right in my face. Real smoke, not from a vape.

I cough, covering my mouth with my hand.

"What the fuck?" I hiss. I'm patient. I'm going to be dead soon. But for the love of all that is holy, that was completely fucking unnecessary.

When the smoke clears, I see him.

Deep blue eyes, a cigarette in one hand, a smile on his full lips.

His face is painted like a skeleton, long lashes raking against the black and white makeup below his dark brows. He has curly black hair, and a strand of it falls over one eye when the wind blows.

"Sorry," he drawls, not sounding sorry at all. "But I think you're supposed to come with me tonight." His eyes snake down my frame.

I don't blush. I've been checked out thousands of times for my job alone. It comes with the territory. But I steel my spine, shake my head.

"You just blew smoke in my face," I point out. I take him in: Tall, lean, wearing black joggers that hug his thighs, a black hoodie rolled up at the forearms, corded muscle visible beneath.

He's probably a few years older than me, maybe mid-twenties. But with the skeleton paint, it's kind of hard to tell.

"Isn't that something Lucifer might do?" he asks, tilting his head. Then he nods in front of us. The light has changed, the stick figure man is flashing.

I start walking.

He takes my hand in his when we're in the middle of the street.

I try to jerk mine away, but he holds firm.

"Don't fight me," he says, voice husky as we reach the other side of the street. He brings the cigarette to his lips and inhales, then exhales as I stare at him, equal parts awe and anger. "I'll win."

I try to pull my hand away again, my eyes darting around us. There's no one out here. This little section of Alexandria is dead. But I have a gun on my thigh. I don't need anyone to rescue me.

"Who the fuck are you?" I ask.

He winks, one midnight blue eye twinkling for a second. "Lucifer," he answers coolly. "And you're my Lilith."

I'm in shock he knows who I'm supposed to be.

His hand engulfs mine, his fingers calloused. I don't pull away again as I stare at him.

"You're in skeleton paint," I point out. "Where are your horns?" I glance at his all-black outfit. That could pass, I guess.

"Lucifer doesn't have horns," he says, eyes finding my own horns. "That's for his lover to do."

I frown. "Do?" I repeat.

"Yeah," he says with a throaty laugh, taking another drag on his cigarette. I take in his sharp cheekbones, the vein visible on his neck beneath his hoodie. He exhales, his beautiful face momentarily obscured by a cloud of smoke. "To stab anyone who gets too close to me."

I sigh and shake my head, but don't bother pulling away again. What's a little more fun before I die? "I'm going to Raven Park," I state. "Either you can follow me there, or you can let go of me. My plans can't change."

It isn't my imagination that see his eyes flick to the gun. He furrows his brow, white and black paint smudging a little.

Finally, he nods. "Raven Park it is," he says with a smile. "But I'm warning you..." Another drag on his cigarette. Another cloud of smoke. "You might die there."

I laugh.

If he only knew.

CHAPTER THREE

Present

I NEVER HAVE a problem with the blood. We're made of the stuff, after all. When Jeremiah first started torturing me, he thought I might faint over the sight of it. He thought, scared girl that I was, it would be the blood that made me run.

Of course, it's not like I can run very far. Jeremiah isn't letting me get away again.

But it isn't the blood.

It's his eyes on mine.

He watches me, and I can feel him waiting for me. Waiting for me to cry. To hurl accusations his way. To run away. Or try to.

But I stare at the corpse at our feet, and I don't move an inch. I'm still not sure, even close to a year after he started bringing me to these viewings, what it is I'm supposed to do here. I've tried everything.

The first time, a man's severed head in a warehouse, I had puked. I had fallen to my knees and vomited, and he had had to drag me away with the help of his men, back to the Rain mansion. He'd tormented me once we got back there, too. Hurling insults, screaming in my face, shaking me by the arms.

The next time, it was just a gunshot wound to the dead man's chest. I had just stood there, waiting for it to be over. I stood there for fifteen minutes. Then I couldn't take it anymore. I'd screamed at him. He'd let me.

Then he'd taken me back to the mansion. More screaming. More grabbing.

Every time, I've gotten it wrong. I know this time will be no different. It's strange. I can still feel him pressed against me, like he was an hour ago at the merry-go-round at Raven Park, even though he's standing by my side. I feel the weight of him. I always feel the weight of him. Right now, he's got one hand propped under one elbow, and it takes everything in me to keep looking at the ruined body.

We're in the man's house this time. A man who wronged Jeremiah in some way. But there are a thousand ways to wrong Jeremiah, each one stranger and more arbitrary than the last. There are a thousand ways to insult the Order of Rain, too. It's funny, how I share his last name. But aside from keeping me on a tight leash, I don't get any of the privileges that come with it.

Blood is oozing on the plush carpet, and the man is completely naked. There are more stab wounds than I could possibly count on his body. I should be appalled. I guess I kind of am, but what is there to do about it? The man is already dead. He was dead the minute he wronged my brother. A dozen times I thought he would be arrested. A dozen times he proved he was above the law.

With the amount of money he has, I'm not that surprised.

I can smell the blood, iron and bordering on rot. I don't know how long ago Jeremiah did this; he never takes me for the kills. I don't even know if he does them all himself. His right-hand man, Nicolas, is usually by his side. He's in the shadows now, along with Kristof, his guard. I can't see them, but I'm aware of their eyes on me.

Finally, I tear my eyes away and look at my brother.

"Jeremiah," I plead, "I see it." I don't know what that's supposed to mean. It's not like I haven't tried this before. It always ends the same way. Every fucking time.

His dark brows go up. He's kept the lights on in this man's living room, to better show the damage. I know that with the state of this body, he's done this. There's no one more fucked up than he is working for the Order of Rain. This is his work, and he wants me to know it.

"But do you feel it?" he asks me.

The hairs on the back of my neck stand on end. I slip my hands into my hoodie pockets, shift a little in my combat boots. I shake my head, confused. My heart is hammering in my chest.

"Do you *feel* it, Sid, that's what I'm asking you?" Jeremiah smooths his hands down his grey collared shirt, cocking his head, staring at me. Waiting for an answer. Whatever the answer is, it'll be the wrong one.

I'm so tired of this shit.

"What the fuck are you talking about?" I ask him. I'm used to striding these lines. Playing the meek sister. The weak sister. And then Lilith comes out to play, like she did that night one year ago.

He grins at me, white teeth flashing. I know that's not a good sign. Nothing good comes from my brother's smile.

"Touch him," he urges me, slipping his hands in his pockets, nodding toward the corpse.

I shake my head without looking back at the guy. "No."

I hear Nicolas cough at my back, warning me. But Jeremiah shifts his gaze to him, and there's silence stealing through the house again. Nicolas is twenty-five. Two years older than Jamie. Five years older than me. But he cows to him like everyone else.

Everyone except me. When I can stand it.

"Did you say 'no'?" Jeremiah presses. He looks delighted. He likes this game. Sometimes, in these moments, he reminds me of Lucifer. Except Lucifer was much crueler. I wonder if my brother knows that. I wonder if he has any idea how he pales in comparison. I think he thinks of all of the Unsaints, he was the worst one.

He's dead wrong.

"I'm not touching him. Let's go." I turn to go. I catch Nicolas's eye.

He coughs into his fist, loudly. Warning me again. But Nicolas can go to hell for all I care. He had tended to me when I'd been in that cell the first two weeks after Halloween last year.

By *tended to*, I mean he force fed me and stood guard day and night. Through everything.

"Your arrogance is astounding, Sid." Jeremiah pauses, letting me take a step. I'm tense, because I know what's coming. But he's keeping me on edge.

I take another step.

Finally, he grabs my wrist, jerking me to a stop. I still. It doesn't surprise me.

"Touch him," he says again, his words brushing against my ear, his voice a growl.

I stiffen. Fear crawls down my spine.

I yank my hand away from his and turn back to the body. The man was probably in his thirties. He's fit, lots of tattoos on his torso, some torn away by the knife my brother plunged into his flesh again and again. He's lying in a pool of his own blood which means my black boots will probably get in it. But his head is untouched. His eyes are unseeing, he's got closely cropped blonde hair, not too different than Nicolas's.

That's where I'll do it. Because I can't keep disobeying Jeremiah. It'll only get worse.

I carefully walk around the body, avoid the coffee

table he's lying a foot from. I crouch down, take a breath, and reach my hand out to the man's clean-shaven face.

He feels weird under my fingers. Not quite cold. Not really warm, either. I stroke his cheek. Then I snatch my hand away and look up, meeting my brother's gaze.

"Are you done?" I ask him.

He smiles. My stomach churns.

"Not even close," he purrs.

I get to my feet. "Fuck you," I say to him for the second time that night. "I'm done, Ja—Jeremiah." Sometimes I forget he changed his fucking name. Changed his name and sold his soul, it feels like sometimes. "Done. Take me home."

But I don't move.

Jeremiah laces his fingers together in front of him, flicks his jade eyes from the body to me.

We're blood. But in these moments, I feel like nothing to him.

"I need you to be strong, Sid." His voice is low. "I need you to be brave. I need you to learn how to look out for your own goddamn self. But if you're not strong, you won't be able to do that, will you? Like you couldn't last year?"

We're not on a merry-go-round anymore, but I still want to puke when I think of that night. When he found me after fourteen years. At my lowest.

I feel that familiar anger growing in my skin. I'm always angry. But unlike the Hulk, it isn't something I even want to control. And it isn't a superpower. Not where my brother is concerned.

I stand to my feet. Beyond my brother, Kristof, meaty and bald, is smirking at me. Nicolas is frowning and he shakes his head. Another warning. I ignore him. I walk around the blood soaking in the carpet and stand toe-to-toe with Jeremiah.

"Let me go," I say, my fingers flexing wide at my sides to keep them from curling into fists. I glance again at the muscle lining the room that my brother keeps with him at all times—even when he fucks Brooklin. But neither Kristof nor Nicolas reach for their weapons or take a step.

It makes me feel a little better. But it makes me angrier, too. My brother has never taken me seriously. Even less so since he found me in that underground asylum, bloodied and hungover, nearly naked the morning after Halloween a year ago. I had been alone. I wasn't supposed to have been alone.

Before that night, I'd been free of him for over a decade. Now, he has me trapped again.

"I tried to let you go, Sid. We know how well that turned out."

Kristof dares to laugh.

Jeremiah turns to him, his eyes narrowed. Kristof sobers up, wiping that smile off of his broad face.

Hell, if he keeps this shit up, the man on the floor won't be the only one leaving this room in a body bag.

"Then give me a different job," I snap, tearing my eyes from Kristof. My brother regards me like he regards everything else: Coldly. His head is cocked to the side, his obsidian watch gleaming beneath the sleeves of his grey shirt. "Let me do something besides viewing your leftovers."

But it's what he says next that's the reminder. The reminder that I'm not an employee he'll kill instead of fire. I'm not someone he will ever let go, in any way. No, I'm his. I belong to him, no matter how much I might hate it.

"My sister won't be food for the wolves." Meaning I can't be an escort again. The only other job under the roof of the Order of Rain that I might be qualified for.

But not quite.

"Housekeeper? Chef? Fucking pool boy? Give me something else. I'm done with this shit, Jeremiah."

"I'm going to let you reconsider what you're asking me right now," he purrs, looking down at his hands. He runs one through his hair. We're inches apart, and I want to reach out and strangle him.

"I'm not going to reconsider. What am I doing here? Why..." I choke on the words. I look down at the bit of carpet between us that isn't bloody. I swallow, the scent of blood hitting me like raw meat kept in an airtight container. "Why do you do this to me, Jamie?" My eyes meet his. I let the name he was born to hang between us. Maybe he'll remember that he wasn't always this nightmare. Whatever the Unsaints did to him, I think it might be worse than what they did to me.

No one breathes in the room. But it's too late to take the words back now. The plea. Even as I regret it already, even as it feels as bitter as the blood in this room on my tongue.

Fuck him. Fuck the Order of Rain. Fuck. This. Shit.

"You want a different job?" He steps closer.

Involuntarily, I step back. Jeremiah isn't just older than me. He's taller than me. Richer than me. Stronger than me. Loved more than me. Or maybe it's hated more than me...it's hard to tell the difference between the two these days. He nods to one of the men.

Kristof. The biggest of the two of them. Blue eyes and arms bigger than both of my legs. Not that that is particularly impressive, considering I'm a stick. But still. I think I know what he's getting at.

My skin crawls, but I don't look away from my brother. There's got to be something human in there still. Something with a shred of compassion.

"Kristof. My sister is yours every night this week. Keep your girl at home. She's *yours*." He reiterates the word, and fucking Kristof can't get the stupid smile off of his face.

I shake my head. "No fucking way."

Jeremiah sighs, glancing up at the high ceilings of this dead man's house. He crosses his arms.

"You don't get to say no," he finally says, dipping his chin, holding my gaze. The tension in the room is getting thicker. And fear finally begins to set in. *Too late, Sid.*

I shake my head and make to step back, but he grabs my wrists.

"Get back down there," he says, nodding toward the body. His grip tightens against my wrists so hard I swear I feel the bones rub together. "Get back down there and lick the blood off of his dick, Sid."

I swear even Nicolas draws a sharp intake of breath.

"Jamie..." I say, shaking my head, my lip trembling. "You don't mean that. You don't want me to do that." I'm pleading with him, because the anger is gone. Fear is setting in thick and heavy, in my lungs. My bones. My heart.

This is my brother.

God, what happened to us?

"I do want you to, Sid." He pulls me to his chest, and I place my palms on him, to keep some space between our bodies. He wraps his arms around my back, trying to press me closer, but I push back.

He laughs.

"Do it, or you're Kristof's," he says, leaning down to kiss my temple.

I shake in his arms.

"No, Jamie." I only learned of his new name last year. When I learned other things about my brother, too. How he had joined the Unsaints. How he had betrayed them. For me.

He turns his head. I hear footsteps, but I can't see anything. And then Jeremiah pushes me. Into Kristof's arms.

They wrap around my body, squeezing me to him.

Jeremiah doesn't even flinch. Jeremiah, who hasn't let anyone in our house so much as hug me. Jeremiah. My own goddamn brother.

He only watches as Kristof's hands rise from my waist, up under my hoodie, under the black cotton shirt, to my breasts, cupping them and running his thumbs over my nipples.

I never wear a bra. I don't have enough for that. I've got no curves to speak of. But right now, Kristof doesn't seem to mind.

My eyes search once more for something human in Jeremiah's as I feel Kristof harden behind me, his dick pressing into my back.

"Jeremiah..." I whisper.

"You don't get to say no," he says, pinning me with his gaze. "When we get back to the house, you're his for the night."

But I squirm in Kristof's grip. I try to step on his foot, as hard as I can in my combat boots. He just laughs. I throw back an elbow and he pins my arms down by my sides, runs his hot tongue up and down my neck.

"Jamie!" I scream, twisting in Kristof's arms. "Get him off of me!"

My brother only laughs. My hair hangs in my eyes, ash brown and cut to my chin, it's too thick to see out of. And I can't move my hands thanks to Kristof. So I don't have to watch as my own brother says, "If she lasts the night, bring her to my office at dawn."

And then he walks out of the house, and a minute later Nicolas's footsteps trail after him. Everyone but Kristof and me. Still in this house.

I thought we'd go back first.

I can't do this. I freeze in Kristof's arms.

Not for the first time, I think of Lucifer. I think of how he's done this to me. How he fucked me over, sent me here.

He had crawled out of the pits of hell on Halloween night and damned my entire fucking life.

CHAPTER FOUR

Halloween, One Year Ago

RAVEN PARK IS full of people.

Still oddly hand-in-hand, Lucifer and I dodge our way through cars parked haphazardly on the gravel lot, the sound of music thudding in the woods ahead of us.

He glances over at me as we walk down a gravel path. I know the gravel will soon end, and this trail will lead us to Raven River. Another to a creepy little merry-go-round. I used to run here, when I gave a shit. But I've had this date marked for months. I no longer give a shit at all.

The sun has set. I see several fold-out tables with drinks and food, and there's a small fire in the center of it all.

A fire.

In the middle of a state park.

Lucifer drops my hand. I turn to stare at him.

"There's a fire." I throw my hand vaguely toward it. "A fire. In the middle of the fucking woods!"

He doesn't laugh. "Buckle up, Lilith. This is hell. That's where fire is born."

Okayyyy...someone took their Halloween costumes a little too seriously. But who am I to judge? I have a real-life gun on my thigh.

Someone calls Lucifer's name. By actually shouting, "Lucifer!"

That cannot be his name.

I would have laughed if it wasn't all so...strange. A guy breaks away from a gaggle of girls and comes striding toward us, a beer in his hand. He isn't dressed up, save for the fact he's wearing a t-shirt that hugs his shoulders with a creepy skull on it.

His eyes narrow my way, but he doesn't speak to me when he says, "And who's this?" He doesn't sound thrilled I'm here.

Lucifer's shoulder brushes mine. "She's here tonight. For Lover's Death."

I arch a brow, but this dude's eyes suddenly light up. The corner of his mouth twitches in a menacing smirk. He nods, takes a pull from his beer.

"Fun," he purrs, and then turns to walk away.

"Atlas," Lucifer calls after him. Turns out they aren't all demons of the underworld here. Some guide the way down.

Atlas halts, turns back.

"She's mine."

Atlas frowns. "That's not how Lover's Death goes, and you know it."

Lucifer takes a step toward Atlas and I swear he almost flinches. "It is tonight."

Atlas looks like he wants to argue but instead he only nods. "Whatever you say." His eyes flick to me. "Shame, though."

He walks away with a shrug and a girl runs over to him, slinging her arm around his shoulder. He turns to look at her and whatever she sees, she moves away. Real quick. She glances at Lucifer and I can't be sure in the dark, but I swear she glares at me.

I look to Lucifer. "Do you wanna tell me what the fuck is going on?"

I know the Alexandria University students have parties here, although I've never seen a fire here before. I know that this is a college town. But I have no idea what 'Lover's Death' is or why the gorgeous dude in skull paint beside me is called 'Lucifer'.

Lucifer smiles. He pulls a cigarette from his back pocket, along with a lighter. He lights up, takes a drag, blows smoke my way. I take a step back and then he finally answers my question.

Kind of.

"You'll see."

This isn't what I had planned for the night.

"Look, I don't really want to party tonight. And it seems all your friends—" I fling my hand toward the horde of people gathered around the fire, some of them definitely staring as us, "—are waiting for you. I'll just..." I cough, "go." I finish. I don't know why, but Lucifer is staring down at me while he smokes as if I've just said something truly amusing.

He watches me for an unnerving moment, blowing smoke out of his full, skeletal lips lazily.

"You're not going anywhere, Lilith."

I feel anger rise up in my gut but before I can tell him to 'Fuck off', he continues, "Tonight, I need you by my side." His eyes flick to the gun on my thigh. "Weren't you planning to go to hell anyway?"

I stiffen. How can he know that? How does he even know this is a real gun?

He can't. He's bluffing. He's referring to my Lilith costume.

"Why do you need me?" I protest. "What is 'Lover's Death' anyway?"

He smiles as smoke comes through his nose. He looks truly devilish. Beautiful and haunting all at once.

"You'll see." He takes my hand and pulls me forward, to the people standing by the plastic tables.

They stop talking as we approach. Only the crackling fire and music from a portable speaker—*Ghost* by Badflower—sounds in the park.

I notice every man here is fucking gorgeous. It shouldn't surprise me. Like calls to like and all that. The women are too, but it seems the men have some sort of sway here. Like whatever this is, they're leading it. It's evident in the way they stand. The way they appraise me as I approach, like I'm their next meal.

Far off from the rest of them is a tall man in a hoodie, pulled down so far over his face, I can only make out a chiseled jaw. He has his arms crossed and his lips are pulled down into a scowl.

Lucifer's voice draws my attention back to him.

"I don't answer questions," he's saying. He has a black plastic cup in his hand and he's pouring an obscene amount of vodka into it.

"But Luc—" a girl is protesting across the table from him. She's got long black braids, and she's wearing a pink crop top and high waisted shorts. It's chilly out here and her arms are crossed, as if she's trying to ward herself away from the cold.

Or maybe the weight of Lucifer's stare. He silences her with a look. He sets the bottle down, screws the lid back on. Still watching her, he opens the lid of a cooler, scoops out ice, dumps it in the cup, puts the scooper back in, and closes it. His hand still resting on the cooler lid, he flicks his brows up.

"Why're you here?" he asks the girl. His eyes snake over her frame. "And why are you wearing that?" His lip curls.

I see her deep brown skin redden as she glances down self-consciously. I don't want to give a shit. But I do. I feel for her.

"I-I didn't know we were dressing up. Atlas didn't say—"

"You didn't ask, doll." Atlas breaks off a kiss with another girl dressed as a vampire at the far end of the table long enough to say those words.

But the girl with the braids is too startled to look at him. She's drowning in an excuse and I don't know why. I don't know why the fuck it matters. This is a public place.

I put my hand on Lucifer's arm, his hoodie sleeves pulled up to his elbows.

He stills under my touch and I swear everyone is holding their breath. I see his jaw clench as his eyes pivot to me.

I drop my hand.

I'm frozen. I don't know what I was going to say. I meant to stand up for the girl but now I'm speechless.

I brush my bangs out of my eyes and I swear something in Lucifer's gaze softens.

"Can I have a drink?" I ask quietly, glancing at the vodka.

For a tense moment, he says nothing. No one says anything, although I hear a girl whimper and I know it's the one with Atlas. He shushes her. Otherwise, it's quiet.

Then Lucifer smiles. He hands the drink to me.

"Of course, Lilith."

People start to chat amongst themselves and I exhale a breath I didn't realize I'd been holding. I take the drink from Lucifer.

He leans down, his lips over my ear as he speaks. "Drink it all," he growls. "Every drop."

Then he pulls away.

I glance at the girl across the table. She's watching me with wide eyes and her mouth hangs open. I have no idea why.

I'm just glad the attention isn't all on us anymore. I give her a small smile. She snaps her mouth closed and returns it with a slight nod of her head, then she scurries away to find some friends.

I notice the guy in the hoodie is still watching me.

I take a long drink, the cup in both hands, then look to Lucifer.

"What did she wanna know?" I try to keep my voice disinterested.

He watches me, like I'm his prey. Like he's trying to find my weakness so he can rip out my throat. The skeleton paint is unnerving. It's fucking with my mind.

I take another drink.

"She wanted to know," he finally says, "what happens next."

I relish the burn of straight vodka trailing down my throat. It'll help me pull the trigger later, I tell myself. Absentmindedly, I touch one of the fake plastic horns on my headband. Lucifer tracks the movement and slides his hands into his pockets.

He seems totally at ease. Yet somehow, totally...eerie.

"What do you mean?" I ask, shaking my head. "It's a party..."

Lucifer flashes me a cruel smile. "Not quite."

Then he turns around and walks away, leaving me staring after him.

I take another drink, watch his tall, lean form, notice-able even beneath his close-fitting hoodie. His black curls are so fucking beautiful, catching on the light from the fire. And when he turns to speak to some chick, I catch his side profile. Straight nose. Strong jaw.

But this girl he's talking to...

She's fucking pregnant. Really, really pregnant.

And the way they're standing so close to each other, I feel something in my gut twist. I pour the entire drink down my throat, quite certain I've just downed four shots of vodka in seconds. I set the empty cup on the table, then wipe the back of my hand over my mouth but I can't stop watching them.

They look like they're arguing. She tosses her long, wavy blonde hair over one shoulder and folds her arms across her chest. She's all baby, wearing black booties, black shorts and black stockings.

Lucifer, for his part, isn't speaking. It's all her.

"Caught you staring," someone whispers behind me.

I jump, startled. It's the girl with the braids. She has two black plastic cups in hand. She holds one out to me.

"I'm Ria," she says with a smile.

I weakly shake her hand and take the drink, even though I definitely shouldn't, but I can't drag my eyes away from Lucifer and the pregnant chick.

"Is that..." I trail off, unsure what to say. This isn't my business. It's not my party. I don't know these people. I had a fucking plan, goddammit.

"Is it his?" Ria finishes for me in a whisper. She's at my

side and we're both watching. It's a drama we can't hear. One I don't want to see. But I can't stop watching.

Wordlessly, I nod.

I see out of the corner of my eye, she shrugs. "No one knows. I'm not even sure she knows."

This does not make me feel better. But what did I think would happen here? Sure, he's fucking gorgeous and his eyes are way too damn blue to be real and he's tall and lean and seemingly popular but...he's also kind of a jerk. And he might be someone else's baby's father. And I don't fucking know him.

I force myself to face Ria.

"So...what is this?" I ask, gesturing around. I assumed it was a party. But Lucifer's words are making me question that.

Ria grins, drinks from her cup. Then she swallows. "It's Unsaints Night."

I tilt my head in silent questioning. I don't follow. And I love Halloween. I've never heard of this shit. And what the fuck is an *Unsaint*?

"Technically, it's not called anything. It's just...the Unsaints do some weird shit here every Halloween night." She takes another drink, and she looks oddly nervous. "You go to AU?"

I shake my head. "Unsaints?" I repeat, confused. "What the hell is that?" My head is spinning with all the vodka but even still, I know I have no idea what that word means. I flip the cup I'm holding upside down and twirl it around my index finger because shit is getting weird and I'm feeling antsy.

"You don't go to AU, then," she says with a little laugh, shaking her head. She tosses one braid over her shoulder. "Unsaints consist of your boy Lucifer—" I blush when she says those two words before his name, but I'm too stunned to say anything, "Cain, Atlas, Ezra, Mayhem, and a new man, Jeremiah."

"Lucifer?" I repeat. "*Mayhem?* I mean, come on, that's not really their real names, right?" What kind of monsters did they have for parents?

She flashes a smile. "I dunno. Just what everyone calls them." She takes another drink, crosses her arms. "If you're not from AU...what do you do? I'm 20. You can't be more than that."

"19," I counter, ignoring her actual question. I look around. Lucifer is still listening to pregnant chick. "Are all these people from AU?"

She shakes her head. "Most. I'm a junior. The Unsaints are seniors. Jeremiah isn't in school."

"What exactly are Unsaints?" I ask, still not following. "I'm gonna need some clarification." I drink more vodka, knowing this is not a good idea. But I'm lost here, and my plans have just been turned upside down.

Someone hollers in the distance and then a peal of laughter follows.

"They're like...they're just close friends," Ria hurriedly explains, but I don't think she's giving me the whole spiel here. "And tonight, they uh...well...I don't actually know."

She lowers her voice, as if what she's telling me—nothing—is secretive.

I nudge her shoulder, trying to be friendly. "Come on. How can you not know?"

She snorts a laugh. "God you really don't know anything about them, do you?" She doesn't sound condescending. She just sounds genuinely shocked.

I rub my hands over my arms, empty cup dangling from my fingers. "Should I?" I ask, amused. Why would I know about these hot weirdos?

"Yeah," she answers, but she doesn't seem amused at all. "They—well their families...they basically own Alexandria."

I nod my head, brows high. "Right."

She laughs, takes another drink. My eyes scan the woods for a quick second. The fire has gotten bigger. Atlas has his hands all over a girl—different from the one he was previously making out with. And my blood runs cold when I realize the dude in the hoodie whose face I can't really make out still appears as if he's watching me. A shiver runs down my spine. I don't know if he's an Unsaint or not. I don't know if it matters. And I don't see Lucifer anymore. Or the pregnant girl.

I don't know why that bothers me.

I force my attention back to Ria.

"I'm serious," she continues. "Their families are third degree, like, Masons or something..."

"*Unsaints?*" I supply sarcastically. I thought the

Masons had 33 degrees but it's not something I really study in my free time.

She doesn't laugh. "No. That's for their evil, hot spawn."

"Okay," I say, the vodka making me bold. "Let's say I believe this bullshit. Which, by the way, I definitely do not."

She laughs again.

"But let's say I do. So, what is tonight all about? The Unsaints are some strange gang? What do they do on Halloween night? Rape and pillage?"

The last part is a joke, but Ria's eyes go wide. "I don't think they'd have to rape anyone, Lilith," she says, eyes going to my horns.

I roll my eyes. "That's a bold, stupid statement."

She smirks. "Have you seen the Unsaints?"

I've seen Lucifer. Atlas. I haven't seen Jeremiah, Mayhem, or the other two whose names I've forgotten.

I shrug. "Whatever. This shit sounds absurd. And besides," I look around the park again, eyes peeled for Lucifer, "this is a public. *Park*." I emphasize the words. No one seems to get them.

"It'll get wilder as the night goes on. If you think the Unsaints are strange...well, girl, you've got something else coming."

"Like what? Are we gonna go for a ride on the merry-go-round?" I laugh, but the truth is it's all making me a little uneasy.

She doesn't even smile. "It's happened before," she admits. "Next morning, it was covered in blood."

She finishes her drink.

My own blood runs cold. It's not that I'm afraid, exactly. I wanted to end this. I'd planned this night for weeks. But still...

"Whose blood—"

The words die on my tongue as arms slide around me, forcing me backward into a hard, warm body.

"No need to ask questions she can't answer," Lucifer says in my ear.

My pulse quickens. I try to breathe normally, but I'm nearly panting.

It's just Lucifer, I tell myself. *And who, exactly, is Lucifer?* myself says back.

What a fucking question.

"Ria," Lucifer drawls.

She looks equal parts terrified and turned on at the way he says her name. I can't say I'm not feeling the same thing.

"Go find your *saint*," I hear the smile in his words. "The games are about to begin."

Ria nods quickly, sets her empty cup on the table where it topples over. With a hesitant look at me—Lucifer's arms still around me—she jogs away, toward the fire.

People are still there, drinking, laughing, making out.

But there's another group, too, Ria bringing up the rear of it, and they're going deeper into the forest. I'm not sure where they're going, exactly. I don't think I've ever ran down that trail.

"Ready, Lilith?" Lucifer purrs.

I shake my head, try to twist in his arms to see his face. He squeezes his strong arms around me tighter.

"Where are they going?" I choke out.

"Oh, love," he says against my neck, "you're going, too."

"Fuck this." I don't know why I'm done now, but something doesn't feel right. Something just feels...all wrong. I twist again in his arms and he lets me go. I toss my cup on the table. "I'm out."

Ria's words come back to me: merry-go-round covered in blood. Unsaints. Something else coming...

Yeah. No.

"It was nice meeting you, but I've got plans and apparently you do too."

He says nothing, his blue eyes locked on mine. A muscle feathers in his skeleton jaw, but otherwise he doesn't move.

And I kind of wish he would. A fucked-up part of my body wants him to stop me.

I turn around, hoping to feel his hands around my waist. Fingers around my wrist. Something.

Nothing.

So, I go, away from the crowd, into the darkness of the forest, looking for a secluded spot to finish what I came here for.

CHAPTER FIVE

Present

"IF YOU FUCKING touch me again, I will kill you."

It's not quite an empty threat, but the way Kristof laughs from his bathroom, it might as well be.

He took me home after all, tied up in the back of the black SUV Jeremiah always takes me to view his kills in.

I'm tied to a chair wearing nothing but a white t-shirt that's three sizes too big, and I'm under no one's protection at the moment—my bastard brother had ordered all guards off of Kristof's hall—but I'm far from fucking defenseless.

After Halloween night a year ago, I made sure I was never defenseless again. I flick the blade from the butterfly knife in my hands, one I'd managed to get to in the car and hide from Kristof because he's dumber than a fucking rock.

Kristof keeps brushing his teeth, and keeping one eye

on him, I begin to saw at the rope he'd cinched around my wrists.

This room is disgusting.

It is, like every room in the Rain house, far too big, with far too many amenities. My brother's *house* was formerly a hotel, and he'd bought the entire thing before it even began to run as one. He'd let the previous owners build it, market it, inlay the floors with gilded marble, the ceilings with mirrors flush above the bed, and the walls with flat screen TVs, and then he'd brokered a deal with them.

By that I mean he threatened to kill them and gave them millions of dollars in exchange for their disappearance and silence. They'd left Alexandria, probably fled north to Virginia. If they were smart, they wouldn't still be in North Carolina.

Jeremiah Rain is a thug of the richest kind. Leader and priest of Order of Rain. He's cruel. Vile. Vicious. He's pushed me to the edge this past year more times than I care to count. I just never thought he'd actually let me be used as a sex toy. But we've been separated far longer than we've been together.

He clearly hasn't developed those brotherly feelings toward me that he should have.

I don't think he's ever developed feelings of any kind, for anyone.

Rumor has it his foster parents locked him in a cage after they adopted him from California, where we were born. Apparently, after he killed his siblings and his parents, he inherited their billions, then became an Unsaint, before he betrayed them. He's never confirmed those rumors.

He's never denied them either.

All I know now is that the Order of Rain deals in murder, drugs, and anything that will put more money into his hands. My own payment is sparse, considering I don't do anything but what Jeremiah says. But I don't lack for anything here.

Except right fucking now.

Right fucking now, I'm going to need someone to come clean up the mess I'm about to make of Kristof's balls. I would never use this blade against my brother.

But I damn sure will against anyone else.

I keep my hands held behind my back, even as they're free now. And I wait.

I wait until Kristof flosses, spits mouthwash in his sink, picks up a towel from the pile of them on the floor to wrap around his waist. Then he turns his gaze to me. There's a bed between us. California king, what once was probably white sheets—clearly, he forgoes housekeeping in this place—and a scattering of weapons. Guns, mainly. A few knives. Handcuffs. I don't know if those are for bad guys or bad girls, or maybe both.

I glance at my reflection in the mirror over our heads.

My grey eyes are smudged with shadows, my short hair simultaneously a mess, and still stick straight. I look skeletal in that mirror, craning my neck back like that.

I shudder. It reminds me of last Halloween.

Of Lucifer.

I force the thought away.

My bare thighs are pale. My entire body is pale.

Everything in here is a shade of white.

But it's about to get splashed with red.

Kristof takes his time striding around the bed, letting his towel slip free from his overly muscled body as he does. I have no idea how old Kristof is. I'm not even sure *Kristof* knows how old Kristof is, but if I had to guess, probably his mid-thirties. Not too old to be fucking a 20-year-old, but old enough to know rape is a serious crime. But everything the Rain family and their associates do is a serious crime.

Hell, we'd just left a corpse.

Kristof stops a few feet from me, leveling his gaze.

"You should know better than to speak to Mr. Rain that way. To refuse him."

I spit on the floor. "Mr. Rain?" I mock him. "Did he take your balls away?"

He narrows his eyes in a momentary rage, but before he lunges for me, he thinks the better of it. Instead, he brings a hand to his cock, stroking himself.

I appraise it for the first time.

It is, unsurprisingly, big. Kristof is big. It only fits.

But I don't want it.

I whistle, pretending to be impressed.

He actually has the audacity to smile, as if this thing between us might become consensual at any moment.

Then he takes a step forward.

I keep the smile on my face.

Another step.

And then I lunge for him.

The blade finds his thigh, and I push it in hard, sinking it in to the hilt, working its way through muscle and tendons. This is the first time I've stabbed a real flesh-and-blood person, and not a dummy Jeremiah lets me practice on. And the good news is, I do it well.

Kristof doesn't expect it.

For a moment, he only stands there. I glance up at him, seeing the surprise in his blue eyes as he gazes down at the blade sticking out of his leg. Blood wells around the entrance, but for just a second, we're both frozen. Me from the strange mix of adrenaline coursing through my veins, heady and intoxicating, and him from, hopefully, the pain.

Then I yank the blade out.

He screams, although from Kristof, it sounds more like a roar.

"You *bitch!*" he hisses, his hands coming to either side of his massive thighs. I dart around him, taking my chance while I have it, the blade in my hand. Kristof might be huge, and I might be little, but that's where my advantage lies. In the running.

The one thing I couldn't do that Halloween night.

I leap over his stack of dirty laundry, my bare feet gripping the marble floor as I land. I dart through the living room, into the area that serves as a kitchen. The door is *right there*, and Kristof isn't close behind me. He has done up the chain on the door, of course, courtesy of the goddamn hotel builders, but that will take me two seconds, and then the other lock will open automatically when I pull the handle.

I don't dare look back, but I hear him coming for me.

The knife is still clenched in one hand, covered in blood. With the other hand, I reach for the chain, slide it back. My hands are shaking. Not so much from fear, I don't think, but excitement.

But this kind of excitement makes me think of Lucifer.

And thinking of Lucifer gets me nowhere.

The chain comes loose. I reach for the silver door handle, smiling like a devil myself. I'm going to be free. Once I get on the hallway, there's no way Kristof will make it down the stairs before me. I'll go to Nicolas. He'd never directly disobey my brother's orders, but he'd also never let someone hurt me, not right in front of his face. Besides, Nicolas doesn't like Kristof.

I push down on the lever. But my mistake is in not calculating the time it would take to pull the heavy door open.

As I pull, something burns at my scalp, and I'm jerked backward.

"You're not leaving this room until I'm done with you," Kristof growls.

I lose my footing, my knees coming down, hard, on the marble floor. Kristof jerks me around by my hair until I'm facing him, a smile on his face. I want to vomit.

Blood is gushing from his thigh, but he doesn't seem to feel the wound anymore. He isn't even trying to stop the flow of blood. Instead, one hand still twining in my hair, he reaches the other for my throat, yanking me to my feet and slamming me against the door. The one I had almost escaped from.

Almost.

I angle the knife, ready to plunge it into his stomach. I don't care if he dies. Kristof means nothing to me. No one means anything to me anymore.

But he grabs my wrist, releasing my hair. My scalp still burns, my head spinning from where he slammed it against the door. And now, my wrist is trembling in his hand, his fingers circling easily around me.

"Put down the knife, Sid, and I'll go easy on you," he grunts, his voice faint.

The wound is getting to him after all. His command has lost its usual bite.

"No," I say, even as he pushes my arm against the door at an unnatural angle. He's going to break it if I don't let go.

But he'll have to do it.

Because I'm not fucking letting go.

"Sid," he breathes against my cheek, hand still crushing against my throat. I can hardly breathe. "I don't want to hurt you."

I choke out a laugh but can't find the words to say he is *already* hurting me. I relax for a second, letting him think the fight has gone out of me. Predictably, his grip around my wrist loosens.

I jerk it forward, angling the knife toward him.

He stops me.

I scream as loud as I can, the sound piercing my own ears. He doesn't let go. He only slams my head back against the door once more, my feet dangling from the floor in his grip.

A sob tears through my throat. But I clamp my teeth together, refusing to let it out. I won't cry for this idiot. Even as his fingers curl tighter around my throat, I won't let the tears spring free.

He slowly lets me slide to the floor, his breathing growing more labored from the blood loss, the knife wound. But even still, he pries my fingers off of my knife, and I have to let him. I can barely breathe with his hand around my neck. He drops the knife to the floor. I hear it clatter, hear his breath, hear my heart pounding in my ears.

He reaches for my thigh, his hand clamping down over it. I want to kill him. I haven't been with anyone in a year. Not since Lucifer. Not since I'd been Lilith.

His hand rises higher, but just before he can touch me *there*, there's a knock on the door at my back. Loud, demanding. Seven quick strikes in a row.

He freezes, and I do too.

"If I have to knock again, I'll kill you both." My brother's cold voice.

"*Fuck,*" Kristof swears under his breath, but he releases me, and I fall to the floor, trying to catch my breath, my hand going to my neck, rubbing at the burning skin. I crawl out of the way before Kristof can hit me with the door as he pulls it open.

I hear my brother laugh before I see him.

"I knew she wouldn't let you," he mutters. The door snaps closed and then he turns to me, his eyes on my hand at my throat. They narrow slightly. "Get up."

Kristof holds his tongue, but my eyes find his, and he's fuming. He's also bleeding and in pain, and he stumbles back against the wall in the foyer, sinking to the floor, not bothering to cover himself in front of me or my brother.

I rub at my neck again, and then get to my feet, tugging down the oversized white t-shirt I'm wearing.

"Why?" I ask, my voice hoarse.

Jeremiah smiles. "Because I can. And you need to learn a lesson." He turns, sliding his hands into his pockets. "Come with me." That order is directed to me. He glances at Kristof. "Get cleaned up. I'm going to need you back on duty tomorrow morning."

Kristof grunts his agreement, which is all he can really manage. I glare at him as I follow Jeremiah out into the dimly lit hall. The door closes behind us, and then Jeremiah pins me against the wall, his hands on my upper arms.

"You cannot afford to disobey me, *Sid*," he growls at me, his eyes wild on mine. "What if he finds you again? What if his filthy fucking friends find you? *That*," he jerks his head to the door at our left, the door to Kristof's room. "Was to teach you a lesson. To help you understand just what could happen to you if you don't trust me fully." He takes a breath, his fingers curling tighter around my arms. "Do you think I *enjoy* tormenting you?"

Even though I know I shouldn't, even though I feel some sick rush of gratitude toward him for not letting it go so far, laughter bubbles on my lips. "Yes," I hiss. "Yes, *Brother*, I think you love tormenting me. Aside from making money and fucking women, I think tormenting me is your favorite pastime."

He blows out a breath, presses his brow against mine. I can feel his words against my lips.

"Sid," he whispers. My heart slams in my chest. My brother is the most dangerous when he's quiet. When he's still. For several moments, he doesn't speak. And then he says, "If you can't get it together, I will kill you. I won't risk letting you crawl around on the streets. I won't risk anyone coming back for you. I won't risk the Unsaints finding you again. I'd rather you be dead."

My heart lodges in my throat, and he smiles.

He pulls back, but still holds on tight to me. In that moment, I'm grateful. Without his grip, I think I might faint. "I know what they do to people that hurt them. And if they were to find out what you are to me...they'd do much worse than Lucifer did that night."

My cheeks heat, and I look away, no longer able to meet his eyes.

He shakes me. "Look at me," he spits, his voice venomous.

Reluctantly, I bring my gaze to his.

"I've seen all of your dirty little secrets, Sid. I know what you did before me. I know that what I saw was the least of what you've done. You're used goods, Sid. This is the best you're going to get." He steps away from me, finally releasing his hold on my arms. "You couldn't really ask for more though, could you?"

Then he turns and walks away, leaving me half-naked on the dim hallway, just outside of Kristof's door.

CHAPTER SIX

Present

THAT NIGHT, I lay in bed, the ceiling fan set on high, spinning like a cyclone above my head. I haven't been able to stand the quiet since that night. Since I had awoken to Jeremiah kicking me in the side, silence ringing out in the forest, after he'd dragged me from the asylum.

I close my eyes against the memory.

But it isn't the memory I want to block out. At least, not all of it.

It's the pain in my chest when I think of *him*. The hole of rage. Grief. Obsession. Even one year later, Halloween quickly approaching in two weeks' time, I can't let that night go. Those blue eyes behind his skull paint, those full lips outlined in stripes of black and white. He's fucking burned into my soul.

All of the Unsaints are.

I sit up, slide against the headboard at my back. It's black, like most everything in my room is. Black comforter, black satin sheets, black marble floor. It's why I chose this room. Jeremiah had given me the pick of them, the ones not used for his staff or himself. Even the bathtub is inlaid with obsidian stone.

I glance out the balcony window, the heavy black drapes open wide. I'm on the seventh floor, and I know Jeremiah is one above me. *Directly* above me. I don't know if that's where his room always was, or if he'd moved his to be closer to me. To keep an eye on me.

I'd asked him. As always, he never answered me. Neither would Nicolas. Although I think that's more because Nicolas has never known where Jeremiah's room is. Only his guards seem to know that, and Brooklin.

Nicolas could be a guard, but he isn't. Not exactly. He's smarter than the others. Not as smart as Jeremiah, or else Jeremiah wouldn't have let him work for him. But smart enough.

It was Nicolas who'd come to my room to tell me Kristof would live, and he'd keep his hands off of me from now on. He'd told me to keep my mouth shut in the kill rooms, as he calls them. To keep my damn head on my shoulders. To listen to my brother.

I told him to fuck off.

Jeremiah never took me to kill rooms more than once a month or so, after he tormented me at Raven Park. I was good for the rest of October. That doesn't mean, of course, that nobody else won't die at his command. It just means I won't have to see the remains. He likes to give me a break. To keep me guessing.

To make me panic.

He's a businessman of the worst kind, if you can even call him that. He operates outside of the law, dealing in things most people wouldn't dare.

Tonight, he'd killed that man before he took me to Raven Park. Our usual sick routine. A reminder of what could happen to me again, if I wasn't safe.

I have no idea why that man was his target tonight. No clue in what way he'd run afoul of my brother. Jeremiah didn't offer that kind of information. He didn't need to. We were sworn to him, to the Order, for the rest of our lives. If we wanted to quit, well, our lives would end rather quickly.

But no one seems foolish enough to come after Jeremiah Rain, to oppose him.

I wish someone would.

Specifically, I wished *he* would. Lucifer. The Unsaints. But he'd vanished that night, the first we met. The last, too. Vanished with the rest of them after Lover's Death. He could be dead for all I know.

I remember the time before Jeremiah and the Unsaints, when I'd spent many blissful years unaware that Jeremiah Rain even existed so close to me. I'd seen the hotel, of course, but I never gave a damn that some billionaire bought it. I didn't know about Lucifer either, or the Society of Six. About Lover's Death. The Unsaints.

It's not that my life had been easy before.

It hadn't been.

It'd been hard.

But it had been *mine*.

Mine to end, until Lucifer convinced me otherwise.

Until my brother came in and took it all away. The choice. The plan. My mind.

CHAPTER SEVEN

Halloween, One Year Ago

THE VOICES GROW distant and the chill this far from the fire wraps itself around me like a living thing. I put my hand on the grip of my gun on my thigh. Before, when I strapped this thing on hours ago—was it really only hours? —I'd felt certain. I'd known what came next. After a series of bumps and bruises and shots to the heart, this final thing was going to be it for me. My own choice, taking my life in my own hands.

Now, though...I'm not so sure. But I don't want to fall back into that abyss of darkness I'd fell into too many times before. That darkness was suffocating. Maddening. I know I can't survive that again.

But can I pull the trigger when the cold barrel of this gun is digging into the side of my head?

I don't know.

The party in Raven Park grows distant and I realize with a start that the fucking merry-go-round is ahead of me. The park opens up into a small clearing, a circle filled in with wood chips for kids to play.

Only right now, it looks like kids should never come here. The merry-go-round isn't moving, but shadows seem to lurk within the small poles spearing the animals: bears, ponies, something that looks like a wolf but with floppy ears. In the dark, it all looks a little grotesque.

I think I see something thick spilling from the white unicorn's side, but I shake my head and it disappears.

Ria's words are just freaking me out. I reach for the horns on my head absently, still walking toward the clearing, and then I freeze.

Someone is watching me.

Standing in the shadows, leaned casually against a lion, it's the man from the party with the hood on. It's still on, down low over his face, concealing his eyes, but I know he's watching me. He's been watching me since the party.

My blood runs cold as I realize he probably followed me out here.

I stop walking and wrap my arms around myself. I think, for just a second, I should reach for my gun, but I don't. I don't want to provoke this guy, and with this much vodka in my veins, my aim would be shit. Instead, I glance over my shoulder, hoping someone else will have floated this way from the party. But there's nothing but dark, empty woods at my back.

I force myself to face this guy again.

But he's gone.

I spin around, heart thudding. I have no idea who he is but for some reason, I can't help but to think he's an Unsaint, too. He's too dark to be anything else.

I know what Lucifer and Atlas look like. Is this Mayhem? Or Cain? Ezra? What was the other one's name? And what does it mean if it is one of them?

I spin around again, eyes darting over the clearing, the woods, the merry-go-round. But there's nothing to see. And there's nothing but silence, too, and the sound of my own breathing. My heart pumping hard in my chest.

I reach for the grip of the gun, and then strong arms wrap around me from behind, blocking my access.

I open my mouth to scream.

A hand come over my lips, muffling the sound.

"Shhh, baby. I won't hurt you if you're quiet."

There's something about that voice that sounds dangerously familiar. But I can't place it. Maybe a client? I don't know.

I close my mouth, but the hand stays clamped over it. I smell clean laundry, the smoke on him from the bonfire.

He pulls me closer into him. I know without looking it's got to be the one that's been following me. And I know, too, that even though I have the weapon, I'm the one who is so fucked right now. Strangely, I long for Lucifer. But he let me go. And I walked right into this.

"Why were you leaving so soon?" the man's words brush against my neck. I'm painfully aware I'm only in a bodysuit and fishnet leggings and I wish I'd thought to grab a coat. Something to cover myself. But I didn't think I'd make it this long.

I try to speak and shocking me, the guy moves his hand, bringing it down to my stomach beside the other one.

"Who are you?" I hear the fear in my voice, but I don't have time to care.

He chuckles against my skin. "I'm your worst nightmare." His fingers dig into my abdomen.

"What do you want?"

He presses his lips against my neck, warm and nearly gentle. "Always the same questions," he taunts me. "As if the answers matter. I always get what I want, baby. And tonight, I want you." He nips at my neck.

I try to turn in his grasp, but he doesn't let me so much as budge.

"Easy, baby. The less you fight, the more fun you'll have."

I feel fear giving way to anger as I glance at the merry-go-round beside us. "Fuck you," I snap at him, knowing as I say the words, they're not very wise. Not for someone in my position. But I suddenly don't care. This Halloween has been a series of fuck ups from start to finish. Might as well go out with a bang.

But the guy doesn't seem angry. He pulls me further into his hard body and runs a hot tongue down my neck. "Oh, you will."

"Jeremiah," a man's voice says warningly.

Ah, I think wryly, so *this* is Jeremiah. What a fucking pleasure to meet him.

But my heart soars all the same. Because that voice...it's Lucifer's.

I can't see him and as he calls the Unsaint's name again, I realize he's behind us.

Jeremiah seems to tense with me in his arms and he spins us both around. I see the familiar skeleton paint, the hoodie, black curls, and as he gets closer, the blue eyes.

I feel a sick relief that Lucifer is here.

But *he* doesn't look relieved. He looks fucking pissed.

"Let her go," he growls to Jeremiah

Jeremiah says nothing for a moment. Then he runs his hand over my stomach, down toward my groin, where he rests it. I struggle to draw breath, my eyes pleading with Lucifer's. But Lucifer isn't looking at me. His jaw clenches and it's almost as if he simply refuses to see where Jeremiah's hand is.

"No can do, Luce. She's mine for the night."

Lucifer shakes his head. "Let her go," he says again.

Jeremiah sighs. His hand slides down my inner thigh, his hot fingers over the skin beneath the fishnet.

"You know how this works," he says, deadly calm. "You left her." He grips my thigh tighter and this time there's no mistaking Lucifer saw it. His eyes narrow into slits. Bright blue, brilliant slits. "Now, I found her. We all get to pick."

Lucifer doesn't back down. But he doesn't say

anything else either. I don't move. Jeremiah's fingers still close around my thigh.

After a moment, he spins me around, picks me up, forcing my legs to wrap around him. His hood is still pulled down low, and I'm too terrified to move as he slides me down the length of his body. I don't imagine a soft groan when my pelvis goes over his hard cock.

I put my hands on his chest, trying to push away, but surprising me, he sets me on my feet. Before I can find my footing, Lucifer yanks me into him, spinning me around. He's got one hand on my low back and the other is pointing at Jeremiah.

"If you touch her again, I'll fucking skin you alive."

I feel his heart beneath my hands and it's strange...his pulse isn't fast. It's steady. Strong. But calm. Even as he keeps pointing at Jeremiah.

Jeremiah says nothing.

And then Lucifer grabs my hand and yanks me past the merry-go-round, back into the woods. I stumble but he keeps pulling at me. I glance over my shoulder and see Jeremiah is still watching us.

It takes me several minutes to be able to speak. My throat is dry, fear still deep in my gut. But finally, as we're enclosed again in the darkness of the trees, I find my voice.

"Stop," I say, digging my heels in.

Lucifer keeps trying to drag me along. I yank hard against him, and although I don't break free, he stops walking and spins around.

"What?" he snarls.

"I told you I don't want to—"

Before I can get the words out, he shoves me against a tree, both hands on my chest. "I didn't ask what you wanted, Lilith. I let you go. You had your chance out of this. It's too fucking late now."

Anger and fear mingle in my blood. "What the fuck is your problem?" His eyes narrow and I shake my head. "I don't want to be here. I don't want to play these games. I don't know who you and your fucking cult friends think they are but—"

His hands go to my throat, and he squeezes, hard. I can barely breathe, but I keep my eyes on his blue ones.

Fuck's sake, I wish he wasn't so goddamn beautiful. It would make it a little easier to hate the feel of his hands on me now.

And I've felt this before. Hands on my throat. I should be more scared. But instead I feel something else. Something that makes my face heat with shame.

Desire.

"*You're* my problem. You became my problem when you walked away. When you found your way into *Jeremiah's* arms." His hands move from my throat to my waist and he presses against me. I have to focus on not pressing back, even though I can feel his cock throb between us. I bite my lip, holding back a groan.

What the fuck is wrong with me?

"You should feel lucky," he whispers in my ear.

"Lucky that I found you. Because I might hurt you. But Jeremiah..." he trails off. "He would kill you."

Lucky.

I want to say something snarky. I want to hit this guy. But that word rings in my ear, and for some sick, twisted reason...I do feel it. Lucky.

CHAPTER EIGHT

Present

I'M DROWNING in cold water. I can't breathe. Can't scream. My body is shivering, my words frozen on my lips. I'm drenched, every inch of my skin covered in icy water. I try to find air. Gasp for it.

For one of the first times in my life, I *want* to live.

"Up, Sid. *Now.*"

My eyes flash open, hands coming up to defend myself.

Jeremiah.

I scramble upright, press myself against my headboard, pull my sheets up to my chin. And only then do I notice the cup in his hand, and the cold water dripping from my face, from my hair, down onto my black tank top.

Rage courses through me.

I fling the covers off and lunge for my brother.

"You fucking threw water on me?!" It's part-question, part-war cry.

We stumble, together, against the glass door to my balcony. The sun is barely up, Alexandria still bathed in pink and yellow, the city stretching out below, people on their morning commutes on what is shaping up to be a sunny Monday morning.

And my own brother has thrown ice cold water on me to wake me up.

I know he's letting me shove him against the glass now. He can stop us both at any time. But a small smile plays on his lips, even as his white shirt is bunched in my fist.

"Are you done?" he asks, infuriatingly calm.

I let go of his shirt, smooth it down.

Then I slap him across the face, making his head spin. Not from my strength, but rather his surprise.

He opens his mouth, cracks his jaw, dark brows raised. When he turns back to face me, he throws his head back and laughs. And then he puts his hand around my throat, squeezing, just as Kristof had.

Just as Lucifer had.

I don't bother fighting back. He won't kill me now. He hadn't gotten up so goddamn early and barged into my room for me to die so soon.

I hold his pale green gaze, hear him breathing in and out, steady. Calm. As if his good side is trying to tell his bad side to let go of his little sister's throat. But Jeremiah doesn't have a good side. He has a bad one. And a worse one.

He just squeezes harder.

My nails find his cheeks.

I pinch him, hard.

He shoves me away, and I catch myself on my bed, then immediately straighten, ready to go at him again if he wants to keep playing this game. He rubs a hand along his jaw, and I see with satisfaction nail marks edged into his tan skin.

"You're a shit, did you know that?" he asks, cracking his jaw again.

I sit on the bed, my hair still dripping wet. I wrap one of the black fuzzy blankets from my bed around my shoulders.

"Why the fuck did you think tossing cold ass water on me was a good idea?" I counter.

He sighs, crosses his arms, and leans against the balcony door, his head tipped back, eyes on the ceiling. He stands like that when he has something he doesn't want to say. Which is almost never. Jeremiah isn't afraid of any word in the English language. Or any language, for that matter. He's fluent in German, and that shit I do not understand. We live in North Carolina for God's sake.

"Spit it out," I growl, ready to get into a warm bath, my throat aching from Jeremiah's and Kristof's hands.

I want to enjoy this Monday.

Observe bodies and get tormented at the park on a Sunday. Relax on a Monday. And the countdown to Halloween is on. Which means the relaxing I'll be able to do is minimal. Jeremiah will be sure of that.

"I have a job for you," he finally says. There's something strange in the way he says it, almost as if he's apologizing. I've never known Jeremiah to apologize to anyone for anything.

I swallow. Hard. And wait. He's making me nervous. He's never had a job for me.

He keeps staring at the ceiling, keeps leaning against the glass door.

The fan still spins overhead, and I'm grateful for the noise. This high up, on the tallest hill in Alexandria, we can't hear the city below. Most days, I wish I could. Especially right now. The fan isn't enough.

But still, I wait. I'm not sure I want to hear what he has to say. Jeremiah never wakes me up. He usually sends Nicolas, or sometimes, when he wants to be a real pain in the ass, he'll send Brooklin. But today, he'd come in himself. With water. The cup had been knocked to the ground in our fight.

I look at it now, bright blue and plastic. Like a kid's cup. It doesn't belong in this dark room.

"A kill."

My mouth falls open as I look back at him.

"I know," he snaps, even though I haven't said a word.

I arch a brow. It isn't his usual snappy tone. It's less dangerous. More on edge. More...worried.

"You're joking?" I give a nervous laugh, bring my knees into my chest and curl into a ball under the black fuzzy blanket. Something is up. He's never offered to let me do anything for the Order, and definitely not this.

I don't think I want to do this.

I'm going to say no.

He's going to make me anyhow.

He still doesn't look at me. "No," he answers evenly. He finally tips his chin down, his pale green eyes on my pale grey ones. "But I don't think you're going to be able to pull the trigger."

I pull my knees in tighter and roll my eyes, blowing my bangs out of my face.

"I don't want it." My voice doesn't shake, but under the blankets, my hands tremble. "I don't want this job. I don't want to do that. I don't care who it is."

He takes a step toward me and I tense. I don't want him to see me shaking. I don't want him to see me squirm.

He stops halfway to me, the rising sun at his back, making him look like some kind of strange angel with a halo. But my brother doesn't wear a halo.

"Lucifer is back."

I still. I want to tell him I don't think he ever left. He was just biding his time.

"And the rest of them," he answers my unspoken question. "They've been here," he admits. "But they kept their distance. Not now."

Now I'm shaking in earnest.

Jeremiah steps to the edge of the bed, his knees against the mattress. He looks down at me.

"You know, I watched the two of you for a long, long time. I couldn't tell if you wanted him or not. I didn't know if it was the Death Oath, or...worse."

A shiver goes down my spine. I know this story, even if I can't remember it. I don't want to remember it. I don't want to talk about it. To think about it. I don't want it to exist.

"I'm not doing it," I say.

He laughs. "Don't play dumb, Sid. It's not a good look." He sighs, slides his hands in his pockets, and then he sits down beside me, his shoulder bumping mine. I try not to recoil. Try, and fail. "You know you have to."

Even as he says those words, he stares at the floor. Then we fall silent.

When he finally speaks again, he still doesn't look at me.

"Turns out, he's even more sinful than the devil himself. And unfortunately for him, and you, he owes me something."

I snap my head up. "Why me? It was one night. I had more than one with many men before he came along."

Jeremiah meets my gaze, his expression unreadable. "Don't bullshit me, Sid. I know you've been pining over him since I dragged you out of the asylum. And now you two will have come full circle. It's almost Halloween, Lilith," he whispers. As if I didn't know.

I feel a blush color my cheeks, but I hold his gaze. "You don't know shit."

He takes one hand out of his pocket so fast I think he might slap me this time. I flinch, but instead, he brushes my bangs from my face, lets his hand linger on my jaw. "I know how Lucifer is. I knew him for years, Sid." He speaks so softly, it's almost as if he cares. But I know better. He wants the shame to burn through me a little more. "I know you called for him in the cell, when I first brought you here. I'm sorry I let him take you from me. But I won't let him do that again." His finger brushes my lip, goes down my chin, over the curve of my throat. Then comes to rest above my heart.

"I should have never let him have you. But I didn't know, Sid." He moves his hand, clasping both of his in his lap. "I didn't know you were mine, then."

"I know you hate being here," he continues, and for the first time I can recall between us, I feel empathy from him. Because I *do* hate being here. I hate that I can't leave, not without him or his men following. I hate that I don't have much money to myself, even though I live in opulence. I hate that I don't have a driver's license. Or a passport. Or even my own car. Because Jeremiah doesn't want Lucifer or the other Unsaints to come after me, for what he did. For taking me from the asylum. Even though they had left me there.

"If you do this, if you kill him..." He sighs. I wait, holding my breath. "Things will change. This can be your only job, if you want it to be. I won't drag you to the sites anymore. You can live your life, Sid. I'll buy you a car. I'll give you a proper salary. Anything you want, if you do this."

I want to punch him. "What part of you thinks I believe anything you're saying right now, Jeremiah? I don't trust you. I've made no secret of the fact that I've never trusted you. And I know you feel the same for me. What would change, with Lucifer's death? And why the fuck do you think I can kill an Unsaint?"

He doesn't look at me. "He's the only one you've ever wanted, isn't he? Because he left you." He laughs, scrubs a hand over his face. "What is it with women and the men that leave them?" He stands to his feet, his back to me.

"What did Lucifer do?" I ask. That, at least, I need to know. I never asked, not about any of the other bodies Jeremiah piled up. Not before. But this is different. What my brother doesn't know is that I would have said yes, no matter what. No matter the car. Or the freedom. Or the money. He can shove those things up his ass for all I care. I just want the vengeance.

Slowly, Jeremiah turns.

"He's looking for you," he says carefully. "They all are." But he doesn't smile, like he usually does when he wants to taunt me. "He burned down Brooklin's house."

I'm not at all surprised. This is Lucifer. This is the Unsaints. This is Cain and Atlas and Ezra and Mayhem. This is the blood brothers from hell.

I didn't even know Brooklin still had a house. I thought once my brother took in a girl, he took everything else from her. Or maybe he just did that with me.

"So what?" I ask. "You don't give a shit."

He shakes his head, as if annoyed. "I don't," he says, but I don't think it's really true. Brooklin has been here a lot longer than most of Jeremiah's women. He cares for her. He might not love her, because I'm not sure the fucker knows how to love anyone. But he cares. "But it means he's trying to get to me. To you." His eyes flick to mine. "And I want to get to him first. To *them.*"

I look down at the fuzzy blanket, brows furrowed together. As if I'm contemplating. As if I'm not going to kill Lucifer no matter what Jeremiah says.

But it must unnerve him, because he says, "What I said earlier, Sid, I swear to you. I promise you, you'll have all of it and more. Just do this for me. Because whatever you think of me, I don't want him to take you. I saw how he left you. And I want him to pay for it. I want to forgive myself for that night. I want to get rid of the fucking Unsaints, and it starts with him."

"Is this about money?" I mutter. Because there's no way this is just about me. He hates them for what they did, especially Lucifer. But they were close before. Closer than brothers, if the stories are to be believed.

Jeremiah scoffs. "I have more money than I'll ever be able to spend in my life, even if I wiped my ass with it every day. I have more money than the Unsaints and the Society of 6 combined."

I wrinkle my nose but say nothing. I'm pretty sure that last part isn't true. The Unsaints and their parents own this town. Even if the spawn had decided to lie low after what happened last year, with me getting away, they still hold sway. It's a miracle they haven't burned this hotel down.

"But whether you hate my guts and whether one day

you might stab a knife in my back—or my front—I care about you, Sid."

I don't believe that for a second. Maybe he's trying to make himself believe it. But what Jeremiah cares about is blood and money.

What I care about is revenge. And I know, too, that Jeremiah's word is good. He's a dick, he can con anyone out of anything. But when he gives someone his word like he just did, he usually means it.

"Okay," I nearly whisper. For the first time in a long time, I feel alive again. I lift my head, no longer feeling the wet strands of my hair. I disentangle myself from the blanket and stand to my feet. I hold out my hand to Jeremiah.

He looks down at it, and he seems genuinely surprised.

"Okay," I say again. "I'll kill Lucifer." *Or die trying*, is what I don't say.

He takes my hand in his, brings my knuckles to his mouth and presses a kiss against them. Then he pulls me in for a hug.

For a moment, I'm stunned.

I can't recall a time we've ever hugged one another.

Slowly, I put my arms around his broad back, savoring his warmth.

"Thank you, Sid," he whispers against my head. "All this time you've hated me...I just wanted you to be mine."

And then he pulls away.

CHAPTER NINE

Halloween, One Year Ago

"WHERE ARE WE GOING?"

Lucifer is still guiding me through the woods, and this time, he has an arm wrapped possessively around my shoulders. He hasn't spoken to me since he shoved me up against the tree, and I've been reluctant to speak.

But now, I want to know.

Because my plan is fading from sight. Adrenaline is coursing through me and although I think I should be terrified, although I think I need to escape, I don't want to. I want to see where this ride takes me. I almost don't ever want to get off.

"You'll see," Lucifer says. His same answer to every question I've asked tonight.

"I want to know now," I counter.

He stops walking, turning to me, eyes narrowed.

"We're going to be late to Lover's Death. You're going to miss the Death Oath. And that is something you *cannot* miss, unless you want to die."

I laugh nervously. "Well, funny you mention it..."

He takes my chin in his hand, tips my head up so my gaze is on his. "I know what you planned to do," he says, his voice low and angry. His eyes trail down my body, to the gun. His hands follow, and he takes it out of the holster.

I reach for it, but his hand slides down my chin, over my neck. He shakes his head. "Don't," he warns me.

He throws the gun. I hear it land, softly, some distance away.

"What the fuck?" I hiss at him, trying to track his aim in the dark. But it's no use. It could be fucking anywhere.

"You're not going to die tonight, Lilith, at least not by your own hand. I want you to stop asking questions. I want you to shut the fuck up, okay?"

My hand comes up, and I slap him.

I slap him so hard, I swear to God the sound of my palm on his face echoes in the forest. I see a smear of his skeleton paint, but otherwise, he didn't even move. My hand probably hurts more than his face, which pisses me off even more.

He smiles at me. It's cold. Malicious.

And then he knocks me to the ground, shoving me and falling with me.

His body is pressed against me, one hand is on my chest. "Violence is never the answer, Lilith," he whispers into my ear, pressing further into me. His mouth brushes against my neck, and then he sinks his teeth into me.

I open my mouth to scream at him, but he clamps a hand over my lips. My neck is burning, and I swear he drew blood.

His lips find their way to my own, and he moves his fingers. I taste it as I open my mouth for him.

Iron.

My own blood.

But I kiss him back. I don't fucking know why, but I do.

His tongue probes my mouth, my teeth, my own tongue. And then when we're both nearly breathless, he pulls back, his eyes searching mine.

"We can't miss this," he says roughly, standing to his feet and yanking me up. "Stop trying to resist me."

And goddammit, I do.

▼

I FINALLY REALIZE WHERE WE ARE WHEN IT'S TOO fucking late to turn back.

An abandoned, monstrous brick building, crumbling stones and a door that's been kicked in one too many times. An overgrown parking lot, and a fenced-in lot set against Raven River.

The former Raven Shores Psych Hospital. Now abandoned in favor of a less creepy location.

But tonight, I'm at the creepy one with Lucifer, and we're not the only ones here.

There's a line of people outside of the door hanging off its hinges, and I see, standing guard at the door, four guys with their arms crossed, watching the crowd of people from the party with stony expressions.

They must be the Unsaints, because I see Atlas among them.

They're all unnervingly attractive, even in the dark. None of them are dressed up, but aside from one guy in a white tank with tattoos up and down his arms, they all wear dark clothes.

I see Ria, too, near the front, her eyes locked on the guy in the white tank.

But the Unsaints' eyes go over the heads of the throng outside of the psych door, and then everyone turns to us.

Silence steels through the few dozen people here.

They're watching us.

Or rather, they're probably watching Lucifer, and I just happen to be in their line of sight.

Lucifer, for his part, keeps tugging me forward, and the crowd, miraculously, parts. Like Lucifer is crossing the goddamn Red Sea or something.

Ria's breath hitches when I get close to her and I toss her a small smile. She grins back, and I'm happy her face is at least a friendly one. Lucifer pulls me up the steps, shoves me behind him and the rest of the guys.

None of them turn to look at me.

I notice Jeremiah isn't here.

So does the guy in the white tank. "Where's J?" he asks quietly. The people below the steps start talking and laughing again. A vape cloud forms in the air over their heads.

"Not coming," Lucifer says. There's no arguing with that tone, and no one dares. "You got your girls?" he asks the guys.

Atlas snorts. "We got 'em. They just don't know it yet."

"Then let's go. It'll be eleven soon." Lucifer turns and grabs my wrist to pull me into the building.

"Luce," one of the guys calls. He's the biggest of them all, hard muscle beneath a dark dress shirt that strains against his chest. He has a shaved head, dark eyes. And right now, those eyes are staring at me. "Be careful with that one. Jeremiah couldn't take his eyes off of her. There's probably a reason."

Lucifer stares down this guy.

"Lay off it, Cain," Atlas says with a smile. "Jeremiah is a fuck."

But Lucifer looks back at me. "Do you know him?" he asks me. "Jeremiah?"

Now all five of them are staring at me. I feel...trapped. I shake my head, not daring myself to speak.

"You trust her?" the guy called Cain asks.

The one in the white tank turns around, his eyes narrowed on me. I see he has an inverted cross tattooed on the side of his face, by his baby blue eyes. "I trust her," he volunteers. "She's too tiny to fuck us up." He leers at me.

Lucifer turns his head to glare at him. "Keep your fucking mouth shut about her, Mayhem, if you don't want me to sew your lips together when you sleep tonight."

Then he turns and pulls me through the door.

My eyes widen when we stand in what used to be the foyer. It's high-ceilinged, and there's fucking torches in the wall like we're in the medieval times or some shit. Torches.

And for a crumbling building, the inside isn't half-bad.

There's another plastic table stacked with drinks and Lucifer lets go of my hand while he walks toward one, flipping two black cups over, scooping out ice and pouring vodka. I hear one of the Unsaints through the barely-there door talking, calling out what sounds like names.

And I hear Ria's name, paired with *Mayhem*.

God help her.

Lucifer shoves a drink in my hand. "You ready?" he asks me.

I shake my head but take a gulp of straight vodka. "No," I answer honestly after making a face. It doesn't even burn that much anymore. It kind of tastes good, which means I'm drunker than I feel.

Lucifer doesn't laugh. Or smile. "Good answer." He tips his cup back and finishes it in seconds. Before I can say anything about it, the four other guys come inside, four girls trailing behind them.

"Time for the Death Oath," Atlas says with a grin. He checks the black watch on his wrist. The skull on his t-shirt catches in the torch light and it almost seems to morph, eerie and unnerving. I drink more, letting the vodka burn away my fear.

I see Ria, and she comes to stand beside me. For some reason, this causes the guys to look our way. But I ignore them and loop my arm through Ria's. Because this shit is weird and it's probably only going to get weirder.

"No use in bonding, girls," a deep voice says. It comes from a guy that's shorter than the rest of them, but built, and still taller than me and the other four girls. He's got dark brown skin.

All of the girls have their arms wrapped around themselves but with smiles on their beautiful faces.

"You're going to be separated soon," the same guy drawls.

And sure enough, Lucifer plucks the drink from my hand and pulls me toward him, away from Ria, who watches me with wide eyes. I glance beside me and realize I'm the only girl standing by the drink table. The rest of them are still crowded around the door, with Ria in the middle, and the rest of the guys on either side of me.

"Not how it works, Lucifer," the guy with the deep voice says. "Put her with the rest." He nods to the girls. "Get on your knees."

I stiffen and spin around to face him. Lucifer's hand clamps down on mine so hard I have to bite down on my tongue to keep from crying out at the pain in my bones, but I don't cry out. I look at the guy with the deep voice.

"Excuse me?" I spit at the guy, my anger barely contained. First Lucifer fucks up my plan to kill myself, then I almost get kidnapped by a merry-go-round, and now these fucking idiots want us on our knees.

The girls are silent.

Everyone is silent.

But the guy holds my gaze and a slow smile forms on his lips. "Lilith?" he asks, as if he knows. Lucifer must have told him. "You clearly have no idea how things work around here, so I'll enlighten you." He breaks rank with the guys, and Lucifer again squeezes my hand.

"Ezra," he snarls, the name a warning.

Ah. The missing piece of the six.

Ezra ignores Lucifer and comes to stand in front of me, his arms crossed. "You don't get to ask questions, Lilith." I can feel his body heat in front of me, and Lucifer's beside me. "This isn't the night for that. I don't know how Lucifer found you," his eyes flick to Lucifer's at my side, "but it's too late for you to turn back now."

"Ezra," Lucifer says again. "Back the fuck up."

Ezra laughs. And he doesn't back up. Instead, he steps closer, his chest nearly brushing my shoulders. "You might have to kill her when this is all over, Luce, you know that, don't you?" Even though he directs the question to Lucifer, he keeps his gaze on me.

I look to Lucifer. Surely this guy is joking. Surely *I'm* joking. I set out tonight with the intention of taking my own life. Now I'm scared of this bonehead?

But he doesn't really look like a bonehead. With dark hair, dark green eyes, and his head cocked to the side as he stares at me, he looks deadly serious. Like he might actually kill me before the night is over.

Before I can think of a response, Lucifer jerks me behind him, and steps up into Ezra's face.

"Back. The fuck. *Up.*"

Ezra stares at him a minute, jaw clenched, and then he does. He backs up. And he turns to the girls and snarls, "On your knees," again. "Lucifer." His eyes flick to his. "Get your shit together."

Lucifer turns to me. "It'll only be a minute," he whispers. And then, before I can ask what the hell he's talking about, he pushes me in line with the girls.

Who are on their knees.

He steps back.

I look around, shaking my head.

"I'm not going to tell you again," Ezra snarls to me.

Ria, on her knees beside me, catches my eye. "Come on, Lilith," she whispers with a grin.

I'm staring at them, my mouth open, when Lucifer breaks rank, comes forward, and pushes me down, his leg hooking around the back of my own knee, forcing me to the stone floor, too.

I twist my head and stare up at him, humiliated.

"What the fuck was that—" I make to spit at him, but he shoves three fingers in my mouth. And I bite down immediately, *hard.*

He doesn't even frown.

He gets to his knees in front of me and shoves his

fingers further into my mouth, down my throat, until I'm gagging.

With his other hand, he pulls me close, his fingers digging into my shoulder. "Stop talking," he whispers. The fingers in my mouth press further, tickling my uvula. I gag again, and the guys all laugh. My face burns.

"Stop talking, or this will get so much worse for you, *Lilith*."

I gag again, and my stomach clenches. I don't remember the last time I ate, but I've had a lot to drink. My head is spinning and even my ears are burning. My knees hurt on the cement, but I can't get up, not with Lucifer trailing his fingers down my throat and holding onto my shoulder.

"Do you understand?" he asks me.

I nod.

He takes his fingers out of my mouth and then stands to his feet, glaring down at me before joining the rest of the Unsaints.

Ezra starts to talk again. He sounds amused.

"The Death Oath comes before Lover's Death. It's the *essence* of Lover's Death." He takes a fucking knife out of his back pocket.

I want to get to my feet, but a girl on my other side with long red hair shakes her head, her gaze meeting mine. Reluctantly, I stay where I am.

Ezra steps up to the redheaded girl, staring down at her, the knife in his hands. If he raises that knife to her, I'm going to get up. I'm going to knock him on his ass. I don't care that he's twice my size.

But as he lifts the blade, he lifts up his shirt. I jerk back, confused. And then I see a skull tattoo on the left side of his abs. In black and grey, smoke pouring from one eye of the skull, a 'U' carved into the other eye.

I see Lucifer watching me. Everyone seems to be holding their breath.

What the fuck is this shit?

Ezra holds the blade to his own skin, above his tattoo. And this close, I can see that he's actually going to do it. He's going to cut himself. I know, because there are pale white scars through the mouth of the skull tattoo. Right next to the line of blood he now cuts into his skin with the knife. He keeps going, until it reaches the length of the other scars, nearly six inches.

My eyes are going to bug out of my head.

What. The. Fuck.

I look to Lucifer. He's still staring at me. I look at Ria. Her eyes are wide, too, and her brown skin has grown pale. Okay, so at least I'm not the only one flipping out here.

Ezra holds the blade out, full of his blood, to the redhead.

My stomach churns.

The redhead seems confused, her brows pulling together.

"Open your mouth," Ezra commands her.

Don't do it, I think. But I can't find the words to actually say it.

She opens her mouth, sticks out her tongue. Ezra runs the flat edge of the blade around it and even though I want to, I can't look away. I can't even blink.

Ezra smiles, then he grabs her by the back of the head, moves the knife away, and forces her mouth to his bleeding wound.

Hesitantly, she licks the blood. Ezra almost groans, and she gets more confident in her blood sucking abilities.

I'm aware that outside the door at my back, there are probably still partygoers hanging out, wondering what's going to become of the five girls that went inside. I'm aware that if I scream really loudly, they'll hear me.

Maybe one of them will call the police.

Or maybe no one will.

And it's that dread that keeps my mouth closed. It's thinking that maybe those partygoers *know* what's happening here.

When I force myself to look away, Lucifer is standing over me, and he has a knife too. I notice all the Unsaints are standing over their girls. I stare at Lucifer's extended hand toward me. Okay, so maybe not everyone gets to drink the blood of the Unsaints...

Beside me, the redhead is still lapping up blood and Ezra groans again.

I want to get out of here. I take Lucifer's hand, and he pulls me to my feet. I keep watching the knife. Thankfully, he puts it in his back pocket.

Ezra breaks out of his trance long enough to mutter to all the guys, "Nothing happens until the blood comes out."

Lucifer nods, and then he leads me down the hallway, tugging me away from whatever fuckery is happening at my back.

The only thing I can think to ask is, "Why did we have to get on our knees?"

He glances at me, the corners of his mouth turning up into a smile. "Subservience," he purrs.

I stop walking right as we come to the end of the hall and a closed metal door.

I yank out of his hand.

"Lucifer..."

He looks at me as he slides his hands into his pockets. He cocks his head. "Yes, Lilith?"

"What is happening right now? What is this shit?"

He takes a step closer to me, frowning. "My friends and I," he begins, "we're into some weird shit."

I don't know what to say to that besides, "I know."

He wraps his hand around the back of my neck and pulls me gently into him. "Don't run Lilith," he whispers against my ear.

I don't know why I ask my next question. Maybe it's the vodka. Maybe it's the rum I had before I left my apartment. Maybe it's because I'm in a psych ward and I feel like I've lost my goddamn mind.

"Is that your baby?" I blurt out, wishing my voice didn't shake when I said the words. Wishing I didn't give a damn. Knowing that I shouldn't give a damn. Why does it matter? There are way more fucked up things going on here.

He pulls away and I watch the vein in his neck, watch him swallow. He still has my neck in his hand, but he puts some space between us.

He bites his lip and I can't look away from his mouth. I might actually start to believe he really is the devil himself. Because in this moment, I don't care what comes next. I don't think I'm going to try to walk away again.

"I don't know," he finally answers me.

I realize I've been holding my breath. Now, I exhale and frown, but I can't bring myself to ask a follow-up question.

He shakes his head, straightens, but keeps a tight grip on me. His brow furrows, a curl falling over one brilliant blue eye.

Down the hall, back from the way we came, a girl moans.

"I don't know," he says again. He brings his other hand to my waist, his fingers digging into the fabric of my bodysuit, pinching my skin. He yanks me to him, and I catch myself on his chest, fingers splayed against him.

"What if it is, Lilith?" he asks me, his voice hoarse. I smell that scent that he seems to be made of: Cigarettes and pine. I relish in it. I've never smoked, never been drawn to smokers. I have no idea how bad his habit is, but right now, I don't care. Life is short. Mine was going to be especially short, nineteen years of wasted time. But if I get to the end of those nineteen years on a night like this, they might actually mean something.

"What if it is mine?" he asks me again, brushing his lips against my brow.

I shudder against him, and he pulls me in even tighter. It almost hurts. But I don't want him to let go.

"Then it is," I finally answer. "It won't matter. It has nothing to do with me." I meet his gaze. "It won't matter because tonight, you're not you, and I'm not me. You're Lucifer. I'm Lilith. We own hell. We can own our own hells, too."

That must be the vodka talking.

He tips my chin up.

"What if I want to be me? With you?"

I make to turn away, but he grips my face tighter, forcing me to meet his gaze.

But there's things he doesn't know about me. Things I clearly do not know about him. And this Lover's Death shit...

And despite the fact that I just watched a man carve into his own skin and force a girl to drink his blood, *I'm* the one feeling insecure.

"You don't want me," I bite out. "Not the real me." I don't want to keep going down this path. I need to get the fuck out of here. But it's like I'm frozen in place around him.

His face darkens. He's angry. "Don't tell me what I want, Lilith." He tips my chin up further. "Don't *ever* tell me what I want."

"I'm not just a lonely girl looking for a one-night stand, Lucifer." His grip doesn't slacken, and my throat is pulled taunt, but I keep talking anyway, making myself get the words out. I don't even know why it matters, but for some reason, it does. "It looks like you might've had enough of those," I spit, nearly shaking. From anger, from lust, from what I'd planned to do tonight, I don't know. "And so have I." His eyes narrow. "I've had more one-night stands than you can possibly fucking imagine. I've had so many—"

He presses his hand against my mouth. Hard

"Stop talking."

I part my lips, but he clamps down more, his fingers digging into the side of my face, his palm keeping my words in.

"I said *Stop talking.*"

I can feel him beneath my own hands on his chest, breathing hard, his heart hammering fast. But my anger rises up to meet his. I just watched a blood ceremony, the first I've ever seen, and yet he can't listen to my sins. My confessions.

He keeps his hand pressed to my mouth, and reaches the other behind him. In his back pocket. It takes me a minute to wonder what he's doing but then I hear the snick of the blade and see it gleaming in the torchlight when he brings his hand up between us.

I make to step away, but he shakes his head, moves his hand from my mouth and catches my wrist, pressing so hard I feel the bones rub together.

"Not so fast, Lilith," he purrs, holding up the knife. It's a short blade but it looks wicked sharp.

I have no idea what he intends to do. Carve up his

own skin, like Ezra? His lips are turned up into an eerie smile, the skeleton paint making him seem nearly deranged. And yet I'm glad he's holding my wrist.

Because part of me wants to run.

But part of me...part of me wants to stay. The part that's fucked up. That's always been fucked up since that first foster home.

"If I let you go, are you going to try to run?" he asks me, cocking his head.

I swallow. Was I? I don't know.

But slowly, I shake my head.

"Don't lie to me, Lilith."

I take a breath, and another. Another. I suck down air as fast as I can get it.

"Are you going to run, baby girl?" he asks again, loosening his hold on my wrist.

I shake my head again. I'm not.

He seems to realize I'm telling the truth. He lets me go, then flips the knife in his hand and before I can say a word, he slices a hole in his black pants.

For a moment, I only stare at the pale skin beneath. He cuts a strip of his pants, lets the fabric fall to the ground. Then I see the tattoo. Same as Ezra's; a skull with smoke and a U. I also see the blood.

I should gasp. Or run now. Maybe ask him what the fuck he's doing. But I don't do any of that. I just watch the cut deepen with crimson, swelling under the skull eyes, then run down his thigh, down his pants. He's bleeding. It's a good three inches or more, and it might be a shallow wound, but it's dripping steadily. He has other scars, too.

He runs the flat part of the blade over the wound, coating it in blood. Then he holds up the knife again between us. I can't stop staring at it, the silver slick with red. He pushes me back against the door.

"Open your mouth," he commands.

I tense, finding his gaze in the darkness.

"Open your mouth, Lilith."

And I fucking do. I don't know why. I could run now. I could scream for help.

But I don't.

I open my goddamn mouth.

He makes a sound somewhere between a sigh and a groan and he presses closer to me, leaving only enough room to hold up the knife.

"Stick out your tongue," he whispers, his voice thick with some unknown emotion.

I stick out my tongue.

"Don't move." The warning rings in my head as he places the flat of the blood against my tongue. I taste copper. Blood.

His blood.

He slides the blade down my tongue, careful not to cut me, but he coats my tongue with him.

"Swallow it."

I do. It's salty and metallic, and I only want fucking more of it. I clench my hands into fists to keep from sinking to my knees, to keep from running my tongue down his thigh. From stopping the bleeding with my own goddamn mouth.

But he pulls me to him by the neck and he crushes his mouth to mine.

We're teeth and tongues and blood and spit and I only want more. He groans against my mouth, then slips something into my hand.

The hilt of the blade.

"Your turn," he whispers against my lips.

CHAPTER TEN

Present

MY FIRST THOUGHT is about the child. I know it shouldn't be. I know I should be a better person. But I can't stop thinking about that girl's belly, sitting tight and plump between her and Lucifer when they were speaking.

And then Ria's words, about not knowing. Lucifer's confirmation, that he didn't know.

I want to know about her. About the baby. So I ask Nicolas.

He's day drinking, because the Rain mansion doesn't follow the natural order of things: breakfast, lunch, dinner. Work in between. No, the Rain mansion specializes in night murders, drug trafficking, and lots and lots of booze.

That and marijuana are the only drugs Jeremiah lets people consume who work for him. They're drug tested. And they know better than to try to fake one.

I'm not. I don't know why. Maybe he doesn't care. Maybe he knows I've never been drawn to drugs.

Not yet.

Anyhow, getting piss drunk before ten in the morning is perfectly acceptable in the Rain mansion, as long as work gets handled.

Nicolas guzzles his beer as I sit across from him in one of the living rooms. It used to be a bar, and it still has a bar. But Jeremiah had wanted a bigger bar. Now there are three in the Rain mansion.

The lights are dim, tinted glass shielding us from the warm, mid-October sun.

I remember, vaguely, California's fall. It was mild, but here...well, North Carolina is still sweltering during the day.

By Halloween, though, it usually cools off. Nights are already dropping in temperature.

Nicolas sets the empty bottle on the edge of the dark red leather chair. I have my knees tucked into my chest, my hands stuffed into my hoodie pockets. Years of dressing up for men left me with a style that screams, "I just woke up". It's comfortable. I love it. No one leers at me this way.

Nicolas's deep brown eyes find mine. Then they go lower. To my throat.

There are purple and yellow bruises there, too high up to hide under my hoodie. Probably from Kristof. Maybe from my brother.

Nicolas sighs and stretches his legs out. He wears dark jeans, a loose-fitting t-shirt that shows off his tan skin, scarred arms. Nicolas hadn't made his way to the foster system as a child. But he should have. Even I can admit he would've been better off. Most of his scars came from his own mother.

"Your brother told me not to tell you any of this," he finally says, looking down at the polished wooden floor now.

I scoff. "Since when do you let my brother order you around?"

He barks a laugh. "Since I started working for his punk ass all those years ago."

When Nicolas dealt on the streets. He was known for his quality goods and his word. My brother had told me as much, during one of the many times he tried to compare me to his more competent men. Even to the Unsaints themselves. Although never Lucifer.

"Yeah, stupid question," I murmur. But even still, I'm not letting it go. "Let's just do a little 'Yes' or 'No'?" I waggle my brows as he looks back at me, a smirk on his face. It was a game we played when I didn't want to talk, and he wanted to let me vent, with few words. We asked 'Yes' or 'No' questions, and no explanation was required. Or, in fact, allowed. All part of the game.

He sighs, lifts his hands in a shrug. "Fine," he growls.

There's a five-question limit unless the party being interrogated agrees to lift it. I feel confident he won't, so I don't press it.

I tap my fingers together, pressing the tips against one another. "Does Lucifer have a child?"

"Going in for the kill," Nicolas mutters, shaking his head. He heaves a sigh and plays with the clear beer bottle on his armchair, twirling it around and around. "Yes."

I feel like I want to throw up. But that will get me nowhere.

"Is he with the mother of that child, romantically?"

Nicolas stares at me, clearly annoyed.

"You know no matter what I say, you have to kill him, right?"

I shush him. "Not part of the game, Nicky," I croon.

He swallows. I watch his Adam's apple bob up and down. "Yes." And then he throws me a bone. "Julie is the mother."

Julie.

Another punch to the gut. If I ask the rest of my three questions, I'll probably kill Lucifer right now, as soon as I can find him.

"Did he really burn down Brooklin's house?"

I know Jeremiah meant what he said when he offered me my freedom. Or rather, my freedom within reason, within the confines of this mansion. But I don't know if he'd lied about the details.

For some reason, Nicolas seems nervous. He spins the bottle faster in his hands, watching it carefully.

"Yes," he finally says. "With the help of his Unsaint fiends." This surprises me. Not the Unsaints, but I thought his nerves had to do with the fact he was going to reveal a lie from my brother.

Two more questions. I shift in my chair, put my hands back in my pockets and clear my throat.

Nicolas raises his brows as if to ask, 'Is that enough?' But it isn't. Not even close.

"Does my brother love Brooklin?"

Nicolas jerks back, nearly dropping the bottle in his hands. He squeezes it in one, fingers blanching against the glass. He didn't expect that one. But I already know the answer before he confirms it.

"Yes."

My throat goes dry, and I don't even know why. If Jeremiah loves her, maybe he'll stay off my back. He doesn't seem to be doing that, though. But maybe I don't want him to. Maybe I like his overbearing cruelties. Maybe they make me feel loved.

My face burns with that thought. I look down at my knees, knobby and full of bruises from God-knows what. Then I remember. Kristof throwing me down on his marble floor. Something my brother had let him do.

One more question.

I take a breath and glance outside, at the neat hedges that line the windows.

I can feel Nicolas watching me.

I don't know if I want the answer to the one question beating against the side of my brain like a wild animal.

"Does he know I'm here?"

Nicolas freezes. His grip on the bottle tightens so much I think it might shatter in his hands. He seems to stop breathing. I think I know the answer.

But shocking me, he shakes his head.

I gasp at him. "You can't lie!"

He smiles, but it doesn't quite meet his eyes. "I'm not lying. He probably thinks you're here. They all do. But if they knew, they'd have tried to get to you before now. Anyway, no more questions. No explanations, *Sidney.*"

I shoot him the bird. My name isn't Sidney. My mom, probably cracked out and half-awake, had written "Sid" on my birth certificate when I was fresh from the womb, still in the hospital.

Well then.

Lucifer might not know I'm here, but he knows something about me. Knows something happened to Jeremiah that night, to make him leave the Unsaints without a word. And Nicolas had given me a hint. He generally showed his emotions around me, but I knew very well he could have hidden them too, when I asked if Lucifer knew where I was.

Nicolas usually kept his feelings to himself, like he had those first two weeks I was here. When Jeremiah kept me in a cell because he didn't trust me in a room by myself.

Nicolas had been entirely mute. Even when he handcuffed my hands behind my back and forced my mouth open, even as my jaw cracked when he pushed soup down my throat.

He hadn't said a word. I thought he actually was the devil himself, until Jeremiah released me. And I became friendly with Nicolas.

We aren't friends exactly. I don't have those. But we're something. And he had given me more than he had to.

I almost want to thank him. But I know better.

I sigh and stand to my feet, crouching down to lace up my combat boots.

"One more question," I say without looking up. "When do I start?"

Nicolas laughs. "It's a one-shot deal. One shot kill. Halloween night only, Sidney. Your brother is a sado-masochist, you know?"

I smile, nod.

I know.

But no way in hell am I going to wait 'til Halloween.

CHAPTER ELEVEN

Present

FINDING LUCIFER IS HARDER than I thought it would be.

For one, I don't have his last name. I hadn't thought to ask Nicolas what it was during our game, and now it's too late for that. When I find Nicolas that night in the gym, he zips his lips and throws away an imaginary key. I roll my eyes and get to running on the treadmill. I work better when I get a sweat in.

I don't listen to music, just the own steady beating of my heart, the inhales and exhales as I run through sprint intervals. I glance in the wall of mirrors in front of me and see the purple and blue bruising on my throat.

I haven't seen Kristof since the night before. I'm glad. If I had, I might have punctured his lung with the long, curved knife I have in the cup holder of the treadmill. I had left the switchblade in his room in the chaos of my brother's interruption, but I didn't need it back. I had more knives in my room than I had clothes.

My eyes flick to Nicolas in the mirror. He's doing weighted burpees at the far end of the gym, wearing a tank top and basketball shorts. I watch his body move for a long moment, marveling at the muscle tone. He's breathing hard, and he runs a hand through his short blonde hair, transferring the hand weights to one hand to do so. He catches me looking at him in the mirror and shakes his head, rolling his eyes.

I laugh, bring my gaze back to myself.

I'm wearing a hoodie, letting the extra heat drench me as I power through another stretch of high intervals. My pale complexion is splotchy and red now, and I glance down at the muscles flexing in my thighs as I run, my long runner's shorts swaying a little with the movement. I take pride in that muscle. It had taken me a long time to build it, half a year after my brother took me from Raven Park. When I'd been an escort, I'd ran, too, but never lifted weights. I didn't practice fighting either or firing a gun or wielding a knife.

All that changed when I came to the Rain mansion. Even inside these walls, where most of my brother's staff lives full-time, it's hard to trust anyone. The only person I did trust was the one at my back, but I know that he would take a bullet for Jeremiah in a heartbeat before he thought to take one for me. I understand that loyalty. Nicolas has been here longer than I have. In truth, he'd known my brother longer, too.

Nicolas hadn't been an Unsaint because his own family hadn't been with the Society of 6. But he'd been my brother's friend even before he started the Order of Rain.

After me and Jeremiah split up, when I was a kid, I had cried for him, even though he'd terrorized me. He was familiar. The devil I knew. The new homes I went to were full of worse monsters, worse devils. When I turned eighteen, found myself with no high school diploma (because I found writing in the library was more fun than writing in class), I had finally tasted freedom.

I'd fallen into escorting after looking for easy jobs on the library computer. I'd worked for an older woman for a few months, learning the trade, how not to get caught, how to avoid the cops. And then I got tired of her taking my cut, so I got out from under her and took my clients with me. They brought me more.

I hadn't been rich.

I should have been. But I undercharged, only wanted enough to pay my bills and buy books and clothes. Then, a year ago, when I decided I didn't even want that, I'd taken the gun I had at the house for some perceived sense of self-protection and thought I'd retire early. Nineteen and ready to die.

Fucking Lucifer. He took that from me, then put me somewhere worse.

Here.

I walk through the low interval, tugging up my hoodie sleeves, wiping the back of my hand over my forehead. Then I power through the last of the high intervals, thinking only of him. Of how now I could destroy him. He might owe my brother something for burning down Brooklin's house, but he owed me more. He had taken my death away.

When Jeremiah had thrown me in that cell, it had been fourteen days of constant suicide watch by Nicolas, and a sub when Nicolas had to catch a few hours of sleep. Even then, he didn't leave my side. Or rather, the other side of my cell. When I'd finally gotten out, I had a woman —the head housekeeper's daughter—at my side. She even slept in my room. I screamed at her. I threatened her. But she was stocky, tall, and this time, *she* had the gun.

I didn't kill myself.

Taking my own life would have taken bravery that on that Halloween night, I'd had. I'd been confident my life wouldn't get better, and I felt good about making that choice. About taking my life and death into my own hands. But by the time I'd finally earned Jeremiah's trust just enough to live alone in the hotel, I hadn't been brave any longer.

I also couldn't get Lucifer out of my head. I still can't. But I never expected to see him again. He had left me in the psych ward, for Jeremiah to find me. And Jeremiah had tried to take me that night himself, before he knew who I was. Lucifer had warned me about him, but turns out, Lucifer was the worst monster.

I'm not just going to kill him for my brother. I'm going

to fuck up his life like he'd fucked up mine when he took away my choice. When I'd sworn that oath to him, and he to me. He didn't keep his end of it.

I'll take my time enjoying his death, like I hadn't been able to enjoy mine.

▼

It's an unlikely source that leads me to Lucifer's whereabouts.

Around midnight, I'd taken the seven flights of stairs down to one of the kitchens, the industrial one that had been intended for serving meals for the entire hotel. It's busy, as it usually is in the middle of the night. People who work for the Order of Rain don't keep normal hours. And the people that aren't working are getting high, and thus, hungry.

One of my brother's guards is down here, sitting on top of a mini fridge, ironically used for the kitchen staff. As if the glistening stainless-steel monstrosity isn't enough. The guard isn't, thankfully, Kristof, so I let go of the knife strapped against my waist band, tucked beneath my baggy black t-shirt under my hoodie.

Trey reaches his fist out to me and I pound it, nodding toward the string cheese in his hands.

"This place serves gourmet meals and that's what you're working with," I tease him. Trey is young, just a year older than me. He shaves his head, and a black stud glistens from above his eyebrow.

He grins. "Cheese is dank," he says with a laugh.

"Why'd my brother let you off your leash?" I duck around the head night chef, Chasity, as she makes her way through, reaching for a spice on the stainless-steel counter. I glimpse meat browning in her pan. I sit down beside Trey.

He frowns at me, his bright eyes narrowing. "You're a bitch, did anyone ever tell you?"

I shrug, slap him on the knee. He has a hole in his too-big jeans. I know he can afford ones that fit, but everything about Trey's clothes are too big.

"Every day, pal," I answer him, stuffing my hands back in my pockets.

I see his eyes flick to my throat, and he shakes his head. I thought I'd pulled up my hoodie enough to cover the bruises but apparently not.

"Kristof is a dick bag," he says, then he chomps off another bite of string cheese.

I frown. "You know, you're supposed to peel off strings of the cheese, not bite it off like a wild animal."

He pops the rest of it in his mouth and chews with his mouth open, right in my face. I laugh, jerking back. He crumples up the plastic wrap and tosses it in the trashcan beside him.

"Did you come here to piss me off or to eat?"

I watch a flame shoot up from Chasity's pan and she whistles. So do most of the staff. I'm not into meat, but it does smell damn good.

My stomach growls, and Trey hears it. His eyes go wide.

"You motherfucker. There's enough food in this place to feed Alexandria and you're starving yourself?" He pinches my thigh, coming up nearly empty-handed. "Besides that, I could break you in half. What's going to happen when Kristof comes for you again?"

I laugh at that. "He won't. Or I'll kill him."

Trey winks, rubs his hands over his jeans. "That's a good girl. But you're right," he sighs, "he probably won't. Because if he does, you *and* Jeremiah will kill him. No one wants to die from both Rains."

I roll my eyes.

"Seriously," he says, punching me lightly on the arm. "What Kristof did was fucked up."

"You mean what my brother ordered him to do?" I counter, brow arched. I cross my ankles, flex my feet in my white sneakers.

Trey suddenly looks uncomfortable. He clears his throat. I've never heard him say anything less than positive about my brother, even though I know he's a monster. We all know. Trey looks down at his own shoes, slip-on Vans with holes in them. He really doesn't give a shit about his appearance.

I can relate.

"Forget it," I mumble, letting him off the hook.

He sighs. "Thanks. He's with Brooklin right now, going to a goddamn drive-in movie like civilized people."

"A drive-in at midnight?" I ask, shaking my head,

surprised at both the time and the activity. But I remember what Nicolas had said. That Jeremiah loves Brooklin. Or something like it.

Trey nods. "He only took Kristof—probably to keep him off you—and the rest of us get off. Lucky assholes, huh?" He rolls his eyes.

My stomach growls again. I had planned to grab some cooked tofu from the fridge; I know Chasity always keeps some down here for me. But now I plan to grab something else.

Trey and I are quiet a moment as people work around us, sizzling and frying and washing dishes. It amazes me my brother funds all of this. He hadn't been born into money, but he'd found it anyhow. I shouldn't be surprised. I don't know if he'd really killed his foster family, but I know he'd somehow fell into some money he didn't really deserve and used it to get into the Unsaints. Although now he's grown more of it. That, I guess, he does deserve.

"You heard about my big job?" I ask Trey, trying to keep my voice even, indifferent.

He blows out a breath. "Yep. How you feelin' about it?" I don't know what he knows about Lucifer and me, but the way he asks, he must know something. And I know he knows of the Unsaints.

I shrug. "I've seen a lot of dead bodies." That much is true. I'm more terrified of the prospect of one day giving birth and—God forbid—raising a child, than I am about taking a life. Especially Lucifer's.

Thinking of paying him back is exciting somehow.

"You know where he is?" I ask. It's a direct question, and if Trey had thought the better of it, he wouldn't have answered me. But he didn't. Not until it's too late.

He laughs, shakes his head, rubs a hand over his jaw. "Yep," he says, nodding. "Motherfucker is making himself an easy target. He's not at his fucking mansion, though. Knows we've got too many eyes there."

I wait, my nerves on edge.

"Know a lot about Raven Park?" he continues, and I feel his gaze slide to mine. But I don't look at him. I don't want him to know how much this information means to me.

Instead, I only nod. "Everyone knows Raven Park." *And I know everything about it.*

"There's a weird ass house on the other side of it. Only one. I don't even know if the place has indoor plumbing. He's staying there."

I can barely breathe.

"It's not, like, his actual house. Nah, dude has a family. But he's there for now. Him and the fucking Unsaints went back there after he burned down Brooklin's house. We followed him. His *gang* is there too."

Finally, I meet Trey's gaze.

And he seems to see what I'm thinking as I hop off the mini fridge. He reaches out, yanking my arm and spinning me around.

"Fuck, I shouldn't have told you that." He stands, towering over me, still gripping my arm. "Look, Sid, you can't go after him. Not yet. You'll get your chance. But if something were to happen to you...Jeremiah would kill me. And you."

I shrug my arm out of his grip. He lets go.

"Don't tell Jeremiah we had this conversation."

I smile at him, then leave, threading my way out of the kitchen without bothering to look for the tofu.

CHAPTER TWELVE

Present

I DON'T WANT to go to Raven Park. Jeremiah takes me there to torture me often enough, and I wonder if Lucifer has seen me. I wonder if he's waiting for me there. The thought scares me more than it should.

But I need to do this, for me. To get his beautiful, midnight blue eyes out of my fucking head.

Leaving the hotel is relatively easy, with a few hassles. I plan to have Nicolas vouch for me, after I threaten to tell my brother about the 'Yes/No' game we played earlier that day, in which he'd told me all about Jeremiah's feelings for Brooklin and all about Lucifer's baby.

He hadn't, of course, but it was true enough I could fuck him.

Still, he argues with me.

"Absolutely not, Sid," he says from his black leather

couch. I sit across from him perched on the edge of a chair. The TV is on, replaying a fight from the night before.

"You can't stop me."

Nicolas barks a laugh. "I can. And I will. Your brother would kill us both if I let you leave here."

It isn't that I can never leave. Just not at night. And definitely not to go looking for Lucifer, when Jeremiah has specifically told me the job is for Halloween.

Besides that, I don't have a car. And my phone has a tracker. Jeremiah claims it's to keep me safe from the Unsaints.

But I don't plan to bring my phone. Or take a car. Raven Park isn't that far. I can run there, and I know how to get to the southern border that edges the lake. That's where the house is. I've seen it myself.

A small part of me wonders how close he knows he is to me. What he and the Unsaints would do to Jeremiah if they knew I was here. Maybe they do know. But I want to know why the fuck they're looking for me. Lucifer had no problem letting me go that night.

"Look, Nicky," I say, crossing my ankles, my combat boots on the seat of his chair. "You either let me leave, keep your mouth shut about it, or I'll tell my brother about our little game."

Nicolas glares at me, tearing his eyes away from the fight. He closes his eyes, lets out an impatient sigh. "You're testing me, kid. But here's the thing." His eyes spring open. "I don't give a damn if you tell Jeremiah about the game. I'll have much less hell to pay for that than if he finds out I let you walk out of here in the dead of night while he was away, without sending anyone with you."

I grin, hopping down from the chair, standing right in front of Nicolas, blocking his view.

He narrows his eyes, waiting for my challenge.

"I'll be back in two hours," I say, crossing my arms. "And you might *think* Jeremiah won't mind if I tell him about our game, and maybe he wouldn't have. Maybe he wouldn't have given a damn, you telling me about Brooklin." I lift one shoulder in a lazy shrug. "Maybe he wouldn't have gave a damn that you told me Lucifer doesn't know I'm here." Then I drop into a crouch, my hand on his knee. "But he *will* give a damn about the rest. About the fact that Lucifer is a father. That he's with his baby's mama. He'll give a damn, because he'll know, then, that it was *you* who pushed me out of this hotel to go looking for Lucifer. Because if you don't *let* me leave, I'll find a way out myself. We both know I will." I squeeze his kneecap, my heart thudding while he watches me.

This might not work.

I will find another way out, if he says no. But having Nicolas get me out is easier. Much less work than trying to scale the roof and sneak down the long driveway, dodging my way past the armed guards.

But I will do it. I'll take out the guards, too, if I have to.

But I'd rather not.

Two hours. That's all I want. Enough time to jog to the park, scope out the house, and jog back. To see what

I'm up against. To see where Lucifer and his gang went after he dumped me in the asylum last Halloween.

"Jesus fucking Christ," Nicolas seethes, scrubbing his hand over his face. That's when I know I have him.

I smile, stand to my feet, and turn to go, shoving my hands in my hoodie pocket.

"Two hours, Sid. If you're not back in two hours, all bets are off. I'll lie to your brother if I have to, and when I find you, I'll kill you myself."

I glance over my shoulder. "Deal. Now zip me up."

▼

CLIMBING OUT OF THE TRUNK OF NICOLAS'S Mercedes and breathing in the still-warm fall air gives me a kick of adrenaline. I'm really doing it. I'd really bargained my way into two hours of free time, even if Nicolas had to stuff me in a body bag to do it. A body bag that he claimed was full of tools when we passed the guards at the door to the mansion. It's no secret Nicolas has a hideaway in the city, and that he's been working on renovating it himself. A place to get away when he has time off, which is almost never.

My brother knows where it is.

Which meant Nicolas had actually put tools in the body bag with me, and on the long, winding ride down the driveway, I'd been smacked in the ass with a hammer and some nails one too many times.

But still...I'm free now.

Nicolas doesn't ask where I'm going. He doesn't want to know. Because if Jeremiah comes after him for this, his ass will be on the line.

But even as he lets me walk away from the parking lot of a dead gas station, I think he knows. Especially as he calls out, "Two hours. Do you have the gun? The watch?"

I nod without looking back, making my way to the sidewalk that lines one of the quieter streets of Alexandria.

The gun is against my hip, concealed by my hoodie. The watch is on my wrist. I glance at it as I walk away.

"I won't let you down," I call out into the night.

Nicolas mumbles something under his breath, but I don't catch it, and he doesn't repeat it. I hear the door to the SUV thud closed, but he doesn't start the car. He's going to wait here, we're going to dump the tools at his hideaway, and then we're going back to the mansion together. Jeremiah doesn't do a roll call every night, but sometimes he does. All the time, though, he lets Nicolas know where and when he's going to be somewhere. And tonight, he'd told Nicolas he wouldn't be back until dawn.

I wonder where he and Brooklin are staying, and why.

I know, though, that my brother likes to get away from the mansion sometimes. From the demands. Demands he'd created, demands he dove into like a fool with the jobs he did.

But none of that is my problem tonight.

Tonight, my problem is Lucifer and the Unsaints.

And I know, without him having told me, that Nicolas knows less about the Unsaints than I do. He might know that Jeremiah used to be one. He might know their parents are the Society of 6. But he doesn't know how dangerous they are, or he would never have let me do this.

I'm fucking glad.

The roads to the forest are quiet. It's Monday night, and even in a college town, people sleep. Not often, and not well, but they do. The flashing lights in the downtown core are far off in the distance. But twenty minutes after I left Nicolas, I walk through the intersection I'd first met Lucifer at.

I hold my breath as I cross the street, pull my hood over my head, like he'd had his when we first met. I don't want to think about that night. About the death he'd stolen from me.

I want to think about what I'm going to take from him.

Because whether Jeremiah approves it or not, it'll be more than his life.

The forest is pitch black, the only sound that of the dirt beneath my feet as I walk down the path in the darkness. It occurs to me too late that maybe I should have just taken Nicolas with me. Whether he wanted to know what I was doing or not is irrelevant; if I had asked him, I think he likely would have come.

But he's long gone, the city at my back, the dark expanse of the woods before me. I wish there were more sounds, more bugs, more animals scurrying about the forest. It would feel more...natural. But there's next to nothing.

Just my feet.

I take a dirt path that forks to the left, brush the hood back from my head and pull the gun out from against my hip. I can hear my heartbeat in my head, and I try to stop looking over my shoulder. If someone is watching me, they'll know I'm nervous. It's not a good thing to show nerves.

I steel my spine, put one foot in front of the other, and ignore the shapes my mind conjures around me; shadows becoming bears which become leering men. And when a bat flies overhead, the flap of its wings startling the shit out of me, it becomes Lucifer himself.

I huff out a laugh.

I have no reason to be scared. It's not like Lucifer is going to kill me, even if he does see me in here. I don't know what he wants me for, but it's probably worse than death.

He's an Unsaint after all.

I've survived worse than death.

But the rest of the Unsaints...they might actually kill me.

I like the cool feel of the gun in my hand, and I brush my thumb around the barrel, a zip of confidence lighting down my arm with the touch.

I'm safe.

I repeat that to myself like a mantra as I edge closer to the river.

The house down here is supposedly a family home, from way back in the day. But I'd never known anyone to live in it. This park is government property. I'm surprised they'd never torn the thing down.

And then, too soon, it looms in front of me.

Utter darkness, the river glimmering beyond it under the light of the stars. I look up at the second floor. There are curtains closed at every window, but even still, there isn't a hint of light anywhere in that house. I can't imagine the Unsaints staying here. They supposedly left town for a while after last Halloween, but they have more money than I'd ever see in my life. They can, and do, afford better lodgings than this.

Maybe Trey had been wrong. Maybe Jeremiah had fed him this information precisely because he knew I'd try to ferret it out of Trey. Maybe no one lives here, and I'm playing into my brother's trap, like I always do.

But maybe not.

I take a step closer, eyeing the wooden porch. There are dried leaves scattered around the screen door, but otherwise, it looks shockingly clean.

I think about turning around.

I think about jogging back down the path, jogging out of the park, finding Nicolas and speeding back to the mansion. I think this might have been one of my worst ideas ever. But before I can spin around, I hear something.

From behind me.

I aim the gun, arm extended, opposite hand on my elbow, and then I turn. But I don't say a word. The dark forest stares back at me.

I try to swallow my fear. I have nothing to be afraid of.

I have a gun and I know how to use it. And besides that, it was probably just an animal. Never mind that it sounded like a boot scraping against gravel.

Or maybe it's Nicolas, trying to fuck with me.

I'm safe.

I say it again and again and again.

Safe.

And then a hand clamps over my mouth.

I know better than to pull the trigger, but I draw my arms in, try to elbow whoever is on my back. But their other arm pins mine to my sides, forcing the gun to point down, useless at the tips of my fingers.

I try to breathe. Inhale. Exhale. Repeat. I try to calm my pulse, try to fucking think. But right now, I can't think at all. My mind is blank, my fear nearly palpable.

Because this person's hand over my mouth, I can smell it.

Cigarettes, but a particular kind. I don't know the brand; I've never smoked. But this scent is burned into my memory like so many other things I want to forget.

"You're scared of me, Lilith?"

Lucifer's voice is as hoarse as I remember it, his words brushing against my ear. I try not to shiver in his arms. Try, and fail.

He breathes a laugh against the back of my neck, then rests his chin on my head. His grip hasn't loosened, not even a little. I don't want to give him the benefit of squirming, of trying to uselessly fight back. Because I might have been trained, but something about the way he's holding me, about the way he's making sure the gun is pointed down...I know he and the Unsaints have been trained, too.

I hold still.

"Ah, Lilith. I've been waiting a long, long time for you to come back to hell." He pulls me tighter against him, and I can feel *him*, wanting *me*, against my back. Bile rises to my throat.

Not because I don't want it.

But because I do.

And I hate that part of myself. I'm not an escort anymore, and I'm not his Lilith anymore, either. There's no Death Oath between us tonight. We are nothing. And whether it's tonight or on Halloween night to appease my brother, I'm going to kill him. And I'm going to make him suffer while I do.

But I still can't deny the fact that some sick part of me likes this.

He moves his hand from my mouth, resting it against my throat. He presses his lips against my hair.

"Don't you have anything to say to me?" he whispers.

I swallow. My mouth has gone suddenly dry. I have a lot to say. But I'm forgetting all of it. Every word.

"You're staying here," is the only thing I manage.

It isn't a question, but he murmurs his agreement against my head anyway. "And you came for me," he breathes. "Did Jeremiah send you here?"

I stiffen. I didn't expect that. Nicolas had been wrong. He knows where I am.

Does he know who Jeremiah is to me?

I shake my head. "No," I answer him honestly.

"Put the gun down." A command.

"No." A defiance. Because I'm done with people telling me what to do tonight. Nicolas, my brother, now Lucifer.

I want to do this my way. And that is *with* the gun in my hand.

Lucifer rasps a laugh. Then his fingers curl around my throat. He slowly increases the pressure until I can't breathe. His fingers dig into the bruises already there, from my brother and Kristof.

A whimper escapes my lips without my permission. I don't want to show any weakness in front of him, not after the year I've spent pining over the boy who left me in the asylum. But the bruises hurt. My face burns.

Lucifer's hand stills, and he lets up on the pressure, but he doesn't let go. "You didn't hurt that easily a year ago, Lilith," he purrs.

I don't dare breathe. I can't draw air into my lungs. The woods are so dark, I feel as if I'm in a dream. This might not even be real. But a cool wind blows through the trees, rattling branches, and I snap back to reality.

This is my life.

I'm in Lucifer's arms, once more. And I have the disadvantage, once more.

Before my mind can catch up with reality, Lucifer spins me around, and takes the gun from my hand. And I let him. My fingers don't work quickly enough to stop him.

Suddenly, he holds the weapon. But then again, he's always held the weapon.

He lets me go, takes a step back from me.

Then arms fold around me, strong and firm and even before I hear his deep voice, I know it's Ezra. He whispers in my ear, "Did you miss us?"

And I gasp, struggling against his grip.

He holds firm and all the while, Lucifer just watches.

"What the fuck?" I hiss to both of them, trying to twist my head, to see Ezra's massive form behind me. But he isn't budging. I stop trying to fight, save that for when I can run away.

"Lucifer," I nearly plead.

I can see his midnight blue eyes blazing in the night, and a lock of curly black hair falls over his brow, from beneath his hood. He wears a black hoodie, like I do, and fitted black jogging pants. But it isn't any of that that makes my breath catch in my throat.

It's his skin.

His face.

We're still close enough to share breath, even if we aren't touching. And I realize this is the first time I've ever seen his skin. Before, he'd had on the makeup. But now... his skin is pale, made more so by the night. His jawline is defined, cheekbones nearly hollow. He's beautiful.

He'd been beautiful that night, too, but disguised.

And as his eyes roam over my own face, coming to rest on my lips, I realize he's seeing me, too, for the first time without the pale makeup I'd worn that night.

His full lips curve into a smile. They're pale pink, his top one slightly bigger than the bottom. They're beautiful. They're dangerous. Just like him.

He holds the gun loose at his side, but I'm acutely aware of it.

And then his eyes go past my lips, and his expression changes. He raises the gun, his arm bent at the elbow, the barrel pointing at the canopy above us. He's frowning, and his eyes are narrowed, his jaw locked.

The hand not holding the gun goes to my throat again, and I wince, ready for him to squeeze. Ezra senses my movements because he tightens his grip around me.

But Lucifer doesn't squeeze my throat. He brushes his fingers lightly against my skin, making goosebumps rise down my arms.

"Are those bruises?" he asks, his voice taking a darker, deadlier tone.

I had forgotten. Or rather, I didn't really expect I'd see him tonight. And I never expected him to see me. And not like this. Not this close.

But with his words, the memory of Kristof comes rushing back. Of me stabbing his leg. Of him slamming me against the wall. My brother stepping in at the last minute.

I try not to think about it. Now is so not the time.

It seems too late, though, because Lucifer cocks his head, his finger trailing up to my jaw. "They are, aren't they?" he murmurs. I can smell his breath, feel it on my brow as I look up at him. He smells like cigarettes and spearmint.

"Who did it?" Ezra growls.

I don't answer him and Ezra snorts, pulling me tighter against him.

I ball my hands into fists, but I'm not going anywhere. Ezra has my arms. Lucifer has my gun. I don't have a chance.

"Why?" I challenge Lucifer. It's time for me to find my voice again.

His hand goes back down by his side, away from my jaw. "Why what, Lilith?"

It feels so good to hear his voice.

And I fucking hate it.

"Why did you burn down Brooklin's house?"

Ezra laughs, but with a look from Lucifer, he falls silent. I can feel his chest rising and falling against my shoulders.

Lucifer smiles coldly, looking down at the ground between us. "That's what you want to ask me?" he says softly, dragging his gaze along my body, up to meet my eyes again. "I think you want to know something else, don't you, Lilith?"

I shake my head. "I don't want anything from you." I dig my nails so hard into my palms I know it'll draw blood. Just like I had that night. The pale white scar on my thigh is there to prove that.

He has a matching one. But he had more, before me.

He seems to be thinking about my own scar now as he glances down at my legs, a smile playing on his lips. "I remember your blood," he says quietly, taking a step closer.

I'm frozen, in between these two Unsaints. Once more, me and Lucifer are close enough to touch. But I won't reach for him. Not even to try to get the gun back. I will never reach for him again. "I remember tasting you," he murmurs, chin angled down as he takes me in. Like he wants to devour me. "I remember everything about you, Lilith. About that night. And the first thing you want to ask me is about your boss's fuck toy?"

Ezra barks a laugh, and I feel his chest rumble behind me.

But that means Lucifer doesn't know I'm Jeremiah's sister. And I sure as hell won't tell him. If he knows, he might go thinking that I mean something to Jeremiah. That he can use me as a bargaining chip in whatever war he's waging with my brother. Because there's more to this than me. The Unsaints aren't here just for me. They wouldn't care that much.

And Jeremiah might get me back if they take me. But he won't pay anything for me.

"This was really brave, Lilith. To come out here by yourself." He slides the gun into the waistband of his pants. I want to tell him that's stupid, but I don't care enough to.

That, and I catch a glimpse of the V leading down into his low-slung pants and I've suddenly gone completely stupid. I remember the tattoo on his thigh.

I snap my eyes to his, but not before he notices where I'm staring. He lets out a little laugh.

"Really brave," he drawls, stepping closer to me, his chest brushing my shoulder. "And really stupid."

I back away, farther into Ezra, who laughs again. He presses his nose into the crook of my neck, and I hear him inhale.

"God, you smell fucking good." He lifts his head. "We should have her tonight, Luce," he croons.

Lucifer's gaze hardens, but he says nothing to Ezra. Instead, his next words are to me. "You can run, Lilith. But you can't hide." He shakes his head. "Not from me."

He nods to Ezra, who pushes me forward, and I fucking bolt, not daring to look back. Adrenaline springs through my body as fast as lightening and my shoes pound in the dirt with every hard step. I can't hear over my own heart, my own heavy breathing, but I don't think they'll follow me. Not yet.

They want to drag this out too. I have no idea why they're mad at me, what's gone down between them and my brother besides Brooklin's house and Jeremiah turning his back on the Unsaints. But I don't care. If they want to play, it'll give me time to run.

I only slow when I'm out of the forest completely, only look back when the lights of the city unfurl ahead.

They aren't there.

I cross the empty street, jog slowly down the sidewalk, to the intersection where me and Lucifer first met. My old apartment complex, my old life, is just around the corner.

I put a hand to my chest, feel my heart slam against my palm.

That isn't me anymore. Lucifer had kept a broken girl alive, only to turn her into a monster. He thought he was bad. He thought I was scared.

He has no fucking idea what I've done in the past year. What I've seen. What I've endured at the hands of my brother. He might fuck with me, but only one of us is going to get fucked. And Lilith is going to take back what's hers.

CHAPTER THIRTEEN

Halloween, One Year Ago

LUCIFER GETS DOWN on his knees.

He'd taken us down the staircase at the end of the hall, and we're underground, in what looks like it might have once been a cell. There's a wheelchair with a bottle of rum propped up on the seat of it, and a twin bed with a surprisingly white mattress. The cement floors are bare. There's rope in the corner of the room. And somewhere beyond this cell, I can hear someone moaning, and the unmistakable rhythmic pounding of two people fucking.

Lucifer rips a hole with his hands through my stockings, and then he looks up at me from the ground, glancing at the blade in my hand.

"Do you like pain?"

I don't know what to say. I can still taste him on my

lips. On my tongue. I want more of that. More of him. But I want him to have me, too.

I nod, hand him the blade with shaky hands. I don't know if I'm shaking from the vodka, from fear, confusion. Something else entirely.

His eyes hold mine as he puts the point of the knife against my skin. "It'll only hurt a little," he promises. And then, still looking up at me, he slides the blade across my skin.

It burns, but it's more than bearable.

He drops the knife, and I open my mouth to protest. To tell him he has to taste me, like I had tasted him.

But I don't get to say the words.

His tongue goes to my thigh, lapping up my blood. It stings, and I fucking love it. His tongue is hot, and his lips brush against my skin as he sucks more blood into his mouth, his hands gripping my upper thigh. So close to where I want his fingers to be. To where I want *him* to be. So close, but he won't give me that.

Not yet.

He runs his tongue tauntingly back and forth over the wound, and then he looks up at me once more.

"Get down here," he growls.

I do.

I fall to my knees on the concrete floor, and his mouth finds mine again. It isn't a sweet kiss. It isn't angry, either. It's possessive. It's dirty. Raw. I taste my blood on his tongue, and I bite his lip, hard.

He bites back, breaking the skin.

I whimper and he groans, his hands wrapping around my body. This is sin. And I never want to be good again.

His hands find my throat, fingers curling around me. He pulls back, then brings his lips to my ear. He kisses that sensitive spot between my ear and my neck, and then he bites me again, roughly.

"I don't care what you've done," he says, his words hot on my skin. "I don't care who you've been with, do you understand?"

My breath catches. We're talking about this again. I thought he would hate this part. I thought he didn't want to hear it. No one else did. It's why I never dated. And maybe he doesn't want to hear it, because I didn't want to hear about the pregnant girl. I don't want to think one of his firsts, one of the big ones, won't be with me. That might make me a horrible person. A crazy person. But I don't care.

I understand.

"Do you understand?" he asks me again, his fingers curling tighter around my throat.

I nod.

He groans in my ear, his breath hot against my skin.

"You're mine now, Lilith. You're mine from now on." One hand still on my throat, he drags the other possessively down my body, until he's *there*, in between my thighs. Right where I want him to be.

He grabs me, hard.

"This. It's mine." His hand goes back up, and he cups

one breast, and then the other, running his thumb over my nipples. "*Mine,*" he growls again.

He pulls away, one hand still on my throat. The other on my chest.

"All of you. You're fucking mine now."

I think of the girl. Of her baby. Of Atlas and the other Unsaints. Of what Ria had implied about them. About what they are. What they do. I think of all of that, but I don't care. Tonight, he isn't *him* and I sure as hell am not me. Because the 'me' that had left my apartment had wanted to die. The 'me' I had been mere hours ago was long gone, because if she hadn't been, I wouldn't be here now.

But I am.

He picks me up and throws me on the bed and I roll over, onto my back.

He reaches for something out of my sight, and then he kneels over, his eyes devouring me, one hand on my chest. He holds up a bottle like an offering.

Rum.

A twisted, sick communion that I won't refuse.

"Before you take this, there's something you have to say." He's still pressing one hand against my chest, still kneeling over me.

"What?" I ask him, curious.

"The Death Oath."

He drops the bottle on the bed and pins my wrists roughly above my head. He leans down, his mouth over mine as he speaks the words I'm to repeat back to him.

I bind myself to you tonight,
No matter the shift of the knife.
Through blood and bone,
Flesh and heart,
Death may come,
But we shall not part.

I repeat every line into his mouth, and keeping my wrists held together in one hand, he reaches for the bottle of rum, unscrews the cap with his teeth, and holds the bottle over my mouth.

"That means you're mine for tonight, Lilith, no matter what I do to you. And I don't feel like playing nice. I want to fuck the feel of every man you've ever had out of you." He runs his tongue down my throat. "Now open wide."

I open my mouth, flick my tongue out, and he smiles. Then he pours the liquor on my tongue, slowly, and I relish in the burn of it.

His mouth meets mine and we drink together, rum spilling over us until he tosses the bottle just like he'd tossed my gun. We don't need those things. Not right now. We're each other's own drugs. Each other's own weapons.

He slides the strap of my body suit down, and then seems to think the better of it. He stops, finds the knife in the floor of this underground room, and holds the blade up between us.

"Don't move," he warns me. "Or you might get another scar."

Maybe I should be afraid. Maybe I'm a fucking idiot. But I do as he says.

And then he cuts a line all the way down from my chest to my thighs. The point of the knife skims the skin on my belly, but I don't even flinch. He puts the knife down, and then pulls apart the rest of the fabric like it's nothing.

And even though I've been naked in front of many, many different men, in all types of positions and various stages of sobriety, under his gaze, I feel as if I might melt. As if the fire in my core could burn us both. His eyes, even in the darkness, are full of a longing, a wanting, that I'd never seen before. Not from any man. It's almost feral, what I see when he sees me.

He nudges my legs apart with his knee, his hands back on my wrists, pinning them above my head. He drinks me in with his eyes.

"Fuck, you have a perfect pussy."

Then he lowers himself onto me, his chest brushing up against mine, his body skimming the length of my own.

"Is this what you want, Lilith?" he asks.

I buck my hips, trying to feel him against me, but he pulls away, teasing me. My wrists burn but I don't want him to let go.

"Not until you've confessed," he purrs against my neck, trailing kisses down my chest. Then, his eyes on me, his tongue swirls against my nipple and I gasp. The world seems to spin. I know I've drank far too much to really enjoy this like I should, but I push that thought aside.

"Confess?" I whisper. I thought I'd already done that. How many more sins does he want to take from me?

He bites down on my nipple, then flicks his tongue over it, soothing the burn. He holds my gaze the entire time. He bites again, eyes boring into mine, and I see blood on the corner of his lip. My blood.

"Do you want to take over the world with me?" he asks, his voice husky, his lips brushing my skin.

I let out a little laugh. "I'd do anything with you."

He picks his head up at that, gazing down at me as if he's searching for the truth in my drunkenness. I see his throat bob as he swallows. I see that delicious vein in his neck that I want to run my tongue over. He lets go of my wrist, yanks off his hoodie, pulls down his pants. He's naked save for his boxer briefs, and his body is beautiful. Sculpted, smooth muscles, and I see his cock straining against black fabric. I see the skull tattooed on his thigh.

"After tonight," he says, voice hoarse, leaning back into me, "what about then?"

I blink. After tonight. I wasn't supposed to survive the night. This is supposed to be the end. Depression had visited me like a ghost in the night as far back as I could remember. I'm done drowning in the darkness. I want to finally die in it.

He grips my chin between his thumb and forefinger. "What about then?" he repeats, his voice cold.

I open my mouth, and he strokes his thumb over my swollen lip. I still taste his blood, and mine. He leans down, until we're nose to nose.

"Say you'll stay."

I take a shaky breath. It isn't a command, those words. It's more like a plea.

"Please say you'll stay," he urges me again, his voice more desperate. "You don't want to die." He makes those last words both a question and a threat.

I hear someone moaning again in the distance of this fucked up place. I swear I hear someone whispering, too. I'm getting dizzy, and Lucifer being on top of me, so close to me, begging me to live, it doesn't help me think.

I've been here before. Not emotionally, not like this with Lucifer. But I've blacked out more times than I'd like to count. And I've had far too much to drink tonight. I'm fading, and some small part of me is pissed off. I'll have to wake up in the morning, and this all might turn into a dream. Lucifer might be gone. I might be alone. And I'll have to find the gun in the morning light and work up the courage to pull the trigger all over again.

He presses a kiss to my lips, softer than all the others.

"Say you'll stay, and I'll always be here. We'll always be like this. You take my sins, I'll take yours."

I struggle to keep my eyes open. I'm not going to last much longer here with him.

"I'm afraid when I wake up, you'll be gone."

I should be ashamed of those words, but I'm not.

I don't want this strange, twisted boy to leave.

He kisses me again. "I'll never leave you," he swears. "And if you leave me...the Unsaints will know how to find you."

I close my eyes, a smile on my lips. "You don't know me."

He kisses my lips, my cheeks, my nose. My brow.

"I don't leave what's mine. We can take forever getting to know each other."

I sigh. "The baby..." I don't know why I say it, but it's one of many things I don't understand.

He runs his finger down my jaw, coming to rest on my throat. I keep my eyes closed, afraid what he might say next will hurt.

"We'll figure that out. With you by my side, we'll figure that out, Lilith."

I smile.

And then the world goes black.

I DREAM OF STRANGE THINGS.

Hands around my throat. A whisper in my ear. Someone screaming, far, far away. The sound of groans, of angry male voices. The feeling of love and lust wrapped into one. Into me. The shattering of a heart. A piercing, guttural cry for someone to "Stop!". But no one stops.

The lights go on.

Someone weeps.

I'm taken away, and the Unsaints are left scattered around the asylum.

CHAPTER FOURTEEN

Present

JEREMIAH SET US UP.

Or rather, he specifically told Nicolas he wouldn't be back until morning to see exactly what we might do in his absence.

And he's fucking waiting when Nicolas walks past the guards at the door, me over his shoulder in the black body bag.

I know Jeremiah is there before I see him. Before he says a word. Because Nicolas stills, his hands gripping me tighter around the waist.

Fuck's sake.

Gently, he sets me down, and I know he makes to unzip the bag when Jeremiah stops him.

"Don't," he says quietly. Calmly.

I hear Nicolas back away. I close my eyes tight,

wishing my brother a slow death. He is going to drag this out. He is going to keep me in here, make me learn my lesson. But I promise myself that if he throws me to Kristof again, I will run away and never come back.

Ever.

I'll still kill Lucifer for him, because it's for me, too. But I'm not going to do anymore of his bidding if he puts me in a position to be raped again.

"Is this what you want?" he asks quietly. From the sound of his voice, and the nearness, I know he's kneeling down beside me.

I roll my eyes, unseen by anyone but maybe the devil himself.

"Fuck off."

Sure, maybe I should keep my mouth shut. It's one in the morning. No matter the hours of the Rain mansion, no one is really themselves in the night. We wear masks when the sun goes down. Our dirtiest deeds come out to play. Our ugly souls. In the night, we are our wildest form.

My brother is no exception.

He yanks back the zipper on the bag and hauls me out by my throat, crushing my windpipe in the process. Even though I know I shouldn't, even though I know it's not how to get out of a hold like this, my hands fly to his fingers, trying to peel him off of me. I'm panicking.

Nicolas has my gun, my knife is in my back pocket, and when Jeremiah slams me against the wall beside the sliding glass doors of the entrance, I see spots.

"What did you say to me?" he asks me, my feet dangling off the floor.

My throat is going to look like a fucking plum when these boys are done with me.

I don't bother trying to speak. I know I won't get a word out.

"Jeremiah, it was my fault. I took her." Nicolas's voice. And then I see him, behind my brother, reaching out a hand. Like he might actually lay one on Jeremiah. His eyes are wide, and I realize he's scared. Guards are scattered about the room, Kristof being one of them. He's watching me with a wry smile. I don't even get the satisfaction of seeing his bandaged leg. He wears pants that cover it.

Motherfucker.

Jeremiah's jade eyes are narrowed. He's wearing a suit, a crisp white shirt under his blazer. In that moment, there's nothing I want more than to get his own blood all over it. Fuck him.

He lets me go, throwing me against the wall one more time before he does. He turns his back to me, starts to pace, his hands clench into fists.

"What should I do with you?" he asks loudly. No one answers. Nicolas looks relieved he let go of me; his shoulders sag, and his eyes flick to mine, his brows going up, almost like he's apologizing.

But this is my mess.

I put my hand to my throat, rubbing at my sore muscles and tendons there.

"Kill me," I answer for him. "It's what I was trying to

do when you dragged me from the asylum last year. Before you and your fucking Unsaints fucked that up. Fucking go ahead and help me out. End it now. I'm nothing but a pain in your ass. I will *always be* nothing but a pain in your ass."

He stops pacing, but he doesn't look at me.

Now Nicolas looks furious. With me. Kristof is leering at me. I'm glad Trey isn't here. He had told me where Lucifer was. I don't want him to get the brunt of my brother's bullshit, too. I wonder where Brooklin is. If she's getting a full-body massage in her suite on my brother's floor. I have no idea how she deals with his bullshit. If he's like this with me, I know he has to be worse with her. He's ordered her around in front of everyone, commanded her here and there. Once, I'd seen him raise his hand as if he were going to hit her, but he hadn't.

That was the only time I'd seen them argue.

But that's because Brooklin keeps her mouth shut. Brooklin is meek. She cows to my brother.

I don't. I won't.

Damn him.

"That's what you want?" he finally asks me. His voice is lowered. But I know that doesn't mean he's calm. It means he's angrier.

"Yep," I say in mock cheerfulness. "Put a goddamn bullet through your sister's brain and bury me with the rest of your thugs." I shrug. "Or burn me. I don't give a shit." I sag against the wall, letting my head tilt back, stuffing my hands in my hoodie pockets. I talk a good game. I really don't care if he does kill me. But I'm fucking tired.

Today has been a *day*. And considering my life, that's saying something.

Besides, Lucifer won't get out of my head. He's right here. He might have always been right here. He's with *Julie*. They have a child. I'm going to kill him.

Jeremiah turns around to face me, finally. He has a smile on his face.

"Okay," he says quietly. Then he reaches inside his blazer and pulls out a gun. He cocks it, aims at my head. "If that's what you want, *Sis*."

Nicolas freezes. He had been rubbing his hand over his jaw, but now he's frozen, staring at my brother with an open mouth.

Hell, even Kristof looks uncomfortable, which is saying something. I feel quite sure he would have no qualms about fucking my dead body. But suddenly he isn't leering at me anymore. He looks like he's holding his breath, his gaze darting from me to my brother and back to me.

Jeremiah hasn't faltered.

I haven't moved. I don't want to. Let him do it.

I try to dare him with my eyes. I won't look away. If he's going to pull that trigger, if he's going to kill his sister, he's going to watch my expression. He's going to stare into my eyes. I will *not* look away. I'll let him see the complete and total *lack* of betrayal in my gaze. I always expected it would come to this. Unsaints are unhinged, and he might not be one of them now, but he was bred one. Besides, this hotel has seen enough death, these people have caused enough of it.

What's a little more to add to the body count?

I count to three in my mind, but Jeremiah still hasn't pulled the trigger.

"Don't pussy out now," I hiss at him.

He laughs.

And then he fires.

The shot rings out in the foyer, my ears ringing, and I jump, startled, but otherwise, I force myself not to move. I'm still staring at him. We share blood. He just shot at me.

But he'd aimed high.

Nicolas is staring above my head. Kristof has gone pale.

I step away from the wall and look up at the cream-colored paint. A bullet hole is lodged in the wall, a foot above my head.

He left a lot of room.

I twist my head back to look at him. He lowers the gun, and I can't tell what he's thinking. He doesn't look pleased. Or arrogant. He doesn't even look angry anymore.

He looks disappointed. And I feel pretty damn sure he's disappointed with himself for not being able to do it. I close the space between us, my boots echoing on the marble floor. When we are nearly nose-to-nose, or as close as we will ever be considering our height difference, I stop.

I lean in close to him, whisper the words against his

neck. "Next time, don't miss." And then I walk away, enjoying the silence that follows me.

▼

I SHOULD GO TO BED.

But I can't. I'm exhausted, but my mind is running a million miles a minute. I'm proud of myself for barely flinching. Proud I didn't try to stop him. That I hadn't moved. I'm still genuinely shocked he had purposefully missed me.

But that isn't what I'm thinking about when I sit on my balcony, the sliding door open at my back. I have my legs stretched out, draped over a black iron chair across from me, identical to the one I'm sitting on.

I had downed a rum and Diet from the minifridge in my room, and I should have had more than one, but I don't have the energy to pour another. Instead, I'd set the glass on the nightstand and walked out here in my pajamas; an oversized shirt and black cotton shorts.

The night is cooler than it was when I was in Raven Park. I gaze out at the lights down below in the city, Alexandria powering through in the middle of the night. The university is there. Someone my age is having their first legal drink down there. Someone is getting fucked for the first time. Someone is having their heart ripped in two, probably not for the last time. Someone is dying.

I feel nothing.

I'm numb as I watch the city.

I lean back in my chair, wrap my arms around myself, and close my eyes. I didn't bother to bring a knife out here. If someone comes for me, well, for all I care, they can fucking have me.

But when I close my eyes, it's no one in the hotel I see. No one here I think about, even though I'm certain most everyone under this enormous roof wants me dead.

No.

It's *his* midnight blue eyes that flash in my mind. Pale, smooth skin. A dimple in one cheek. A sharp jawline.

My eyes fly open, and instinctively, they fall on the silver scar on my thigh. Three inches wide, pearly white. I run a finger over it, but the edges are smooth. I wish they weren't. I want to feel the jaggedness of that knife.

I want to feel some physical representation of what Lucifer did to my heart. And now he's playing with me. He's waiting for me. Does he know Jeremiah wants me to kill him? Did he burn down Brooklin's house as a message from all of the Unsaints, to tell my brother they're coming for him? Or for me?

And why?

The betrayal?

My brother refuses to talk to me about the Unsaints. About Lover's Death. About the Death Oath. About what exactly he saw that night.

Burning down Brooklin's house had been a message.

A warning.

She never stayed there anymore. No girl ever stayed apart from Jeremiah once he decided to make them his.

They never lasted this long either, and aside from a few brawls and knife torture, I'd never known Jeremiah to seek retribution against someone who had offended his girl. He replaced them too quickly to develop that kind of feeling. He was protective in that he didn't want to share what was his, but aside from *me*, I'd never known him to be up in arms possessive. He tossed them aside, in the trash.

Literally. At least, I wouldn't have been surprised. I certainly never saw any of his exes, and I couldn't imagine he'd let them live after what they knew.

Jeremiah and the Order of Rain is always under investigation from the police. The Rain mansion as a whole is always under investigation. But the thing about police is that they like money, too. And if you pay enough, they'll look the other way. And if you take care of their families, they'll pretend to be deaf to the rumors.

And Jeremiah paid better than anyone in Alexandria. In the whole goddamn state, probably.

Except for, maybe, the Unsaints themselves.

They're above it all.

If he'd killed me downstairs in that foyer, no one would have known except the people in there. And no one would have cared.

Even Nicolas would have moved on. He'd seen death on repeat since he'd started working with my brother. Probably before then, too.

Kristof would've toasted Jeremiah later on in their "club"; the biggest bar in the hotel that was for "boys only".

Fuck them all.

I glance down at the pavement below, the marble fountain of a gargoyle. I wonder if I'll die if I jump. I'm only on the seventh floor, but there are about twenty more above me. I could climb to the top.

I glance up at the stars. It's strange to know that Lucifer might be looking up at the same ones. Might be thinking of my death, too. He might be wondering what it would feel like to snap my neck in his hands.

Or he might be remembering what my blood tastes like.

Like I'm remembering his.

I wonder if he has more kids with Julie. I didn't think to ask Nicolas that. I'm not sure I want to know. But it'll make it hurt a little more. It'll twist the knife in a little deeper, and maybe that's exactly what I need. Because even though I will kill him, and gladly, I can't stop fucking thinking about him.

The taste of him.

His hands on me.

His voice in my ear.

His scent.

His blood.

His lies.

I press my palm against my forehead.

I want him out.

You can run Lilith, but you can't hide. Not from me.

Same to you, Lucifer.

Same to you.

CHAPTER FIFTEEN

Present

I WAKE up the next morning on the floor of my balcony.

At first, I don't know where I am. I scramble to my feet, and there's a sharp ass pang in my foot. I wince, looking down. Shattered glass. I had had more drinks last night, and now, judging by the trail of blood pooling down my foot, I'd just stepped in it.

My face hurts. I touch my jaw, flexing it. I'd slept out here, on the hard concrete of the balcony floor.

The sun is rising, the city just waking up. Or going to bed.

Glass is everywhere. In moments like these, I'm glad my asshole of a brother has an entire staff of housekeepers. Part of me wants to dig my hands into the glass, to see more of my blood paint this balcony. To remind me of Lucifer.

But part of me wants to never think of him again. It's why I'd drank so much last night, all by myself. That, and the fact that my own brother almost killed me.

I limp into the bedroom, leaving the balcony door open, letting the cool October air rush in. I am, technically, *off* until Halloween night, when Jeremiah wants me to get rid of Lucifer. But I'm not going to be that kind.

Today, I'll find Julie and the kid.

Today, I'll remind Lucifer of all those promises he'd made a year ago.

But first, I need to get the glass out of my foot and get dressed. Because Jeremiah is going to have to let me do this my way.

I walk into the bathroom, black marble and bigger than most people's living rooms. I sit on the edge of the tub after grabbing some tweezers, and I get to work, digging in my skin to find the edge of the sliver I can see glistening in the lights from the bathroom.

The blood makes it difficult to see it all, but I find a good angle and clamp the tweezers down, ready to pull. The sliver is tiny, but it can't stay in there. If it does, I'll be dealing with more than blood on my hands.

Swiftly, I yank it out, gasping with the relief of it, and holding up the sliver to the light. Tiny, jagged, painful. I go to stand, but the world seems to spin around me. I certainly haven't lost enough blood to make me dizzy, but I'm dehydrated, and exhausted. I stumble against the counter, setting the tweezers and glass down as I do, catching myself on the marble.

I turn on the sink, splash water on my face, in my mouth.

There are circles under my eyes, which are red and look eerie. The silver of my iris against the veins of my eyes make me look like a monster from a horror movie. I smile at myself.

Good. I want Lucifer to know a monster is coming after him.

I tilt my chin up, take in the state of my throat. The bruises are ugly, splotches of purple and blue. I'll be damned if anyone else puts their hand around my throat again. Unless I want them to.

"Good morning, Sis."

Jeremiah's voice makes me flinch, and I bite my tongue to keep from crying out. Bite it so hard I taste iron.

I glance at him in the mirror. He's leaning against the frame of the bathroom door, his arms crossed. He's dressed in a long-sleeve black shirt, and basketball shorts. Sweat has dampened his dark hair.

"Came to visit me after your morning workout?" I ask, keeping my tone even and looking back at myself in the mirror. "I feel special."

Then I turn to him, leaning against the counter and crossing my arms, mimicking his posture. "Or did you just come to finish what you started last night?"

His pale green eyes don't falter. He holds my gaze. Nothing about him suggests he feels bad about what he did last night. I still think he probably regrets *missing* my head.

"If I wanted you dead, Sid, you'd be dead."

I can't argue with that. I'm sure it's true. At the very least, he believes it to be true.

"Then why are you here?"

He glances at the floor, the trail of blood from my foot, which is still bleeding. Band-Aids aren't my favorite thing, and I'd wanted to shower first.

"What happened?" he asks me, cocking his head.

I want to bash it against the wall. I shrug. "Accident."

He turns, glancing at the open balcony doors, no doubt seeing the shattered glass outside. He sighs and looks back at me.

"Long night?"

I huff a laugh. "My brother tried to kill me. I got hauled around in a body bag because he doesn't trust me. And my throat looks like a thunderstorm. So, yeah," I lift one shoulder in a lazy shrug, "I guess you could say that."

He smiles. It looks strangely genuine. "A thunderstorm?" he echoes, eyes flicking to my throat.

I swallow. "Yeah. Black and blue with strikes of blinding light, reminding me why it's best to stay away from storms."

He's quiet a moment and then he takes a step toward me, tipping his chin up, looking at the ceiling. He's going to say something he doesn't want to say. I wonder if he's left his guards outside for this very reason. Or maybe they're in my foyer, hanging onto every word. Wondering how much they'll be able to rough me up and get away with it now that Jeremiah and I are at odds again.

But we've always been at odds.

"Whatever it is you want to say, *Brother*, spit it out."

He angles his head down and holds my gaze. "I'm sorry."

I can't possibly have heard him right. I frown, shaking my head. "Didn't quite catch that."

He slides his hands in his pockets. "I'm not going to say it again, Sid. But last night was too far. It shouldn't have happened."

I'm not quite sure my brother isn't having some sort of seizure. He can't possibly mean what he's saying. I shake my head, looking for his angle. Waiting for the next ask. The next thing to make all of this make sense.

But it only gets weirder.

He jerks his head to the edge of the tub.

"Sit," he says.

"No."

He rolls his eyes and pushes past me, into the walk-in closet off of my bathroom. "Where are your medical supplies?"

I snort. "Medical supplies? I don't have those."

"Band-Aids? Nothing?" he asks, rifling through the cabinet that has normal things like pads and tampons, but no *medical supplies*. Before I can tell him to fuck off, he finds the box of Band-Aids I must have had tucked away against the wall in the cabinet.

He pulls them out with a smile and then glances around the rest of my closet. It's not stuffed full of shit, but what's in there is a plethora of hoodies, jeans, and sneakers.

"Do you need more money?" he asks me, frowning. "These clothes...this is literally all you wear?" He tugs on the sleeve of a bright pink hoodie.

"Fuck off," I say, relishing in the opportunity.

He clucks his tongue and lets the hoodie go, coming to stand at the tub again.

"Come on, Sid, sit there, please."

Please.

My brother never says please. I throw up my hands, wondering if maybe his next tactic is to drown me in the tub, and I sit on the edge, extend my bare feet into the empty porcelain.

He slips out of his shoes and socks and steps over me, sitting on the opposite edge, close to the wall. He grabs a washcloth from the ledge and sets the box of Band-Aids down.

"Here," he says, indicating his thigh. "Put your foot up."

"Why are you doing this?" I ask without moving, leaning against the wall opposite him, my feet firmly planted in the tub. "Are you going to inject some poison into my cut?"

"You really are testing my patience, Sid. Just give me your fucking foot."

There he is. The real Jeremiah peeking through.

I gingerly lift my foot, examining the dried blood, and

the wet blood, still coming from my inner arch. I set my heel on his thigh, and he reaches over to turn on the faucet, testing the temperature of the water as he does so. When it's sufficiently warm, he puts the washcloth under it, rings it out, and then, carefully, starts to clean my foot.

I never knew my brother could be so careful. I'd never known him to be gentle, *ever*.

We sit in silence as he works, the white cloth turning red. He rinses it out, rings it, and starts all over again. When the dried blood is taken care of it, he rinses it again, and then holds the cloth to the wound, pressing gently, stopping the blood.

I cross my arms over my chest. Something tight is in my throat, and I swallow it down before I speak.

"Why are you doing this?" I finally manage to ask.

He doesn't look up from my foot, the cloth still pressed against the wound. "I should've taken better care of you," he says quietly.

I stiffen. He notices, and with one hand still holding the cloth, with the other, he draws circles softly against my ankle, then works his hand up my calf, massaging me. His hand goes back down, then up again, and I slowly relax against his touch.

"I should've been better," he continues. "I should have found you, when we were separated." He finally meets my gaze. "I went through hell, Sid. But I don't even know what you went through. Where you went. I tried to find you when I got free. When I found my place with the

Unsaints." I watch him swallow and wonder how much of his lore is true. Had he killed his family? Had they locked him in a cage? For the first time I can remember, my heart hurts for my brother.

"I had been looking for you for a long time. I knew you had somehow made it to North Carolina, too." He shakes his head at the miracle. He sighs. "I always remembered you liked Halloween, when you were a kid."

I did. I had begged our mom to take me costume shopping, every single year since I could talk. She never did, but I found shit around the house to be a witch or a cat or anything that wasn't me.

"When I found you at the asylum..." He blows out a breath and shakes his head, finally removing the cloth from my foot. The bleeding has stopped, but I don't move. He keeps a grip on my ankle. "I didn't know it was you, before then. If I had known...I would have never let you go, Sid. I would have never let Lucifer have you." The leader of the Unsaint's name comes out like a growl. "Lucifer was the worst of us. And I was so angry. So goddamn angry that I'd let you get *there*. That it had taken me so long."

I bite my lip, tears welling up in my eyes. I brush my hand roughly over my face, trying to hold them back. He had shot a gun just above my head, just last night. I'm looking for the trick in this, because the truth is...I want what he's saying to be true. I want a big brother. A real one. One that cares. That doesn't let men like Kristof put their filthy fucking hands on me.

"And I took it all out on you," he's saying. "I punished you with the bodies and the death because I was terrified that would be *you*, if you weren't careful. I'm terrified they'll come for you. They never forgive. And I put all that pain I'd felt for you, all that regret I had about you, and I just unleashed it. On *you*." His eyes are shining. I've never seen my brother cry. I've never seen him come close to it. But his green eyes are glittering with tears. He strokes my ankle again, pulling his lip between his teeth before he lets out an unsteady breath.

"I'm sorry, Sid. I don't want things to be like this."

I can't speak. I don't know what to say. I realize my hands are shaking, and I clench them into fists. I just stare at Jeremiah, trying to find the trick. The nasty surprise. But his face is open, unguarded, probably the only time in his entire fucking life.

He slowly sets my foot down and then he stands, crossing the space in the tub between us. He kneels before me, between my legs, his hands on my thighs. He doesn't know it, but his hand covers that pearly white scar Lucifer had given me. Maybe he does know it. Maybe he doesn't want to think about it.

"I love you, Sid. I've always loved you. And I missed you every day we were apart." His hands squeeze my thighs, gently. "I want us to be different."

I shake my head. "Why?" I croak out. "Why now?"

"Last night I aimed a gun at your head, to teach you a lesson. To show you the monsters that are outside these walls. But I was the fucking monster last night. I'm so sorry, Sid." He reaches out a hand, puts it gently around the back of my neck and pulls me to him. I press my brow against his, looking down at him.

My beautiful, cold brother. Crying at my feet.

I nod, my lip trembling. "Okay," I manage to say. "Okay. Let's do this differently."

And then I can't hold back the tears anymore, and for the first time in my life, I cry on my brother's shoulder.

▼

Jeremiah himself has the glass on the balcony taken care of. And it's Jeremiah I stand beside when he holds a gun in his hands, pointed at someone else entirely when we are in the meeting room. I usually don't go in here. Jeremiah calls me *after* a corpse is created. Before one, he briefs his men here. I have no part in that.

But he had asked me here this morning, after I had taken a shower and bandaged up my foot. He'd called me to watch him take care of someone.

I didn't know what to expect when I slid into my seat, across from Nicolas at the table. Brooklin sat at the head of the table, one leg crossed over the other, looking bored. But she'd actually bidden me good morning which has never happened once before in the six months we've been living under the same enormous roof.

I only inclined my head in response, but it was something. I didn't know what type of epiphany Jeremiah had

had last night, or if Nicolas had said something to him, or if he was on drugs. I liked it, but it made me uneasy. I felt like I was walking on eggshells. Like anything I did slightly wrong would disappoint him and make this all disappear.

And right now, I feel as if I'm holding my breath.

Three guards, Trey included, stand around the room, but Jeremiah is pointing a gun at his best guard.

Kristof.

Kristof is wearing a suit, his own gun at his hip, and he's holding his massive hands up in submission, shaking his head, darting his eyes to me and back to the gun as he stumbles over excuses.

"I'm sorry," he's saying, "I didn't mean to hurt her. You told me...you told me that she was mine for the night—"

"I didn't tell you to rape her," Jeremiah replies coolly. His gaze flicks to mine. "Look at her throat," he purrs. "Tell me what you see."

Kristof does. He isn't surprised, of course. Even in the hoodie I wear now over my jean shorts, the bruises are, unfortunately, visible. I had thought to wrap a scarf around my neck, but then thought the better of. No need to hide war wounds here in this mansion.

"I see..." Kristof trails off, his shoulders sagging, his face scrunching up as he looks back at my brother. "I'm sorry, Rain, I didn't mean to—"

I roll my eyes. We all know he did, in fact, mean to. We all know he would have finished the job, too, even after I stabbed him, if my brother hadn't intervened. But

I'm not sure what Jeremiah's next move is. He's a murderer. If he pulls the trigger, I won't be all that surprised. But to do it in front of everyone like this...it seems rash.

He sighs, but still aims the gun at Kristof. Everyone in the room seems on edge. Even Nicolas's thigh is bouncing up and down under the table. The only one who doesn't seem to care is Brooklin, glancing at her manicured nails as if she can't wait to get the hell to spin class or a waxing appointment or to trim her pixie cut or some shit.

"Sid, what do you think I should do?" Jeremiah asks me, his eyes trained on Kristof.

I shift in my seat. What the fuck? "I don't know, Jeremiah. Whatever you think is best."

His lips twitch into a smile and I see Nicolas bite his lip. "But what do *you* think is best?"

I consider the question. What do I think is best? Obviously, Kristof is a piece of shit. But so is every single person in this room, for different reasons, me included. None of us are saints. We're the opposite of saints. We're all *unsainted*, whether we're the spawn of the Society of 6 or not.

I drum my fingers on the table. "Let him live," I finally say.

Nicolas exhales across from me and nods in my direction, as if I made the right choice. I guess even unsaints have some sort of twisted moral code.

"Really?" Jeremiah asks, sounding surprised. But he still doesn't look at me. He's enjoying watching Kristof squirm. I think that letting Kristof live might present a problem for my brother in the future. Kristof will be resentful of this little show. He'll start to hate Jeremiah, if he doesn't already. That might not bode well for my brother.

But for now...

"Why not?" I ask. "Let him live. Let's move on for now."

I think for a split-second Jeremiah is going to pull the trigger anyway. His mouth is pressed into a thin line as he glares at Kristof, and Kristof actually whimpers, flinching as if he's getting ready to die.

But then Jeremiah lowers the gun.

"For now," he agrees, tucking the weapon away. "But if you touch my sister again"—he looks around the room now as he speaks—"if *any* of you touch my sister, I will fucking blow your head off."

Silence greets his words.

I smile. "Let's get started?" I ask, cocking my head. Surely there's something else we all came here for.

Jeremiah nods, and tosses a smile my way. Then he sits down opposite Brooklin, at the other end of the table. Kristof tries to get his composure back, tugging on his blazer as he takes up his position on the wall. He looks down at his feet.

"Let's get started," Jeremiah echoes. He looks to me. "I've got another job for you, before your big Halloween night. If you want it."

I stop drumming my fingers, place my palms flat on

the table. "Oh?" I ask, trying to keep my expression bored. Disinterested. But something twists in my gut. Something is warning me I'm not going to like what my brother has to say next.

Jeremiah nods, rubs his hands together. "One of our guys was killed this morning." He gives that information without a hint of emotion.

"Which guy?" I ask.

He shakes his head. Clearly someone I don't know. "Doesn't matter. A runner." For drugs. "And the shipment was stolen, over the border." Mexico. I don't know much about Jeremiah's jobs, outside of the ones he showed me the result of, but I know what those words mean. They mean war.

"Who did it?" I ask.

He flashes me a smile. "Lucifer. The Unsaints."

My heart sinks. But I had seen Lucifer last night. And while neither Nicolas nor my brother had bothered to ask me where I had gone when I snuck off, I'm sure they might have had an idea.

"Lucifer himself?" I press. "Which one?"

Jeremiah shakes his head. "One of the devils," he replies easily. "One of their people."

I swallow. "Okay," I say. "What do you want me to do?"

Jeremiah exchanges a look with Nicolas. "Find his baby. Find his girl."

I wait, holding my breath.

"Kill the girl. Kill all of the fucking Unsaints if you find them, too."

This motherfucker. No wonder he'd played the big brother card earlier. No wonder he'd held a gun to Kristof's head. He wanted to show me he'd do anything for me, and in turn, I should be willing to do anything for him. But what he doesn't know, what he doesn't seem to get, is that I'm as fucked up as he is. As ruthless.

"Okay," I say, lifting one shoulder in a lazy shrug. "Tell me where they are."

Silence greets those words. Even Brooklin's mouth drops open, and I see the bright pink gum on her tongue. But she doesn't dare say a word.

Jeremiah, for his part, looks impressed. He nods, as if confirming something to himself. "You'll meet with Nicolas around noon, he'll give you all the information."

"Do I have to wait for Halloween to do this, too?" I ask.

Jeremiah shakes his head. "Open season." He stands up, pushes his chair in, and presses his fingertips to the table, leaning over. "Alright, let's go," he says, looking to Nicolas. He glances at Brooklin, then clears his throat.

His gaze slides to me.

"Before you meet with Nicolas..." He nods toward Brooklin. "You'll have brunch with her."

I stiffen, my eyes darting from Brooklin to my brother and back again. "Why?" I ask, staring at her.

She laughs. It's fake.

I force myself to face my brother. He never tried to

make me and Brooklin like one another when he brought her home six months ago. For good reason. I didn't want to be friends with his fuck toys. I still don't.

"She's going to tell you all about the Unsaints, Sis."

I think I might faint. I hounded him with questions about them in the first few months I was here. Nicolas, too. They wouldn't tell me a fucking thing. I knew that Jeremiah had always been the one on the outside; the Unsaints hadn't cared that he hadn't made it to Raven Shores for the Death Oath. They hadn't waited for him. And Lucifer had threatened him in the park, by the merry-go-round. I knew, too, that my brother hadn't been born here. How he'd found his way into the gang, I still didn't know. No one would answer anything for me.

How the hell would Brooklin know?

She flashes him a smile, and I note it doesn't look fake.

She stands, her cheetah-print dress hugging her hips, and she sashays toward the door, blowing my brother an air kiss. Then she looks to me. Waiting.

Nicolas's and Jeremiah's eyes are on me too, along with hers.

I don't quite believe this, but I'm too greedy for information to argue with my brother. I stand on wobbly legs and cross the room. Brooklin pushes the door open and holds it out for me.

I give her a nod, and we walk out together, a guard that isn't Kristof trailing behind us.

The door falls closed.

"You wanna drink before you hear this shit?" Brooklin

asks me. Probably the most words she's ever spoken to me at one time.

I swallow, open my mouth. Close it.

Then I nod.

"I want more than one," I say, and together, we head to the bar.

CHAPTER SIXTEEN

Present

I TOSS BACK my second shot of whiskey.

Brooklin sips on something bright purple and twirls the paper straw in her glass. We've said about three words to each other since we've been sitting here, and I'm waiting for her to get to the fucking point. To tell me what I want to hear so I can get away from her. It isn't fair to her, my awkwardness around other women. It isn't fair to women in general. But here we are.

I motion to the bartender, Monica, for another shot. Monica shakes her head, her lips tugging into a smile.

She brings it to the table, sets it down, and folds her arms over her chest. "You Rains are exactly the same," she says.

Both me and Brooklin glare at her.

I bristle against those words. She tucks a strand of

honey-colored hair behind her ear, a piece that had fallen from her low ponytail. She pushes the shot toward me. Her hands are flat on the table as I throw back the shot, relishing in the burn, aware that both her and Brooklin are watching me.

"No, we're not," I answer her, slamming the shot glass on the table.

She arches a brow, refolds her arms. She's probably in her early thirties, if that. I have no idea how she'd come to work for Jeremiah. I don't know how most of his people came to work for him, but I suppose we all had one thing in common: We had been strays. He'd plucked us up off the streets and put us in this fancy prison instead.

"Look around, Sid," Monica says, glancing around at the empty bar, meeting Brooklin's gaze briefly. "Your brother is the same. Drinks at the worst times."

"Worst?" I ask, shaking my head. "There's no such thing."

"Agreed," Brooklin chimes in, glancing at her nails and taking a sip from her purple drink. She has a bleached blonde pixie cut, and she ruffles it with her hand, blue eyes swiveling back to Monica.

Monica smiles, and her eyes light up with that smile. She could've been something more than my brother's bartender, if she'd wanted to be. I know she, like everyone else here, gets paid well. But still, she's beautiful. She could be a model. An actress.

But maybe she hadn't wanted to be any of that at all.

"You can't run from your demons in a bottle, Sid," she

says quietly. She turns to Brooklin. "That goes for you, too."

I frown. "Who said I'm running?" I twirl the shot glass around, watching it catch the low lights of the bar.

"Only runners drown."

I sigh. "Haven't you ever heard of the Ironman? Those people, they'd probably beg to differ."

She rolls her eyes and slaps the cleaning rag that had been on her shoulder on the table between us. "You know what I meant," she teases.

I shrug. "Maybe."

She winks at me and turns, heading back to the bar.

The three shots have warmed me up. I place my hands on the table and lean in toward Brooklin, who sips on her drink. She's only halfway done. She needs to hurry up.

"Tell me," I demand. "Tell me about the mother-fucking Unsaints before I lose my goddamn mind."

She chews on the straw, licks her plumped lips, and then leans back in her chair. She has giant silver hoop earrings on and she fiddles with one now. She's beautiful, which is no surprise. My brother has a type.

She finally sighs, crosses her arms. "The Unsaints really do own Alexandria," she says, echoing Ria's words from a year ago. I don't say anything. I want to hear it all. She glances out the window, at the manicured lawn round the back of the Rain mansion. "Kids of the Society of 6." She shrugs, still not looking at me. "The Society is made of all kinds of rich ass people. A chairman of an investment conglomerate, CEOs of billion-dollar companies, heirs of fortunes that would bring you to your knees." She shakes her head. "Doesn't matter, really. The kids are worse than the parents."

I swirl the dregs of my shot glass. There's nothing really in there except a few drops of whiskey, but I have the urge to lick it all up. I resist.

"How do you know all this?" I ask Brooklin. There're obviously things I don't know about my brother, but I can't imagine he'd tell her any of this.

She meets my gaze. "I'm Mayhem's sister."

I stop fucking around with my glass. "What?" I ask her, sure I've heard her wrong.

She sighs, taps her perfectly manicured nails on the table. "Mayhem is one of the Unsaints—"

"I know who he is," I say, brushing off her explanation. She seems surprised that I know, but says nothing. I wonder what my brother told her about how he found me. "But you...then why the fuck are you here?"

She frowns. "Mayhem and I love each other a hell of a lot less than Jeremiah and you do."

Which is to say, they must really, *really* hate each other.

I arch a brow, waiting for her to continue.

"He's my older brother. I was always trying to follow him around to the Unsaint ceremonies. I went to Lover's Death one night, when I was fifteen, he was seventeen. I snuck out, followed him to the park." She trails off, working her lip between her teeth. I wonder if her story is as fucked as mine. "I got caught up with Atlas, took the

Death Oath. But I wore a mask, covered my whole face. Atlas didn't know it was me, his blood brothers' sister." She shakes her head and sighs, looking at the ceiling. I marvel at how much my brother is rubbing off on her.

And then I realize why my brother is keeping her around. She's probably a boon of information.

"When Atlas found out, after he, um, knocked my mask off, he told Mayhem immediately." She closes her eyes. "Mayhem lost his shit," she whispers. "Beat the fuck out of Atlas on that merry-go-round in Raven Park. His blood was all over it. Then Mayhem told my father. My dad...he kicked me out."

I feel rage bolt through me on her behalf. I think of Ria's story, about the merry-go-round. Turns out it was fucking true. "What?" I ask, slamming my palms on the table. "Why?"

"Girls aren't allowed in the Unsaints. They're like... the Masons, you know?" she asks, looking at me again. She brings her drink to her lips but doesn't take a sip. "And for me to be tainted by one..."

"Tainted?" I spit out, angry all over again. "What the fuck?" I see Monica glancing at us from behind the bar, where she's rubbing down a clean spot. But what else is she supposed to do? It's an empty bar. And I'm sure as hell not going to lower my voice.

"Look, Sid, I know you were...an escort..." she says it like it's a dirty word. "But my family, the Astors, we don't...it's just not done for girls. They're old school."

I swallow back the angry retort I have for that, trying

to empathize. I find I can't. "But wouldn't that be a *good* thing, for you to fuck one of the Unsaints? I mean, it's a super-secret club for naughty rich boys. Your brother was *in it*. What's the problem?"

"The problem is no one fucks anyone's family in there without permission. I forced Atlas to break his own oaths to Mayhem."

I see tears glimmering in her eyes. This shit is fucked. It makes no sense. But I swallow back all of that. It won't do any good for me to say it now. Either Brooklin gets it, or she doesn't. But there's no use arguing with her on some shit her family did to her.

"Where does my brother come into this picture?" I ask quietly. That's what I really want to know. I get the Unsaints are fucked. I know they like blood oaths. I know they're misogynists. I just want to know how Jeremiah Rain ended up running with them when he'd been born on the other side of the country. "I mean, they're all old school families from Alexandria, right?"

She nods, wiping at her eyes with the back of her hand. "Yeah," she sniffs, taking a sip of her drink then setting it down, spinning the glass. "Yeah, they are. But your brother's last foster family was from here. They were richer than everyone else, save for Lucifer's family." Her eyes flick to mine with his name. I don't comment. Of course, Lucifer would be the wealthiest fuck among them.

"Did he really kill them?" I ask. Because if my brother killed a family *that* rich, I have no idea how the fuck he isn't in prison.

Shocking the shit out of me, she nods. "He killed them. And the blood kids."

My mouth falls open. "What." It isn't really a question.

"When he was seventeen. They'd left him locked up for two weeks at that point," she explains, and my blood grows cold. "But not their kids. They just didn't like him. Maybe because he was always getting in trouble at school. Bad attitude." She laughs a little at that, and I do too. I don't even know why. It's not amusing. My heart is hurting for my brother, but I can't stop the laugh anyway.

"One of the girls—both of them were older than him, by the way, a nineteen-year-old and a twenty-year-old—let him out, and he grabbed a gun from his foster dad's bedroom and shot them all." She shrugs. "The will deemed he got the money, because the family was fucking stupid and never updated it. It just went to the remaining kids, him included, evenly distributed. He was the only one left. He hired a good lawyer. Self-defense. It didn't even go to trial. Because that's what that kind of money can do."

"And the Unsaints just let him in after that?"

She laughs. "Are you kidding me? They would've killed to have him. I was already out on the streets then—"

"On the fucking *streets*?" I ask her, bewildered. I knew she said her dad kicked her out but...

She nods, lip trembling again. This is clearly a sore spot for her. I can't blame her. "Yeah," she says, "they wrote me out of the will and gave me a few thousand for a hotel, and that's about it."

I let loose a breath. "Wow," I say, shocked. "Continue."

She frowns but does. "The Unsaints wanted him. They all more or less hate their parents. They thought what he did was cool. But obviously, he was always on the outside looking in. Even though he'd been in for a few years by the time *you* came into the picture, he still wasn't fully one of them. These kids had grown up together. They'd started the Unsaints when they were just kids, and their parents supported it. Encouraged it, even. So Jeremiah didn't quite fit in. And you...well...when he saw what Lucifer did to you..." She lowers her voice, as if that'll take away the fucking hole in my heart. "He couldn't stay in it anymore. He left, after that night. He had nothing to do with them. He already had this place, already had his people who were loyal to him and not the Unsaints. He became the Order of Rain, and," she shrugs, "here we are."

I sit in silence, letting it all digest.

It doesn't make sense.

There are things I still don't get.

"Why are they coming after him? After you?" I ask, gesturing toward her. Finding out Mayhem is her brother blows my mind. It makes burning down her house all the worse.

"I'm surprised they took this long. But you don't just get to leave a gang like that and survive to tell the tale, Sid. They came for me as a warning. I met Jeremiah at one of his clubs. They would have had eyes and ears all over the city. They *do* have eyes and ears all over the city. I'm dead to Mayhem. He wouldn't lose sleep after burning down my house."

I need another shot but I'm momentarily speechless. A cult of rich pricks that are loyal to one another to a fault but abandon their true family over something as ridiculous as sex and made-up oaths on Halloween night.

I drum my fingers on the table, staring at nothing in particular.

"Sid?" Brooklin whispers.

I incline my head in her direction, wondering what fresh new wave of information is coming.

"If you hurt Julie—"

"I'm not going to *hurt* Julie." My eyes snap to Brooklin. "I'm going to kill her."

Brooklin visibly recoils. She might be the estranged sister of an Unsaint and my brother's current toy, but she clearly isn't suited to this life, even after what her own family did to her.

"If you do, Lucifer and the rest of them will come after you."

I flash her a smile. "I hope to God they do."

CHAPTER SEVENTEEN

Halloween, One Year Ago

THE FIRST THING I feel is the pain.

My head is spinning, my mouth is dry, my tongue sticks to the roof of my mouth. And my legs *ache*. I try to open my eyes, but they're so unbelievably heavy, it takes a herculean effort.

When I finally manage to pry them open, I close them again, immediately.

The light is too bright.

I register that I'm lying on the forest floor. And everything from the night before comes rushing back to me in painful waves.

The gun on my hip, now gone. The walk from my apartment. My plan that had been torn to pieces. Lucifer. His mouth. His tongue. The knife. His voice. His scent.

The Unsaints.

The pregnant girl.

Ria.

The fire.

The rum.

The asylum.

The Death Oath.

Oh God.

I try to open my eyes again, but then I feel something dig into my side.

"Good morning, sleeping beauty."

I recognize the voice, and fear ripples through me. I need to move. I need to *get up*. But I can't. Everything hurts. I grit my teeth, and push myself over, rolling onto my back, so I can at least *see*.

A man stands over me.

It isn't Lucifer.

"*Lucifer,*" I whisper anyway, hoping he'll come out from the trees. Surely, he's still here. He had promised me he would be here.

I swallow past the dry knot in my throat, and taste blood. I wonder if it's my own, or his.

The sky is pink and blue above me, and I shiver. It's only then, as a breeze hits my chest, that I realize I'm not wearing *anything*. My bodysuit is in tatters on the ground beside me, and even my boots have been ripped off. I can't feel the weight of the horns on my head, and my hand flies to my face, but I don't know what I'm checking for.

Bruises? Cuts?

The man standing over me smiles. It chills my blood.

I know him.

Jeremiah.

The one who followed me last night. The one Lucifer took me from.

"You're in one piece," he croons. "But barely." He's wearing a hoodie, but the hood is off of his face now. I squint up at him, trying to think. Trying to put together the pieces of what happened last night.

But the only thing I remembered after making promises to Lucifer is...blacking out. I'd blacked out. I don't know if he had known that; I know sometimes people can't tell. It isn't the same as passing out. I have no idea what happened after that. But I'm naked. I feel dirty.

The man standing over me seems to sense my confusion. He crouches down beside me and grips my hand. I let him hold it, but I don't squeeze back.

"Do you remember me?" he asks.

I make to shake my head, to pull my hand from his. To cover myself. But then I see his eyes.

Pale green, like the lightest jade. Like a blade of new grass. And his hair, dark and thick. Heavy brows, perfectly arched, like my own.

I bite back a gasp.

"Jamie?" I whisper. My throat hurts with his name, but I need him to tell me it's true. I need to know.

My brother's hand on mine tightens. But a shadow crosses his face. "Yes, Sid. Yes."

HE HAD CARRIED ME OUT OF THE ASYLUM IN HIS arms. At first, he had had to drag me away. I had scrambled to stay, to look for Lucifer. To fight. But there's only Jamie and two guards with him—the latter of whom thankfully has clothes for me to pull on. I had willingly worn the hoodie and sweatpants, looking at the scraps that remained of my bodysuit on the forest floor.

But I didn't want to leave.

There's blood in patches of grass and dirt among the ground. I don't know if it's mine, or Lucifer's, or Jamie's. My brother won't tell me anything. I had hit his back as he tossed me over one shoulder, as if I was nothing. I had looked for the gun. For the entrance to the asylum. For anything to tell me that last night had been real. That it hadn't been a dream. A hallucination. But I'd seen nothing. We were deep in the woods. There was nothing to confirm that anything at all had happened last night, except for the fact someone had cut off my bodysuit.

I remember Lucifer doing it. I remember him on top of me. And I had seen the cut on my thigh, which was streaked with blood.

That had been real.

But what else? What else had happened? How had Jamie found me? After all that time...fourteen years. Over a decade, an entire country had been placed between us.

Jamie says nothing.

And last night, they had called him *Jeremiah*. I also hear one of the guards call him as much.

He says nothing. He offers no explanation. Instead, he

takes me into the hotel, puts me in the bathtub, takes off my new clothes himself and scrubs me clean. I scream at him. I cover my breasts with my hands. But he is clinical, methodical, scrubbing me down with a loofah. He hasn't spoken a word, but he has nearly scrubbed my skin off. I'm pink by the time he's done with me.

His eyes linger on the cut on my thigh, but he doesn't ask about it.

He yanks me to my feet, pats me dry with a towel, and puts me in a white robe. Then he sits me down on a leather chair in a hotel room, and he starts to pace in front of me.

One of his guards comes in and offers me a glass of water. I want to throw it back in his face. I want to scream at the top of my lungs. But instead, I take the water and drain it, then set the glass on the coffee table.

The guard looks to Jamie, who gives him a curt nod, and then he leaves.

Jamie stops pacing.

He's grown up. When we were separated, he had been a boy. Eight years old. Now, he's a man. Broad-shouldered, muscular, still dressed in that hoodie and dark jeans. His jaw had angled out, his neck is corded with muscle.

"How did you find me?" I ask him. I want to scream at him, but I don't have the strength. I can't get to my feet. Humiliation washes over me in waves. From the way he found me to the way he had scrubbed me clean as if I were impure. To the fact that Lucifer left me. He had broken me and then he had left me.

Jamie tilts his head up to glance at the ceiling. The hotel has to be a five-star one. I've seen it before, beyond a hill past my apartment. But I've never wondered about it. I met clients in my home or theirs, but I didn't do hotels. I wanted the profits. I needed them. Besides, most of my clients couldn't afford both a hotel and my services. They had to pick one, which was fine with me.

What I don't understand about this place is that... Jamie seems to own it.

"I searched for you," he finally says, chest heaving as he stares at me. *Glares* at me. "I searched for you for a long, long time, Sid. Where the fuck have you been?"

And that propels me to my feet. I leap at him, my finger poking into his chest. "Where the fuck have *you* been?" I growl, anger lighting my veins. "Where the fuck have you been, Jamie? You were supposed to look out for me! You were my big brother! Where the fuck have you been? How did you find me?"

He catches my wrist in his hand and lowers it between us. "Don't do that."

"Don't do what?" I hiss. I'm nineteen now, and he's twenty-three. But in that moment, I feel like his kid sister again, five years old and screaming his name as social services pulled us apart. We never came back together.

Not until now.

"Don't blame me," he says, shaking his head. He's still holding my wrist in his hand. "Don't do that." His expression seems...anguished. Some of the anger in my chest melts away. It turns into grief. "Where were you, Sid? All this time?"

I close my eyes. He pulls me closer to him, and when I meet his gaze again, we're close enough to share breath. "I was moved here, right after we were...right after we were separated. Then I..." I swallow, wondering how the fuck to sum up fourteen brutal years in one sentence. "I bounced around. Last year, when I turned eighteen, dropped out of high school and moved out. Got my own place."

His eyes darken. "I've been looking for you," he says quietly.

"I've been here," I answer him. It isn't exactly true. I'd moved from Raleigh to Alexandria when I moved out of my last foster parent's house. A house I'd only stayed at for six months before I dropped out of school. They'd wanted the extra money they'd get from the government for giving me a closet-sized room to stay in. I barely remember their names. "How did you find me?" I ask again.

But it isn't what I really want to know. What I really want to know is something deeper. Where is Lucifer? What happened to me in the night? There was no sign of the party when we had left, but I'd seen the fire pit on our way out of the park, surprisingly burned down to nothing. It hadn't been a dream. The cut on my leg...

But my entire body still aches, as if I've been run over by a truck. There are bruises all over me.

"I need to know what happened last night," I finally whisper. "What happened to me?" I swallow down the lump in my throat. "Why were you with *them*?"

He lets go of my wrist and I think he's going to turn away from me. I think he's going to leave me again. But instead, he wraps his arms around me, and pulls me into his hard chest.

I resist, at first, stiffening under his touch. I don't rest my head against him. Not at first. His scent swirls around me, fresh laundry and cologne, but something else too. Something like smoke. Bonfire smoke. From the night before.

When did he find out it was me? How long had he watched me while I was unconscious?

A sob creeps its way into my throat and I give in, resting against his shoulder, letting him hold me up.

"What happened to me?" I ask again. "What happened to me, Jamie?"

He tightens his hold on me, pulling me closer, trying to keep me from falling apart.

"I'm so sorry," he says against my hair. "I'm so sorry I didn't find you sooner."

I know that whatever happened, it's going to be hard to hear. Maybe I don't want to know. I'm not sure I'll ever want to know.

CHAPTER EIGHTEEN

Present

LUNCH WITH NICOLAS starts with drinks. I'm already buzzed by the time I drop down into the seat across from him at one of the restaurants in the hotel. This place really is like its own village, for the sick, twisted, and afflicted.

But Nicolas has a drink waiting for me, what looks to be a rum and Coke, and I'll take that affliction any day. He also has iced water, and I nod my thanks to him for both before I reach for the alcohol.

"You might want to slow down, kid," he warns me. I want to tell him I'm not a fucking kid, but instead I just take a drink.

He rolls his eyes, rests his forearm on the table. No one has come to take our order yet, and I'm glad. I want to get this out of the way first. Then I'll know if I'll be able to eat without vomiting.

Nicolas is wearing a white dress shirt, sleeves rolled up at the forearms. He gives me a crooked smile as I finish my drink and reach for the water, but the smile doesn't quite meet his eyes.

"What's going on with you and Jeremiah?" he asks me.

The question takes me by surprise. I let the ice-cold water make its way down my throat, cooling the burn from the rum. "Why didn't you ask him that?"

His eyes narrow into slits. "I did. But now I'm asking you."

I lean back, take the cloth napkin from the table and unfurl it, draping it over my lap for something to do, even though there's no food on the way yet.

I clasp my hands in my lap. "What did he say?"

Nicolas scrubs a hand over his face. "You two are more alike than you think," he says, groaning. "You are definitely brother and sister. One hundred percent Rain and one hundred percent assholes."

I laugh out loud. "We're not alike," I argue. I don't want us to be alike. We *can't* be alike. I don't think I'm a saint, by any stretch of the imagination. But Jeremiah is worse than Satan himself.

"He would have shot Kristof for you, this morning," Nicolas says, suddenly serious, looking at me through his blonde lashes. "He would have killed him in that meeting room and had someone burn the body. Do you know that?"

I wave away his suggestion that somehow Jeremiah has had a real change of heart toward me. I want it to be true.

But he'd only pretended to, to get me to agree to getting rid of Julie and the Unsaints. *And Lucifer*, I remind myself.

"Whatever. He aimed a gun at my head just last night and pulled the fucking trigger. Or did you forget that?"

Nicolas's expression is serious. "No," he says, his voice clipped. "I did not forget. And I won't." He leans forward, both elbows on the table. "But I don't think Jeremiah will forget either. I think he regrets it."

"Is that what he said?" I ask, knowing he hadn't.

Nicolas doesn't look away from me. "No," he answers truthfully. "But I know him. More than you. More than nearly anybody. He regrets it. And he regrets he's putting you in this position, to do something he knows will hurt you—"

"Woah," I interrupt, shaking my head. "Who said it will hurt me?"

Nicolas leans back and clears his throat. "Jeremiah knows about Lucifer. He's the one that found you, remember? Or have you forgotten?"

"He doesn't know what happened before he found me."

I don't even know what happened before he found me. I remember learning my brother was no longer called 'Jamie'. That he had morphed into Jeremiah. I remember waking up in the park, deep in the woods, far from the asylum. My eyes burn with that memory. But I didn't know what had *actually* happened.

No one did.

No one but Lucifer.

And he had run away, like he promised he wouldn't.

I push that memory aside. I have no time to think about that shit now. It's far too late for regrets, from either me or Jeremiah.

"If he feels so damn bad about it," I snap, trying to clear my head, "then why is he making me do it?"

Nicolas raises his brows. "You really don't know?"

I shake my head, my temper rising. "No, I really fucking don't."

He sighs and motions at the bar for another drink. I notice he only has water, but I don't care. I can spiral out of control. Jeremiah can pick up the pieces or let me die. Either one is fine with me, so long as I can get out of my own goddamn head.

The bartender, a man I barely know, sets the drink down. I don't usually come here. This is Jeremiah's and Nicolas's spot. Usually reserved for the men.

I take the drink without looking at the man, who walks away.

"Because he wants to let you have your vengeance."

It takes all of the self-control I possess—which is already on short supply as it is—not to fling this drink against the wall.

"Fuck that," I seethe. I take a sip, set it down, cross my arms on the table. "Fuck that. You and I both know that's not why he's doing it. He's doing it to punish me. Because he thinks, for some reason, that there was something between Lucifer and me. But he has no fucking clue. None. There was nothing between us. So I'll do this job," I rake my bangs out of my eyes, "and I'll kill whoever the fuck it is he wants me to kill. But don't you dare fucking pretend this is for *me.*"

Nicolas watches me from hooded eyes. I'm breathing fast, the anger like a living thing in my blood. I'm not angry at Nicolas, not exactly. But if he actually thinks my brother—conniving, manipulative, fucking batshit crazy— is offering me these kills as *vengeance,* he's lost his goddamn mind. He's drank from the Kool-Aid for far too fucking long.

The longer he watches me, the angrier I get. Until I'm about to stand to my feet and walk out. But he must sense it, because he finally opens his mouth to respond to me.

"You forget so easily." He runs his tongue over his teeth, and stares past me, as if he's remembering. As if I had forgotten. As if I could forget. God, I want to. I want to forget it all. More than putting the pieces together, more than *remembering* the holes from that night, I want to forget it all.

"You forget that *Lucifer* raped you."

I flinch at those words.

"You forget he left you, naked, in a fucking insane asylum. You forget he didn't give a shit about you, about what happened to you. He used you like a piece of fucking trash, Sid, and you don't want to make him pay for that? Because I fucking do."

I scoff. "You would've let Kristof rape me," I counter, my hands curled into fists.

Nicolas shakes his head. "I knew Jeremiah wouldn't

let it happen," he says firmly. As if he believes it. I sure as hell don't. "He wouldn't have, and if I had thought he would, I would have been there to stop it myself."

I laugh, loud and low. "You're an idiot."

Nicolas slams his fist on the table. "And you're a fucking stupid little girl," he snarls at me, leaning across the table to get in my face. "He. *Raped.* You. Your brother saved you. All that you've been through, all that you had to do to survive, and you still act like nothing more than a child."

I try to calm my temper. I try to breathe in through my nose, out through my mouth. I try to relax. "If you're so fired up about this, about defending my honor, why don't *you* kill them?"

Nicolas's fist uncurls and he shifts in his seat, holding my gaze steady, aiming. Ready to pierce my heart. "Because you need to grow the fuck up, Sid. Jeremiah won't always be around to protect you. One day, you might lead the Order of Rain. One day, you'll have to deal with the shit he goes through on a daily basis. One day," he gestures around us, "this might be yours. And if you're going to be in charge of something like this, you need to grow some fucking balls."

"I don't want this place, Nicolas. What don't you get about this? I was ready to fucking die that night before my brother dragged me out of the asylum. I still am!" I stand to my feet, swipe my hand across the table, knocking my drink to the floor, the sound of shattering glass piercing the quiet of the nearly empty restaurant. "Did he tell you that?"

Nicolas is so angry, his hands are shaking. I know he probably wants to punch me in the face. I want to do the same to him. We've never physically fought, not since those two weeks I spent in a cell and he had to force food down my throat and fresh clothes on my body every day. But I'm ready for it now.

"You told us," he spits, standing to his feet now too, staring down across the table at me. "You fucking told us. You screamed at me every fucking day in that cell that you wanted to die. That you had tried to die. That Lucifer had saved you and you didn't want to be saved."

My face burns with that memory. I'd conveniently forgotten it. Everything after that night had been a blur, for a long, long time.

"Lucifer fucked you over, Sid. In more ways than one. I know what Jeremiah asked you to do this morning isn't easy, no matter what you might say to the contrary. He's also not expecting you'll follow through on all of it."

My mouth drops open, some of the anger washing away. "What?" I hiss.

Nicolas shakes his head, pounds his fist against the table. "Obviously, I'm not supposed to tell you this shit. But kill all of the Unsaints? You, who have never killed anyone in your life? No, Sid, you're not going to take all five of them. He knows it. But he wants you to get Julie before you get Lucifer. To let Lucifer panic. To let Lucifer get some of the payback he deserves."

Despite myself, I can't hide my smile at that.

"And who is going to help me kill all of them?"

Nicolas shrugs. "We will."

I bite my lip, biting back against the pain. Pain Nicolas has no idea he's causing me. Because I might not remember the rape, I might not remember the worst of that night, but I remember our promises. What Lucifer and Lilith had sworn to each other in the darkness.

But he'd broken those vows as soon as he made them. The Death Oath didn't mean shit to the Unsaints.

I'm going to fucking enjoy breaking him, too.

"Tell me what I need to know to get this shit done."

Nicolas stares at me a moment, reading me. Trying to gauge my mood. But it's impossible to do that. I don't even know my own mind in this moment. I just know what I want. What I'm going to take.

What I fucking deserve.

CHAPTER NINETEEN

Present

I HAVE to hand it to Lucifer. He'd hidden his girl and his baby boy well. Not in Alexandria. Not even in the state of North Carolina. No, he'd taken them north, to Virginia. A small town just outside of Roanoke called Acid City.

Fitting, really.

Acid City is a four-hour drive, which was his first mistake. That isn't far enough. Especially not for a Rain. Nowhere would have been far enough, but this just makes it easier.

His second mistake is staying at that house in Raven Park. It means my brother can keep an eye on him, make sure he has no idea anything is amiss. I don't know what kind of war him and my brother have, what exactly it means for an Unsaint to desert, but Lucifer wants to hurt Jeremiah just as bad as Jeremiah wants to hurt him.

That much is obvious when one of my brother's clubs, Dead Weight, burns down in the middle of the day, right after Nicolas and I finish our lunch. It's a loss that my brother takes lightly enough; he has more than half a dozen clubs in and around the city. But to be so brazen about it, to bypass the security cameras completely...it's bold.

But it means Lucifer is still around.

And Jeremiah knows it had to be him; he'd left a skeleton mask at the entrance to the parking lot. Motherfucker.

When afternoon comes, while Jeremiah deals with insurance and restoration and adjusters, Nicolas and I leave. We take one of the spare cars, a black Porsche SUV with blacked out windows and wheels. I think that in itself might be conspicuous, but Nicolas reminds me this is Alexandria.

A portion of this city is fucking made out of money.

Which reminds me of the Unsaints. Atlas, Cain, Mayhem, and Ezra. I wonder if they're all with Lucifer at the house in Raven Park. I wonder if they're that stupid.

Trey had stashed knives and guns in our black zip-up bags in the backseat. I make Nicolas run through a drive-thru for a large iced coffee, and then we're on our way.

I flip on *Upperdrugs* by Highly Suspect from my phone and turn it up. Nicolas glances at me from behind the wheel as we merge on the highway.

"You know," he says, speaking loudly over the music, "it is possible to be a gangster and still keep your hearing."

I laugh, shaking my head to the beat and singing out loud. "Don't think so," I call out after my favorite part passes. "And besides," I add, "what's the point?"

Nicolas laughs and rolls down the windows. I relish in the cool air ripping through my hair, my bangs obscuring my vision. It's sunny this afternoon, but finally turning cool. Finally changing with the season. Halloween will be here soon, and once I burn Lucifer's body, I'll fucking dance on his grave.

Nicolas turns down my music when the song ends, and I'm about to protest when he puts a hand on mine.

"You seem excited," he observes over the wind blowing through the vehicle.

I crisscross my legs in the seat and he looks over and laughs, shaking his head. "I wish I could do that," he murmurs.

"You're driving," I point out, squeezing his hand. "You need a foot on the gas."

"Fuck, Sid, even if I wasn't driving, my legs would never fit in the seat like that."

"Chop them off," I deadpan.

He bursts into laughter again.

I feel light. Even though I know we're carrying more weapons than can possibly be legal. Even though I know we're about to do something very *illegal*, I feel lighter than I have in ages. I'm not going to see my brother's leftovers. I'm not going to be forced to touch their corpses. No, I'm going to do the job this time.

It doesn't matter that I've never done it before. My

anger, seething beneath my skin this past year, it's enough to get the job done. And for practical matters, Nicolas is with me.

I only wished Lucifer would be there to watch me pretend to deliberate over the decision to end Julie's life.

This is going to be fun, with or without him. I might even bring Julie's head in bag to throw at his feet.

I don't know much about Lucifer. But the one thing I know for sure is that he's a psycho. And yeah, so am I. So is Jeremiah. Maybe Nicolas, too. But Lucifer isn't a psycho on my side, and that makes him dangerous. He's a threat to me and the fucked-up family I've built over the past year. Maybe Jeremiah had only been manipulating me this morning when he cleaned my foot, but I believed Nicolas when he said my brother would have killed Kristof. I kind of believed him, too, when he had said Jeremiah wouldn't have let Kristof get to me, in the end.

And he hadn't. In the end.

Jeremiah and I will never be close, we'll never be like normal brothers and sisters. But we love each other, in our own sick way. And Lucifer is going to see what that love looks like. Lucifer might have ruled hell, but Lilith made it burn. And tonight, he's going to find out just what that means.

▼

I FALL ASLEEP ON THE DRIVE, EVEN AFTER THE coffee. I had leaned far back in my seat, the music was on high again, my hands were stuffed in my hoodie pockets, and Nicolas had left me to my music and my thoughts. I'd dozed off, and when I wake up, it's completely dark outside.

We're on a two-lane road, the only car I can see around us. My playlist has started over, *The Old Me* by Memphis May Fire is playing, and I have to turn it down. It's a song I love to hate, because it hurts. I'm tired of hurting.

"How much further?" I ask.

Nicolas is drumming his hands on the wheel. "You sound like a kid," he jokes.

I shoot him a glare and the bird.

"We're coming into Acid City now." He looks around, brow furrowed. "Funny. I don't see anything good to trip on."

I scoff. "That was a fucking dad joke if I've ever heard one."

"What do you know about dads?" he counters.

"Wowww," I say, exaggerating the word. "Just, wow. You are an *asshole;* did anyone ever tell you?"

He shrugs one shoulder. I watch his tricep flex under his black cotton shirt in the lights from the dash. "A time or two."

"When you get married, your wife better make fun of you all the fucking time or I'll have to divorce you two. Someone has to remind you that you ain't shit."

He blows out a breath. "Good thing I'll never get married, Sid."

"But don't you like steady sex and stuff?"

He shakes his head. "Yeahhh, we're not having this conversation."

But I know he has that private apartment. He's right, though. I don't want this conversation either.

I stretch out my legs, rotate my neck. Up ahead, I see lights. When we round a corner, there's a lonely gas station with one car at the pump.

"Need fuel?" I ask Nicolas.

He shakes his head. "I stopped while you were knocked out. We'll be there in five minutes."

I frown. "There's absolutely nothing in this town. Why would Lucifer stash his family so far from *people?*"

Nicolas shrugs. "It'll make it easier for us. She won't be able to call for help."

I nod. "True." It's a good point. The flipside, though, is that if she *does* call for help, the police will easily spot us. This town is deserted. And we, along with the Unsaints, might have the Alexandria police in our pocket, but we don't usually cross state lines for our worst crimes.

I fiddle with the strings of my hoodie, keeping an eye on the empty, curving road. I wish we were here to go camping. To have a bizarre family vacation. For fun. Something I haven't had in way too fucking long. But every nerve in my body seems on edge, my blood pumping hard through my veins. This isn't for fun. This is part of the war.

I see, out of the corner of my eye, Nicolas glance at me.

"You okay?"

I want to say something rude. Toss his worry back at him. But the truth is, for some reason, I'm not exactly *okay*. I don't know why. Or rather, I do know. But I should be more excited about this. Extracting vengeance.

It's not even the kid.

I'm not going to touch the kid.

Something just feels...*off*.

"No," I answer Nicolas honestly. His eyes are back on the road, and so are mine, so I keep talking. It's easier to talk when I'm not looking at him. "I just have a weird feeling."

He slows the Porsche, and I see a gravel driveway to my right, leading far off the road, thick trees obscuring our vision of what might lie ahead.

"Did you map this area out?" I ask, turning to Nicolas. He hasn't said anything about my weird feeling. He'd probably dismissed it as soon as the words came out of my mouth.

But he's staring at me, and he hasn't turned down the driveway. He cuts the lights, and we're just off the side of the main road, but he makes no move to get out.

"Why do you have a weird feeling?" His eyes are intent on mine. He's taking this too seriously. Hell, I shouldn't be taking it this seriously.

I shake my head, reach for my door handle, but he locks the doors.

"It's nothing, Nicky," I say with a laugh. "Let's go. Did you want to walk down there?"

"Feelings mean something, Sid. I know your brother would like you to believe otherwise, but they do."

I know that. I'd been a sex worker for a year, and it didn't just involve juggling clients' sexual preferences. It involved a multitude of far too many feelings. I keep my hand on the door handle, which is still locked, but I twist back around to look at Nicolas.

"It's probably nothing." I blow out a breath. "Honestly. What could go wrong? If we can't get in tonight for some reason, we leave, come back another day." I lift one shoulder in a shrug. "Right?"

Nicolas scrubs a hand over his face, but he seems to agree.

"Right. But we're driving up." He glances down the long driveway. "This is creepy. Like a scary movie. I want the getaway car close." He smiles, but it doesn't meet his eyes.

He keeps the lights off as we drive down the bumpy road, and I have to admit, it *is* creepy. Nothing but darkness and trees and gravel as far as we can see. But I'd ran into a forest in the middle of the night a year ago, right into the arms of a man who clearly wanted to harm me. This is a mother and her baby. How scary can it be?

We round a corner, and the house looms off in the distance. Full of lights. Because this is Lucifer we're dealing with. Lights are deterrents. Even in the middle of fucking nowhere.

At least, they're deterrents to most people.

But Nicolas and I...we aren't most people.

I'm Sid Rain. If my brother has taught me anything, it's to get the fucking job done, no matter the cost.

We pull off beside a line of trees in the expansive front yard, and Nicolas turns the SUV around, so it's facing the road out. The house itself is moderately sized, a long, white porch out front with rocking chairs. Two stories. There's a shed beside it, a red wagon's handle propped up against it. And a Jeep, parked right out front, the doors to the car almost lining up to the red door of the house. A quick getaway.

I know that isn't Lucifer's car. None of the Unsaints would drive a Jeep, if they're as rich as everyone says.

Shockingly, I don't hear or see any dogs.

I had begged Jeremiah for dogs at the hotel. Said they would be great guard dogs. He told me he didn't want another mouth to feed and that's what guns were for. Guarding.

Seems he and Lucifer share that sentiment.

My eyes linger on the wagon in the side mirror as Nicolas and I sit, waiting. To see if anyone notices us. To see if we see any movement of the curtains from the windows.

My gut twists.

Julie.

Lucifer's kid.

He hadn't known, he said. Although that could very well be bullshit. He hadn't known, but he had stuck around. Meanwhile, he'd left me naked in an asylum, full of bruises and a permanent scar.

My fists clench and I reach for the black zipped bag behind my seat.

Nicolas catches my arm.

I shrug him off but don't grab the bag, narrowing my eyes at him instead. "We can't sit here all night."

His brows flick up. "I know. But what do you want to do? After Julie is dead?"

I don't know why, but it suddenly occurs to me that Lucifer doesn't know my real name. If he has one, I don't know his either. Which is good.

I want to stay Lilith. It's the only way I'm going to get through this.

"What do you mean *what do I want to do?*" I snap. "I want to get the hell out of here and go home." But I see the red wagon again. I know what he's asking. I just don't want to deal with it.

"Sid, look, I know you hate this guy. You should. He's a piece of shit for what he did to you. All the Unsaints are pieces of shit. But that doesn't change the fact that inside that nice little white house is a baby sleeping soundly in a crib or a tiny bed and we're about to murder his mom. So I'll ask you again." He grounds the steering wheel in his hand, I watch as his knuckles blanch. "What do you want to do afterward?"

I throw up my hands. "You and Jeremiah should have thought about this before *now*. We can't kidnap the kid.

We won't live that down without spending time behind bars."

He snorts. I know what he's thinking, but the truth is, murder is easier to get away with. For us. Kidnapping a baby...no police station in America will let that shit go. And Jeremiah will kill us if we bring a kid back into the hotel.

Nicolas drums his fingers on the steering wheel, staring at the house in the rearview mirror, thinking. I have no answer. This should have been planned better, but I was so eager to get back at Lucifer, to keep my brother pacified, to prove myself, that we'd made this drive without working out all the angles.

This was a mistake, and we can't afford to make mistakes. I already made enough of those as it is, according to my brother.

"If you don't want to do this," I taunt Nicolas, "we can always go back home and tell Jeremiah we pussied out."

Nicolas frowns. "I'm not scared of your brother, kid." I actually believe him, although he'd be the only one, save for me. Most days, though, if I'm being honest with myself, I'm scared, too. "We'll deal with the mom, then we'll call 911 from inside the house, and then we'll go. First responders will deal with the kid."

He unbuckles his seatbelt. As if that settles it. As if that makes sense. Murdering in the night is beneficial because it will give us much more time to get the hell away from the victim's house. Calling the cops while we're still *inside* the home seems like a horrible idea. But I also don't have any better ones.

"Okay," I agree. "I guess we gotta do what we gotta do."

I open the car door, close it quietly. On the other side of the SUV, Nicolas does the same. Suddenly the vengeance I'd imagined taking against Lucifer is a lot more complicated than it should be.

I open up the rear door, Nicolas opens the opposite one.

"Which?" I ask, glancing at the black bag.

Nicolas shrugs. "Gun is quicker. Knife is more painful." His eyes flick to mine. "Which do you want it to be?"

"I want to get out of here."

Nicolas nods. "Got it." He unzips the bag, tosses me a pair of gloves. When we both have them on, he hands me a Glock, and I take it by the grip. He gets the same, and then we duck out of there, pressing the doors closed to avoid any unnecessary noise.

We stand outside of the pool of lights for a moment, looking the house over before we make our way in.

"The back?" he asks me.

As if I know.

But I nod. He's letting me think this through. Letting me feel in control. There are lights around back, and we could have just as easily went in through the front. But most homeowners take more precautions with their front doors. As if criminals won't have the audacity to scuttle around to the back.

Criminals have the audacity to do most anything when they're already planning to break into a house in the middle of the night.

We circle around the house on opposite sides, keeping out of the pool of light until we absolutely have to step in it. I take the side of the house away from the shed. I don't want to see the fucking red wagon again.

We meet in the backyard, both nodding that the coast is clear. Here, there's a forest beyond the backyard, an endless landscape of trees that goes God knows where. The back porch is smaller than the front, just a few steps leading up to a screen door. There's an aboveground pool with a tarp over it, and a few toys scattered across the lawn.

Together, looking around, guns drawn, Nicolas and I walk silently up the steps. He pulls on the screen door. It's unlocked. I see a smile flicker on his lips. Less mess.

The back door itself, of course, is locked tight.

Nicolas hands me his gun, pulls out a lockpick from his pocket and goes to work. I don't know shit about breaking into houses. I don't know shit about murder, except the bodies my brother leaves behind. I am wholly unprepared for this. But it's a little too late to back out now.

The lock clicks, and Nicolas pushes the door open, pocketing the tools. He takes his gun back, and we wait, there on the threshold of the door. Wait for an alarm, a dog, a cat. Anything. We wait thirty seconds. Then we go inside, and I guide the door gently closed.

We stand inside the kitchen, shrouded in darkness.

It smells like someone has baked something recently, cookies or something like it. It smells good, and my stomach growls. Nicolas shoots me a look, but there isn't much I can do about it. I shrug in the darkness.

As my eyes adjust, I see bottles in the sink, a highchair around a gleaming wooden table off of the kitchen, in the dining room. And just past the kitchen are stairs leading upward. Nicolas had told me bedrooms are almost always upstairs.

I jerk my head in that direction, nearly holding my breath. There's some noise upstairs, like a sound machine or a fan, but otherwise, it's silent. I can hear my heart thudding in my ears.

Nicolas takes small steps through the kitchen, testing the floor out. It's creaky, so he distributes his weight almost comically, creeping like a cartoon burglar across the dark wooden floors.

This place is a home. There's no marble here. No shine like at the hotel. It actually feels...*cozy*. But I shove that thought aside.

I follow in Nicolas's wake, glancing behind me as I do, looking around the hallway once we get to the bottom of the stairs. I can see the front door, and a living room just before it. Darkness. Silence.

Yet that feeling hasn't left. The weird one. I thought it was because there's a baby in this house. But I get a prick on the back of my neck, like I'm being watched. As Nicolas tests out the stairs, thankfully *not* very creaky, I look behind me, at the door we had come in from.

Nothing.

I'm paranoid.

I am, truth be told, always paranoid. But that's not going to help me now.

I take a breath in through my nose, out through my mouth, trying to calm my racing heart. We're in. That's half the battle. Now we just have to do the other half, and then we can get out.

Nicolas is halfway up the stairs when I realize he's glaring at me. I haven't moved. I clench my teeth together to keep the apology on my tongue from bubbling out through my lips. I follow him up, glancing at the walls ahead of him, on the landing. No photographs that I can see. I'm hopeful I won't have to see any pictures of Lucifer's smiling face with Julie and this child.

We reach the landing, the both of us, and wait again. Listening. The sound is a fan, coming from a closed door at the end of the hall. Probably the baby's room. Right off the top of the stairs, there's another door that's wide open. At my back, there's a small bathroom.

Nicolas nods toward the open door, and he walks quickly over to it, standing flush against the wall before he pokes his head in, twisting around like they do in cop movies when they're clearing the rooms.

He twists back around, and I see on his face.

Something is wrong. He's frowning, his eyes wide.

I come closer to him, standing just in front of him, and do as he had, looking inside the room. It's a bedroom, and underneath the blue comforter is Julie—blonde tendrils splayed on the pillow, her face away from us—and the baby, snuggled up against her chest, wisps of hair sticking up at all angles, facing against his mother.

I try to breathe as I duck out the room and slide past Nicolas, flattening myself against the wall, too.

We don't look at each other. Not for a long moment.

"I'll do it," Nicolas finally says, words against my ear so I can hear him.

I swallow the lump in my throat. This is not right. But I've never been right. Nothing about me is right.

I squeeze my eyes closed. Jeremiah might be pissed it isn't me that does it. He wants to teach me a lesson in all of this. But I can't. I know I can't. I'll only fuck it up.

I nod, and Nicolas nods toward the stairs. He wants me to go down before he pulls the trigger.

I want to argue, but now is really not the time. We can't speak any more than we already have, and I'm not about to fuck this up more than it's already fucked. So much for bringing Julie's head back to taunt Lucifer.

My gun still drawn, still in both hands, I make my way down the stairs on tiptoes, looking at my feet, careful not to trip. When I get to the bottom, I glance up at Nicolas, and he's staring at me. I pull my brows together, confused. He needs to move. We need to get the fuck out of here. The longer we stay, the worse the bad feeling gets.

But when he moves, it isn't into the room.

It's toward me. He opens his mouth, about to say something, when I feel a hand over my own mouth.

I try to move, to swing around to whoever it is, but Nicolas is the one to speak.

"He's got a gun. Don't move."

He says it quietly enough, but I hear it loud and clear.

I freeze.

"I told you that you couldn't run, Lilith."

CHAPTER TWENTY

Present

I NEVER THOUGHT anyone could scare me as much as Jeremiah did. My brother is ruthless, cold, unaffected by basic human emotions. I thought, at times, he was a psychopath. I thought he was a combination of the worst of nature and nurture. Abandoned by a mother that never cared for him, given to families that only wanted to use him. But he had had the darkness in him from an early age. I was scared of him even before we were separated.

But I'd been wrong.

Because when Lucifer drags me outside, into the back-yard, and Nicolas comes after me, I'm terrified.

Lucifer still has me against his front, an arm wrapped around my chest. But I can see the gun in his hand. It's aimed at Nicolas, and Nicolas, for his part, is aiming right back, his eyes focused on Lucifer.

I don't care much about what Lucifer might do to me, even though I know it will be horrific. I had almost just helped kill his precious Julie, after all. In the same bed his child slept in. But I don't want Nicolas to die.

He's one of the only bright spots for me at the Rain mansion.

"Let her go." His voice is calm, his hands steady as he aims at Lucifer, but his jaw ticks. He doesn't dare look at me.

Lucifer laughs, raspy and hoarse. I can smell him. Cigarettes and pine. I can feel the warmth of him at my back, feel the strength in his arm slung around my chest. My own gun hangs limply at my side. I could turn it around. Somehow find a way to aim at Lucifer behind me. But I don't. I don't want to provoke him. I want Nicolas to live.

"You come into my home, plan to kill a mother and child, and you dare give *me* a command?" Lucifer doesn't sound angry as he speaks the words, which is even more unsettling. He sounds as if we're discussing the weather. Chilly, with a light breeze. Dark, clear skies. Lots of stars visible overhead.

"Let her go, and we'll leave. We can call it even." I know Nicolas doesn't mean that, and Lucifer knows it too.

He doesn't laugh again. But he rests his chin against my hair, and I see Nicolas inhale, deeply. Trying to calm his anger.

"I'm not letting her go. But you'll leave. *Now.*" Lucifer

keeps the same conversational tone, his chin still resting on my hair.

Nicolas takes a step forward. Lucifer doesn't move. Doesn't even tense. Nicolas notices, and takes another step. I'm not sure how he thinks that approaching closer with his gun still drawn is going to get us the fuck out of this mess, but I can think of nothing to say. Being this close to Lucifer again, being flush against his body...I can't think at all. He makes me stupid.

"If you don't let her go," Nicolas says through clenched teeth, "I'm going to kill you. Then I'm going to kill *them*," he jerks his head back toward the house, "and I'm going to make it slow. Especially for the child. I don't know if he can talk yet, but either way, he'll be fucking begging me for death."

I know he won't. Nicolas won't harm a tiny hair on that kid's head. But Lucifer doesn't know that. Even still, he doesn't react.

"Do you think they mean something to me?" he asks instead. He tightens his arm against me, sliding his hand up my shoulder and coming to rest it against my neck. "They don't. But this," his fingers curl around my throat and Nicolas's eyes narrow. I see the gun tremble in his grip, just a little. "This does. Did you have any part of this?"

I don't know what he means at first. I have no clue what he's getting at.

But then I remember. The bruises. He had seen them in the forest. But what the fuck does he care? He had left me in an asylum, unconscious, soon to be dead for all he knew. I know he hasn't suddenly grown a heart. He never had one.

Nicolas doesn't play into the bait. "Let her go."

Lucifer sighs. I feel his chest expand against my shoulders. Then the gun is withdrawn from my view. And I feel the cold barrel of it against my own head.

I stiffen. Now might be the time to use my own gun. I shift a little in Lucifer's arms, and he is surprised enough to let me do it. Then I press the gun to his thigh at my back.

He laughs. "That will hurt," he acknowledges, "but it won't kill me." He digs the barrel of his own gun in a little deeper to the side of my head. "This though, this will."

Nicolas is full of barely contained fury. But he knows as well as I do that Lucifer has just turned the tables. There's no way, even if both Nicolas and I fire at the same time, that we can get Lucifer down before he puts a bullet in my brain.

And I have no doubt he would. He's already fucked me over once.

For the first time since this standoff began, Nicolas and I lock eyes. I keep the gun pressed awkwardly against Lucifer's thigh, but I speak first.

"Go," I say. "Go and tell Jeremiah. He'll figure it out."

Lucifer laughs darkly behind me. "I doubt that, Lilith."

Nicolas shakes his head. "I'm not leaving without you."

"You'll go," I say, my voice rising, "and you'll get the fuck back to Alexandria and you'll tell Jeremiah. There's no other option." I hate saying it, especially as Lucifer chuckles again, but it's true. There's no other way to get out of this. I can handle myself. I still have a gun, after all.

"Listen to her," Lucifer croons. "Or I'll put a bullet through her precious little skull."

I swallow the lump in my throat, my eyes still on Nicolas's.

He shakes his head again. "No."

"Goddammit!" I hiss, my temper rising. I want this gun away from my head. Once, I thought I'd wanted it. Once, I'd planned to do it. Some days, I thought of other plans. Like jumping from a balcony at the hotel. But right now, I don't want to die. Not before I kill Lucifer first.

"Shh, baby," he whispers in my ear. "He'll do as you say." He moves his face away from me. "Won't you?" he challenges Nicolas.

"Jeremiah will kill me," Nicolas says. I know that isn't his first concern. But it's a valid one, nonetheless. I don't know what to say to it. Maybe he will, after he finds me. But I'll fight for Nicolas. Just as I'm fighting for him now.

But it's Lucifer who speaks before I can console him.

"Jeremiah can go fuck himself," he hisses, the first signs of anger creeping into his tone. "Jeremiah left her when she needed him. Jeremiah has done worse to her than even I could do."

"What the fuck are you talking about?" I ask. My first words spoken to him since we've been out here.

Jeremiah is a dick. He had almost killed me. What Lucifer is saying isn't exactly untrue. But my brother hadn't raped me in an abandoned building and left me for dead.

Lucifer laughs. "He knows."

Nicolas frowns. He shakes his head. "Fuck you."

But he doesn't deny it. He doesn't deny that he knows something.

Lucifer keeps the gun against my head, his hand gentle on my throat. "If you don't go running back to your master, I'll tell her. And then I'll kill her."

I twist my head. I don't care about the gun anymore. I want to see Lucifer. But he presses the weapon harder against the side of my face, not letting me see him.

"What are you talking about?" The words come out too quiet. I feel as if the world is spinning around me. They both know something I don't. About my brother. About me.

"You don't know what you're talking about," Nicolas snaps to Lucifer. But there's something beneath those words. Like he's trying to convince himself. And his eyes... they're back on me. And they look almost sorry.

Lucifer sighs. Then he whistles.

I frown, and Nicolas spins around, aiming everywhere he turns. My pulse flies, and I can feel it everywhere. In my chest. My wrists. My head.

Then I hear it.

From the woods, four people emerge with a quiet rustling of leaves. They have skeleton bandanas pulled up over their noses and lips, only their eyes are visible. But I know who they are.

The rest of the Unsaints.

Atlas. Cain. Ezra. Mayhem.

They all have guns. They aren't aiming at anyone, but they walk slowly to stand beside us, and I see out of the corner of my eye, they glare at Nicolas.

"Nice to see you again, Lilith," one with a deep voice says. Ezra. My skin crawls and a whimper escapes my lips.

"So you're not all that stupid, then, huh?" another one asks. I'm not sure who it is. Maybe Mayhem. Maybe Cain. In the dark, I can't get a good look at them.

Lucifer's hand twitches against my throat, a low growl comes from *his* throat. The Unsaints don't speak again.

Nicolas looks like he's going to scream. Instead, he slowly lowers his gun. One of the Unsaints chuckles.

Nicolas hangs his head. "I'm so sorry, Sid."

"*Sid?*" Lucifer purrs. I feel anger harden in my veins that now he knows that about me. He knows my name. I don't know if I know his.

"I'm so sorry," Nicolas says again, sighing. He picks his head up and meets my gaze. "I'm coming back for you. You know that, right? I'll always come back for you."

Lucifer stiffens at my back. "*Go,*" he commands harshly.

I lower my own weapon. My wrist hurts from twisting it to aim at Lucifer's leg. My hands are sweating in my gloves.

"Go," I echo him, nodding toward Nicolas. "I know you'll come back. I'll be waiting for you."

"He'll be waiting a long, long time," Lucifer snarls. Another chuckle from the Unsaints beside us.

Nicolas looks at me with pleading eyes, but I nod again.

And he walks away.

"That's a good boy," one of the Unsaints whispers. Nicolas either doesn't hear him or pretends not to. He keeps walking, without glancing back. And when he reaches the side of the house, he breaks into a run. We can see, off the side of the house, he gets into the Porsche, starts it, the lights on this time. And then he fucking flies down the driveway. I hope to god he doesn't get in a wreck before he can get back to my brother.

And I hope to God my brother doesn't kill him before they find me.

But Lucifer whispers in my ear, and I remember God doesn't give a fuck about me.

"Welcome back, *Sid*." His words are hot against my skin. "I've been waiting for you for a long, long time."

CHAPTER TWENTY-ONE

Present

WE DON'T GO BACK into the house. Instead, Lucifer shoves me forward, toward the woods, after ripping off my gloves and discarding them somewhere I can't see. I don't try to resist. The boys come with us, and there's no way I can fight them all off. One stops Lucifer by standing in front of him, a massive form in a black dress shirt and jeans, the skeleton mask still pulled up over half of his face.

"What, Cain?" Lucifer snarls at him.

Cain grabs the gun from my hand, then nods. I let him do it. I don't want to put up a fight. I have no idea where the fuck I am, where the fuck we're going.

No one speaks as we enter the woods, and I stumble over branches as Lucifer still holds me to his back and shoves me forward.

I wonder if Julie is his wife now. I wonder how she can sleep through all of this bullshit happening yards away from her own child. I know I'm wondering the wrong fucking things.

The only sounds are of the guys' footsteps, my own breathing, and my heart still hammering away in my chest. I see up ahead a clearing, and vehicles, black and white paint shining beneath the moon. That's why we didn't hear them. I wonder if my brother will be able to find me.

"Where are you taking me?" I finally ask. Because I need to ask something.

Another dark laugh from someone in the Unsaints.

"You don't get to ask questions," Lucifer murmurs.

"Aren't you going to kill me anyway?" I ask.

He abruptly stops walking at the edge of the clearing. There's a white Range Rover, and a black car. A blacked-out BMW M5, I see from the back of it. The vehicles are parked at angles, the rear-ends toward one another.

The Unsaints circle around me, their skeleton masks pulled down, and I see their guns are away. Probably in the back of their pants. I know Atlas, backwards hat on, directly across from me. I know Ezra, too, because he's the shorter of them, which isn't saying much. They're all like giants. I recognize Mayhem, too, from his white tank and black pants, tattoos covering every inch of his arms. One on his face.

Cain is wearing a dress shirt, his head shaved on both sides, longer on top.

Their expressions are unreadable, since I can't see most of their damn faces.

Lucifer has been in my nightmares. Both awake and asleep. But I don't know him. I don't know these men, either.

I thought, that Halloween night, that maybe I'd fallen in love with him. I thought miracles happened. I'd started to think, before I drifted off into blackness, that he had been some sort of dark angel, a true *unsaint*, sent to me in the night to keep me here.

But then I'd woken up naked and alone, save for the tormenter that is my brother.

Lucifer hadn't been an angel. Not even a fallen one. He'd really, truly been the devil.

I look down at the forest floor. I can't think while I look at them, while I feel Lucifer's warm body behind me, clutching me to him.

"I'm going to kill them," he answers me. "Everyone in the Order of fucking Rain. But probably not for the reasons you think."

Fear steals through me. Not for myself. For Nicolas. Even, although I'm loathe to admit it, for my brother. I would normally never be scared for my brother. Never think anyone could get to him. But Lucifer has me, and while Jeremiah might not love me in the conventional sense, he'd never allow anyone else to have me. Especially not after what Lucifer did to me. Not after how Jeremiah found me.

My eyes drift to Lucifer's forearm across my waist, the cut muscle, his long, pale fingers digging into my sides.

"Explain," I whisper. I try not to feel his body flush against mine. Try not to smell him.

I don't want to think about how he had met me at that intersection, slipped his hand into mine.

"You don't want to know the truth." He shifts against me, and I realize he had pulled a cigarette from his back pocket as his hand comes up from my waist and he lights it. He takes a drag, exhales the smoke over my shoulder.

I smell that familiar scent of whatever brand of cigarettes he smokes. I like it, although I'll never admit that out loud to anyone.

I close my eyes. I don't want to see the Unsaints' focus on me. They're so quiet, it's freaking me out. And Lucifer seems in no hurry to get into one of those cars.

"Who hurt you?" he asks me quietly.

My eyes snap open. I almost laugh out loud. *You*, I want to scream at him. *You fucking hurt me. You ruined my already fucked-up life. You left me at the hands of a monster.*

I bite back those words. I don't want him to know how much he'd fucked me over. I don't answer him. He doesn't deserve an answer. He doesn't deserve anything.

"I can make her talk," Ezra says, his deep voice rumbling through the forest.

"Chill out, Ez," Atlas says, rolling his dark eyes. "She's gonna have to talk, one way or another."

Lucifer shoves me to the ground. I catch myself on my

palms, the forest floor damp. I scramble around, sitting upright, but there's no where I can scuttle to. They surround me. And from the ground, they look so fucking big. They could tear me apart.

But it's Lucifer I look to.

And I don't know why, but I do. I meet his brilliant blue eyes. He's wearing a black, fitted t-shirt and ripped black jeans.

He sighs, exhaling smoke. "I don't want to ask you again, *Sid*," he sneers, as if my name is a curse. "Who hurt you?"

I laugh. It's bitter and broken, but it's a laugh. "Would you have cared if you had two kids?" I ask him, banking on the fact that Julie's is the only other he has. Hell, he could've fathered a child in all fifty states. Fuck do I know.

I don't know what I expect him to do. And it isn't true. I took Plan B, brought in by Jeremiah. But I want to fuck with him a little, like he's fucking with me.

"The fuck is she talking about?" Ezra growls. I don't look at him, at my back.

Lucifer looks angrier than I've ever seen him. Which, considering I haven't seen him much shouldn't be saying something, but it is. The vein in his neck seems to throb and he grips the cigarette so hard between his thumb and index finger that I think he's accidentally put it out.

"What." It isn't a question.

I meet his glare. This is his fucking fault. "Don't act so surprised," I snarl. "You should have figured out how it works by now."

His gaze doesn't falter. He tosses the cigarette to the ground and stomps on it. "You were pregnant."

I want to drag this out. I want to fuck him where it hurts. Because it seems like it might hurt. But I shake my head.

"No," I spit at him. "But I could have been."

"Fucking psycho bitch," someone says behind me. I think it's Cain.

Lucifer snaps his gaze to him, and his lip curls. Cain doesn't say anything else.

"You fucking left me," I hiss. I swallow, biting back tears. Slowly, I stand to my feet, very aware that five Unsaints circle me right now and I'm screaming at the guy who seems to be their leader. "You fucking left me!" I scream at him, lurching across the space between us, my hands flying to his chest. He just stands there, solid as a rock. "You left me in the middle of the goddamn woods, in a fucking insane asylum. You piece of fucking shit!" I'm screaming at the top of my lungs, all the pain from the past year coming out in a rush. My hands are shaking against his chest, my fists are clenched so hard. I make myself unclench one, point a finger in his face. "You raped me—"

One of the guys whistles.

Lucifer reaches for my wrist, gripping me so tightly I feel the bones rub together. Anger gleams in his eyes; his brow furrows as he clenches his jaw.

"Who is Jeremiah?" he asks me.

I suck in a breath and try to jerk my wrist out of his grip. It's fruitless. He holds tight. "You fucking asshole.

You can't stand it, can you?" I sneer, the anger still coming in waves. Still pouring through my broken heart. "You can't stand to hear what you did. You can't stand to see me. See this."

"Who. Is. Jeremiah?" he repeats. "To you?"

"I told you we should have never trusted that fucker," Atlas says through clenched teeth.

I try to pull my wrist away from Lucifer again, and again, he holds firm.

"Fuck you."

Someone sighs. "If you don't fucking tell her, bro, I will." Cain.

Lucifer looks like he wants to say something to Cain, but he forces his gaze back to me. He bites his lip, and I remember biting it before, too. I remember his blood. How it tasted on my tongue. How being with him felt.

He lets me go, shoving me away. I stumble back, and into someone's lean arms. This is Mayhem. He's built similar to Lucifer. He holds me against him, and I see his inked arms.

"You wanted to play with us, *Lilith?*" Mayhem teases. I wonder how much they've talked about since that night. How much they've laughed at my pain. How much they know about me. Not enough, apparently, if they don't know Jeremiah is my brother. "You might not make it out of this alive, Angel."

"Mayhem," Lucifer snaps, voice cold. "Get her in the fucking car and then get the fuck out of here."

There're some grumbles among the group, but no one

argues. This is the Unsaints at work. Mayhem takes me by the elbow and drags me to the M5, opens the door, and shoves me into the leather seat, doing up my seatbelt, too.

"Don't run, Angel. You'll only make it worse." His baby blue eyes bore into mine and then when Lucifer slides into the driver seat, Mayhem slams the door closed and walks to the Range Rover.

CHAPTER TWENTY-TWO

Present

THERE'S a dirt path surrounded by trees that Lucifer cruises down, the boys in the Range Rover behind us. We make a few turns once we're out on the main road. We don't speak. He doesn't smoke. I try not to think. The tears I've felt coming behind my eyes have dried up. I'm done crying over him. I'm done with him. I've spent a year hating him, but I don't care anymore.

Let them kill me. Let them cut my body into pieces.

Fuck it.

Minutes pass, and then he turns down a long driveway, which seems to be all the rage in Acid City or wherever the fuck we are. I haven't seen any sign of civilization since we left Julie's house.

Julie.

Her name feels bitter in my brain.

The house we pull up in front of is bigger than Julie's, a large brick house, three stories high. The driveway here is paved, and there's a three-car garage off a brick pathway a little distance from the house. Lucifer doesn't bother to park in one of the three. Instead, he stops the car in front of the porch and kills the lights and the engine. The Range Rover parks beside us.

"You know Jeremiah will come for you." It isn't a threat I whisper to him in the dark. It's just the truth. "He'll come for you, and he will kill you."

There's a long stretch of silence between us. I wonder if he'll get out, yank me out with him, and not say a word. I wonder what he plans to do to me. What he can possibly do that's worse than what he's done.

He brushes his thumb over his lip.

"I hope he does come for me," he finally says. Then he gets out, snatches up the gun from the side of the door, and slams it behind him. In seconds, he's on my side, opening the door and unbuckling my seatbelt before he hauls me out, over his shoulder. He might be lean, the leanest among the Unsaints, but he's fucking strong. I feel weightless in his arms.

Weightless and insignificant.

"I can walk," I grind out. The Unsaints get out of their car and laugh at those words. Lucifer doesn't bother putting me down as he walks up the steps on the porch, fishes a key out of his pocket with the same hand that holds his gun. He unlocks the door and squats a little to bring me in the house without banging my head against the doorframe.

The rest of them walk in behind him and someone shuts the door, and I hear the click of the lock. Then Lucifer sets me down.

It's dark inside the foyer. A staircase bisects the entranceway, and beyond that, there's an open plan living room with leather couches and a television that looks like it was built into the wall. The place doesn't smell stale, like it's been kept shut up for a long time. Instead, it smells like cigarettes.

His cigarettes.

But I can't imagine this is his home. It's not as opulent as I imagined it would be.

He's behind me, and neither of us have moved since we came in. The Unsaints make themselves at home here, sitting on the couch in the living room, save for Mayhem. He stays at my back, by the door.

I turn to Lucifer, crossing my arms over my chest.

"What do you want with me?"

He smiles, his dimples flashing. I marvel at how smooth his pale skin is. The only sign of any imperfection on his face, in the symmetry of his features, is that his top lip is bigger than his bottom. But it only serves to make him more beautiful.

He sets the gun on the table by the door, a mirror hanging above it. My eyes don't leave his.

Then he reaches for me, spins me around, and shoves me against the wall beside the door, Mayhem watching us.

Lucifer moves his hands from my chest to either side of my head as he glares down at me. Like *he* is angry. But he doesn't have any right to be. Sure, maybe I'm going to kill his girlfriend. Maybe I'd broken into that house, whosever it was. Maybe I'm going to fuck him over as hard as he's fucked me over. But he had started this chain of events a year ago. He had taken my chance to get out of this hell that was my life, and he'd pushed me into the arms of a monster who was nearly as bad as he was.

Nearly.

But not quite.

"I'm not afraid of you," I breathe, my hands down by my sides, clenched into fists. It's a lie. I know he knows it's a lie. But I don't care. I'm not going to admit to my fear. And Jeremiah really will come for me. I might only be able to count on him for pain and anger and vengeance, but I *can* count on it. Which is more than I can say for Lucifer.

I can't count on him for anything at all.

"You're a bad liar, Lilith."

Mayhem laughs softly under his breath. The three boys in the living room are whispering to each other, low murmurs. I can't make out what they're saying.

I tense at the name Lucifer called me. I'm not Sid right now. But he's still Lucifer. He's always been Lucifer.

His finger trails down my jaw, coming to rest on my throat. His eyes flick there, to the bruises. I feel my face burn with shame.

"Who did that?" he asks me quietly.

I don't answer him. He trails his finger down lower, to

the edge of my hoodie. He pulls at it but makes no move to take it off. Beneath, I have on a black sports bra. I don't want to undress in front of him. I don't even want to be near him. But even so, I can't get myself to move. To say something. Being so close to him clouds my judgement.

This man took advantage of me. He left me. He lied to me.

I try to repeat those things over and over again in my mind. Like a chant. A ward against the other feelings that are resurfacing at his nearness.

"Did you want it?" he tries again, eyes flicking to my throat.

I swallow. Anger lights through me, but I suppose it's a fair question. Sometimes I do want that. Sometimes I had. But these marks weren't sexual.

Although he doesn't know that.

I still don't say anything. I'm not sure what sins I might confess tonight if I do. I don't want to give him any more of mine. I don't want to take any more of his. I can't.

His hand runs down my body, like it had that night. He stops at the hem of my sweatshirt, staring at me. Then he slips his hand beneath it, his fingers splay on my skin. His touch is like fire. A fire I want to burn me.

I try to force that thought away.

"Get your hand off of me," I snarl.

His fingers dig into my skin, one hand still on the wall beside my head. "Who hurt you?"

I sigh. He isn't going to give it up. But how can I tell him? And why would I?

"That's not your business. Who hurts me, who pleases me, who fucks me. None of that is your business. It never was."

"Lucifer, get your girl under control," Ezra drawls from the couch at his back. "We probably don't have much time."

Lucifer's eyes narrow, long lashes nearly reaching his dark brows. He presses his brow against mine. "Lilith," he says, and I notice there's something like a plea in that word. "Please. Tell me."

Please.

Him and my brother are more alike than they probably know. Both manipulative. Both seductive in their darkness. I wonder if they got along well, those few years they ran together. I marvel at the fact they lasted that long.

I marvel, too, at the fact that my brother walked away from them. From this. Over one night. He chose me.

I bite my lip, and Lucifer's eyes go to my mouth. Something flashes in his gaze, something besides the anger. The coldness. Something warm.

I turn my head away from him, and his fingers dig a little deeper into my abdomen. He doesn't move his head from mine.

I close my eyes tight, trying to not feel him. Trying to get my mind away from this moment.

"It doesn't matter," I say softly, the fight going out of me for a moment. "It doesn't matter."

His hand slides further up my torso, coming to rest on my heart. "It matters to me," he whispers.

I shake my head. "Someone that works for Jeremiah. And..." I swallow against the lump in my throat. I don't know why I'm telling him. But it won't make a difference for anyone, anyway. "Jeremiah himself." I spit my brother's name out like it's poison. In some ways, he had been poison to me. But he'd also been my antidote. Lucifer had fucked me over, had taken away my choice to die. But Jeremiah had tried his best to bring me back to life, even if his methods were unconventional.

I feel Lucifer's hand tense on my heart, over my breast. The touch isn't sexual. It's...comforting in a strange way. I keep my eyes closed.

"Look at me," he commands.

I don't.

He sighs through his nose, his brow still on mine. "Lilith," he pleads. "Sid." It's the first time he's said my name, my real name, without disdain. "Sid, look at me."

I open my eyes, turn to face him. He pulls back a little, to take me in fully.

"Who is Jeremiah to you?" he asks me again.

"Why do you get to ask all the questions!" The words erupt from my lips in a growl, but he doesn't even flinch. As if he expected them. As if he was used to my darkness, just biding his time, waiting for it to come out and play. "Why do you get to ask anything at all? What am I even doing here? If it's money you want, you won't get it. Jeremiah doesn't love me that much. He'll kill you, and he'll take me back, and that's it."

He breathes a laugh, my chest heaving beneath his

hand under my sweatshirt. "I don't need his money. I have plenty of my own."

"That's for damn sure," one of the guys says. Atlas, I think. I keep forgetting they're here. I wish they weren't. I wish they weren't watching all of this.

"Then what?" I ask, shrugging my shoulders. I want this shit to end. I want to forget Lucifer ever existed. I don't even care if I don't get to kill him. If he would just let me go, let us live separate lives. Stop fucking with my brother. "Why did you burn down Brooklin's house? And the club? Kill the runner? What do you want from us?"

"*Us?*" he hisses. "You let him fuck around with other women, and you still align yourself with him?"

I flash him a deadly smile. He doesn't know. I don't want him to know the truth. It's more fun this way. "You only got my first name, earlier," I point out. He watches me carefully, as if I'm a bomb that might detonate at any moment. I swear everyone in this house is holding their breath, even Mayhem beside us. "But my last name..." I trail off and lick my lips, enjoying his angst. "My last name is Rain."

He looks at me for a long moment, and then he pounds his fist against the wall, beside my head, and tears his hand from under my shirt. I think I know what he's thinking. I want him to think it. He thinks I took Jeremiah's last name.

He turns around, running his hands through his dark hair. I watch his back muscles flex beneath his shirt, how his hips narrow, how his jeans fit him so well.

Satan.

Lucifer.

The goddamn devil.

I stay against the wall, enjoying this moment. The moment I have something on him. For some reason, even if he hates me, he still wants me to be his. He wants to claim me. Own me. Before he destroys me completely.

The boys have stood up in the living room. They take steps toward us.

Lucifer whirls around to face me. "How could you?" he asks, shaking his head. "How could you?" His hands are still on his head, and I see the line beneath his bicep.

I force myself to look at his face. "I could ask the same of you. You left me in that forest. You fucking left me and you—"

Lights flash through the glass pane of the door at my side. I stop talking, my mouth snapping closed. More lights. Multiple vehicles.

Lucifer acts first, taking the gun from the table by the door. The rest of the Unsaints crowd around us, and Mayhem shoves me behind them. They peer through the glass pane, and Lucifer's hand cups above his eyes to see better. I wait with bated breath. There's no way Nicolas got to Jeremiah and back so fast. That would be impossible.

I stand off to the side, and Lucifer's expression is unreadable as I stare at his side profile. His straight nose. Full lips. I want to bash his head against the glass and break that beautiful fucking face.

"It seems your owners came back early," Cain mutters, smoothing down his dress shirt, muscles bulging beneath it.

I ignore the quip and shake my head. "Alexandria is too far."

Lucifer glances at me. "Jeremiah didn't want you to get too far away from him though, did he?"

It hits me. My brother had followed us here. Given the circumstances, I can't exactly blame him for that.

"It's okay, though," Lucifer continues in his gravelly voice. I feel a chill slide down my spine. "I'd like you to be here for this."

I frown at him. I see all five of the Unsaints, guns in hand, expressions tense, muscles flexing beneath their clothes. They're not going to let my brother walk out of here alive. He left them. After they let an outsider into their little cult for his wicked crimes, he betrayed them. They probably took worse than a Death Oath to one another.

Not that the Death Oath meant anything. At least not to Lucifer.

As one, they all step back from the door. It's eerie, how they move together. Lucifer yanks my arm until I'm in front of him. Mayhem reaches out and slides the lock free of the door, yanks it open, then rejoins the ranks.

Lucifer is in the middle with me, two boys flanking either side of us.

I see Nicolas first, rounding the sidewalk, and then my brother at his back, and fucking Kristof and Trey behind him. They all have guns. All of them except my brother.

I roll my eyes, but my heart leaps at the sight of them. Even fucking Kristof.

I want to get out of here. I want to get way from this shit. From my past. From what happened. I'm ready for it to end.

The four of them walk through the door one at a time, and Trey kicks the door closed behind him.

We're thrown into darkness, muted only by the lamp on in the living room at our backs.

"We can do this the easy way," my brother drawls, "or the hard way."

Lucifer takes us back a step, and I hear the rest of the Unsaints shift with him. Lucifer isn't aiming the gun at me, or them. I'm certain the others are, but I don't take my eyes off of Jeremiah's, even though it isn't me he's looking at.

"You can let her go now and we all walk away from this, or I'll cut your son into pieces and feed them to you, one by one."

No one says anything. Silence rings out after my brother's words. No one is looking at me, save for Trey. He looks almost apologetic. But now is not the time for that.

"You piece of shit." It's Ezra's rumbling voice that breaks the silence. My brother's eyes snap to his. "You motherfucker. You abandon us, break your fucking oath, and *you dare* to make demands of us?"

Lucifer chuckles darkly, and when he speaks, I can

hear the smile in his words. "You keep mistaking me for someone who cares about that child. About Julie. You got all of that wrong. It's why you're here, in this position."

Nicolas spits on the floor and works his jaw. "Wrong?" he counters, tilting his head, gun aimed at Lucifer at my back. Kristof's and Trey's are, too. "Funny, for a guy who doesn't care, you were waiting in the shadows of the kid's house. You dragged Sid out at gunpoint for him. Brought your cronies out for him. That doesn't seem like someone who doesn't care to me, *Lucifer.*"

Lucifer has one arm around my front, and he tightens it against my chest. "Before I consider your request," he says calmly, "what happened to Sid's throat?"

Kristof's gaze darts to me and Lucifer notices. The fucking idiot just gave himself away. I feel Lucifer tense behind me.

"I'm going to kill you," he says quietly to Kristof.

"Let me go." That's my voice joining the fray. I'm sick of being used as a pawn. "Let me go, *Lucifer.* You don't want to kill me. Sure, you might want to fuck me again. To use me. But you don't want to kill me, and they know that."

"Careful, Lilith." Atlas's words. "I wouldn't tell Lucifer what he does and doesn't want."

"Fuck you," I snarl to Atlas. This earns a disapproving click of the tongue from Cain. I twist in Lucifer's arms to meet Atlas's dark eyes at my side. "Did you know?" I ask him. "Did you know he was going to rape me that night?"

Atlas's gaze doesn't falter from my stare. "Rape?" he

mocks, a smile curling on his lips. "Seemed like you wanted it to me."

I lunge at him, but Lucifer keeps his grip firm around my chest.

"I will fucking carve out your tongue and shove it so far down your throat you're going to choke on it." That comes from my brother. For once, we're on the same side.

But Atlas smiles fully now, turning to my brother. "You never told her, did you?"

That makes me pause.

"I'm sick and fucking tired," Lucifer begins, his voice low against my ear, but loud enough for all of them to hear, "of asking you the same fucking things over and over again, Sid. Who is *he*," and I know he's referring to Jeremiah, "to *you*? You have the same last name, but I know Jeremiah. I know him probably better than you. He's fucking filth. You wouldn't marry shit like that, no matter how rich he was. Who is he to you, Lilith? And don't fucking lie to me."

His breath against my skin makes goosebumps form on my arms. All along my body. I meet Jeremiah's gaze in the darkness. His brows are furrowed, and there's a frown on his face. He actually looks worried.

I have no idea why.

I have no idea what it matters, at this point, what I am to Jeremiah. That I'm his sister. It's very clear, based on the amount of muscle and guns Jeremiah has brought here, and based on the fact he'd followed me here, that he would kill for me. He might not pay a ransom or concede his territory or his business, but he'll fire a gun into someone's brain for me.

That should be enough to Lucifer and the Unsaints.

But the way Jeremiah is looking at me, and the amount of times Lucifer has asked the question...I want to know. I want to know what it matters.

"He's my brother," I whisper.

CHAPTER TWENTY-THREE

Present

NO ONE MOVES, but the entire atmosphere in the room changes. It's as if someone has taken the air from the house, closed everyone's lungs. Choking us all. The tension is heavy but loud, like beating rain. And there's a storm brewing, even as not a single word is spoken after my confession.

And that's what it feels like.

A confession.

I have no idea why.

I turn, to see Lucifer's face. And he lets me. His arms are still around me, but he lets me turn to him, and I tilt my head up to meet his gaze.

Shock. That's what's written on his face. I'd expected triumph or joy or cold calculation, knowing what I am to Jeremiah. Knowing we're blood. He doesn't know how shallow that blood runs. Although he must know we were separated, since he knew Jeremiah for several years. Even still, I expected, knowing our tie, he would be elated.

But the shock doesn't morph into anything like elation. It morphs quickly into horror and then anger. He clenches his jaw, and he looks away from me, toward my brother. He aims the gun at Jeremiah with one hand.

Atlas swears under his breath.

None of my brother's men say a word.

But it's Ezra that moves first.

He barrels past all of us, straight into my brother, knocking his head against the door at his back. He flips his gun in his hand when they're both on the floor and starts pistol whipping Jeremiah in the face.

"You—sick—son—of—a—bitch!" he snarls, every word punctuated by the gun smashing into my brother's face. I hear every hit, and I feel it, in my gut, jarring me. I make to run toward them, but Lucifer grabs me by my collar, yanking me backward into him. I fight against him with all that I've got, shoving and kicking and hitting. He only holds me tighter and then he pushes me into Mayhem's arms, which lock around me in a grip it's nearly impossible to breathe from.

Lucifer kneels down next to Ezra, who is still attacking my brother. Nicolas, Trey and Kristof are screaming at Ezra, telling him to put the gun down, and I'm terrified they're going to shoot one of them, and I don't know why I care that they might shoot Ezra, but I do. Even as my brother's face turns into nothing but a bloody pit, I'm terri-

fied for Ezra, too. A man I don't even know. And now
Lucifer is in the fray, gripping Ezra's face.

"Stop," he's saying, his voice low, but Ezra keeps going,
even though he can't see, because Lucifer won't let go of
his head. "Stop," Lucifer growls again.

"I'm going to fucking blow your head off!" Kristof
snarls, cocking the gun.

I freeze as Cain holds a gun to my head, Mayhem's
arms holding me in place.

"No, you're not," Cain says.

Lucifer looks up, his eyes dark. But he doesn't seem to
care that one of his Unsaints is holding me at gunpoint.
Why would he? Fuck, he was just holding me at gunpoint
himself.

Lucifer grabs Ezra's shoulders and shakes him. But
Kristof sees the gun at my head, and he, along with
Nicolas and Trey, fall silent. Although no one lowers their
weapons.

No one except Ezra.

Ezra's chest is heaving, I can see from behind him, his
back rising and falling. Lucifer hauls him up, and Ezra
seems to just stand there, limp in Lucifer's arms. Lucifer
drags him back, and Ezra's gun is dangling from his
fingers. His hazel eyes are unseeing as he stares at the
floor, and my eyes snap to my brother's face.

Trey and Nicolas crouch down over him while Kristof
keeps aiming his gun in the Unsaints' direction. In *my*
direction.

Lucifer stands in front of me, facing me, Ezra now

with one arm flung against Atlas, who is looking at him with concern, but not speaking. Ezra's chest is still heaving.

"Tell me why I shouldn't kill your brother," Lucifer says.

"Leave...her...alone." My brother's voice is hoarse. I'm surprised he's still speaking.

But something is wrong. There's something everyone in this room knows that I don't.

Cain doesn't lower the gun, but I notice his finger isn't on the trigger. Mayhem still has me in a tight grip, Kristof is still aiming at us, and Trey and Nicolas are trying to help my brother sit up. Lucifer's back is to them.

"Lucifer." His name comes out as a whisper. His eyes soften when he hears it.

He shakes his head. "Sid," he begs me, "tell me why." He has a gun in his hand. It's tapping against his thigh.

"What's going on?" I don't know why my voice shakes. Nothing has changed since I told him the truth. Nothing at all. Jeremiah was my brother before I said the words. He's my brother now, after I've said them. But a quick glance at Atlas, who squeezes his eyes shut for a moment before glancing at me and then back at Ezra at his side, tells me everything has changed.

I remember Mayhem's father kicked his sister out, for her fucking Atlas. I remember this is a tangled web. There are things I don't know. Things I don't understand.

"He's fucking with you, Sid." But Jeremiah's garbled words don't ring true. He's lying. But about what?

Lucifer swallows. I remember the skeleton paint I first saw him in. I remember the hood over his curls. I remember his hands all over me. The knife. His teeth. His mouth. Our blood on our lips when we kissed.

How he saved me, maybe without even knowing it.

But I remember other things, too. How he passed me drink after drink. How he poured it down both of our throats when he laid on top of me in the underground asylum. I remember his last words to me. The last ones I remember anyway. *With you by my side, we'll figure that out, Lilith.*

I remember some of my last words to him, too. *I'd do anything with you.*

"What happened, Lucifer?"

Lucifer's eyes are angry. *He* is angry.

But I don't look away from him.

Someone is going to fucking tell me what all nine of these men are holding their breaths about. Someone is going to tell me what I need to know.

Lucifer's face actually crumples. He frowns, squeezes his eyes shut and runs his free hand over his jaw, then presses the palm of his hand against his eyes.

"I've been looking for you," he whispers, lowering his hand but not meeting my gaze. "I've been looking for the past year. I've been looking fucking everywhere for you, Sid." I watch the vein in his neck move as he swallows. "But I never got your name. I fucking never got it."

"Because you left me."

Atlas scoffs, and Mayhem snarls behind me, but they don't say anything.

"That's right," my brother chimes in from the floor behind Lucifer. He's leaning against the door, Nicolas and Trey still crouched around him. But his voice is gaining strength. Before, he had seemed hesitant. But now he's back in command. "He left you. He fucked you over. I took you in. Step back, Sid. Come to your brother, so I can put a bullet in this motherfucker's brain."

Lucifer's eyes snap up to mine. I notice, even in the darkness, that I can see them shining. "He's lying," he chokes out. He shakes his head, bites his lip. I realize Cain's gun is not pressing against my head anymore.

Whatever Lucifer is about to say, he doesn't want to. I feel like I might faint. "He's lying. I never left you, Sid. I would have never fucking left you. That night, when I saw you at that crosswalk, fuck. I saw the gun on your thigh. I knew it was real. When I spoke to you, I had an idea of what you meant to do. And I couldn't. I didn't know you. You didn't know me. But I couldn't have let you do it. And I would have never left you."

"That's enough bullshit," Jeremiah's voice rings out in the quiet house. He's pissed. He makes to stand up, but Nicolas and Trey hold him down.

Atlas aims his gun at my brother, one arm still slung around Ezra.

"If you shoot me," Jeremiah tells Atlas calmly, "you will die. You do understand that, don't you? You're not actually as dumb as you look?"

Atlas smiles. For the first time, I see the coldblooded monster in him. The same that's in Lucifer. In my brother. Kristof. Ezra. Mayhem. Cain.

Me.

"I will," Atlas agrees. "But you'll be dead too, asshole. That'll be enough for me."

My eyes are locked on Lucifer's. I don't care about the pissing match between Jeremiah and Atlas. I don't care about Mayhem's arms around me. I actually need him there, because I feel suddenly far too weak.

"I woke up," I say, my lip trembling. "I woke up and you were...you were gone. I was..." I choke back a sob. I take a breath in through my nose. Out through my mouth. I feel like I'm falling. I feel like I'm falling, and no one is going to catch me. Not this time. "My clothes..."

Lucifer's jaw tightens again. So does Mayhem's grip, although it doesn't feel menacing. "I'm so sorry, Sid. I'm sorry I couldn't save you. I'm so fucking sorry." Lucifer nearly sobs the words out.

"What. Happened?!" I scream the words. Lucifer actually flinches. No one moves. It feels like no one is breathing.

"It won't change anything," Jeremiah says coldly. "It won't make this better. You do understand that, don't you? We can settle this between us. But you won't make her love you."

"It wasn't me, Lilith." Lucifer looks equal parts anguished and angry.

I need to know what the fuck happened that night before I decide how I'm going to change this.

"It wasn't me. It was *him.*" His eyes flick to Jeremiah at his back, narrowing into slits as he turns his head. With an effort, he tears his gaze away from him, focuses back on me. "He found you. At the merry-go-round." I remember. "But he didn't know, then, I don't think, who you were. He just wanted you. We never trusted him, but we tried. God we fucking tried. He would've been the only one that could've fucked us on Unsaints' Night. The only fucking one." He cradles his head in his hands for a second. Then he looks up.

He bites his lip. I see blood gleaming on it when he starts to speak again. "He should have fucking killed me. My God." He covers his mouth with his hand, smearing the blood. Then he lowers it. "He...he tried to hurt you, Sid." He shakes his head and his voice trembles. "He came back. He tried to hurt you." The last words come out as a growl. "He made me watch it happen. You...you were barely conscious. Barely awake. But you thought he was me. You let him, because you didn't know. Oh my God, you didn't know. He made me watch. I couldn't move. He had drugged all of us. Fucking all of us." I remember the table with drinks in the foyer of the rundown asylum. "Then he smashes a bottle over my head and tied me to a goddamn concrete pole. He waited until I was awake."

His chest rises and falls, faster and faster. He swipes his face again, as if he can get the memory out of his head. "He waited. I tried to get to you." He lifts his shirt, and I see scars along his perfect abs, thick and silver. The shape of something that looks like rope.

He lets his shirt go, and my eyes snap back to his.

"I tried to get to you. But he didn't...at some point, he realized who you were. He didn't get all the way, Sid. Fuck if that's a consolation, but he didn't. He must have recognized you because he stopped. He stopped and he hit me again and dragged you away. But I thought I could find you. I didn't know he was...I never knew he was your brother. I'm so fucking sorry, Sid. I'm so fucking sorry."

I don't move. I'm barely breathing. My head is spinning. My mind tries to save me, tries *not* to think of that night. So I don't. I don't want to remember. I don't want to think about it. To think about Jeremiah. His hoodie. About him towering over me. Waiting for me to come to.

About him taking me to the hotel. Washing me. Scrubbing my skin raw.

I don't want to think. I don't want to *be*.

I don't dare look at him. No one speaks. My brother says *nothing*.

I slam my head back, against Mayhem's chest. He's a rock wall behind me. "Fucking kill me," I order Lucifer. I slam my head against Mayhem again.

Lucifer shakes his head. "No, Sid." I watch him swallow again, watch him try to pull himself together. "No, Sid. No. Don't let him win this."

I rear my head back again, slamming it into Mayhem. "Someone fucking pull a trigger. You're Lucifer, after all. Send me back to hell."

"Don't let him win this, Lilith."

Something about that name makes me snap. With one last glance at Lucifer, I twist out of Mayhem's arms. He lets me go. I sidestep Lucifer, and my brother's eyes are on me. His face is white. Ghostly. At least the parts of it not covered in blood and already starting to bruise. He looks lost. I have no idea what he's thinking, but he doesn't move, and neither does Nicolas, Kristof, or Trey, as I make my way to my brother.

I raise my fist, cock it back, and I punch him as hard as I fucking can in the face.

His nose crunches under my fist; his head snaps back. When he twists back to look at me, I see tears welling in his eyes, blood dripping from his nose. From his face. His mouth, where Ezra got to him. I don't know why Ezra snapped, but I don't have time to think about it. I still hold my fist up. I cock it back again.

"Sid." Nicolas's voice.

I look to him. He's still leaned down next to my brother.

"Did you know?" I ask him quietly, not lowering my arm.

He looks away, for half a second. And I know.

My mouth falls open. I lower my arm.

He knew.

He had known.

I look to Kristof, to Trey. They knew too. They had to have fucking known. They knew my own brother nearly raped me, drugged the Unsaints, and then lied to me about it after he kept me prisoner in his hotel.

"Sid." I can't look at Jeremiah as he speaks. Instead, I stare at Nicolas. He had known. He had fucking known the entire time I was in that cell.

Jeremiah keeps talking. "Sid. I didn't know you were unconscious. You were...you were blacked out. But I didn't do it. It didn't go that far. I saw...who you were...my little sister."

I punch him again, but this time, he ducks his head and grabs my wrist.

"Sid, I didn't know..." Blood is everywhere. But I realize, in this moment, that the leverage the Unsaints had is gone. I'm in Jeremiah's grip now. Any of his men could pull the trigger and kill all of the Unsaints.

I relax. Jeremiah's grip on my wrist loosens, but he doesn't let go yet. His pale green eyes bore into my own. He had almost fucked me.

Bile rises up in my throat.

I'm going to be sick.

But I can't. Not yet. "Why didn't you tell me?" I ask instead. Because I have to know that. "Why did you make me think..." I close my eyes against the memory. "Why didn't you confess?" I meet his gaze again. "And why...why did you want me?"

I remember him staring at me at the party. Remember him following me to the merry-go-round. The same one he uses now to torment me. To make me *strong*.

He lowers my arm but doesn't let go. Not yet. "I didn't

want you to hate me," he whispers. In this moment, I believe him. But what he doesn't know is that I already hate him. Even before tonight, I'd hated him. Even if I loved him before, even if I love him still, I hate him too.

I nod. He lets go of my wrist. I seize that moment and dart away. Someone's arms come around me.

Lucifer's.

I can only think about him having to watch. Of those scars on his stomach. Of what he'd tried to do to save me. Of my brother, ruining both of our lives in one night. Of betraying these boys.

"Leave here," I spit at the four of them, the Order of Rain, meeting each of their eyes. They are sick. They are wrong. We are all unsainted, but they are the worst of us. "Get the fuck out of here and never come back. I don't want to see any of your faces, ever again."

My brother shakes his head, struggling to his feet. He looks like he's going to lose his goddamn mind. He grabs his hair, growling under his breath, his face caked with blood and bruises. "I'm not leaving without you, Sid. You're my sister. I waited too long to find you."

"You weren't looking for me," I spit.

"He was." Nicolas. "He was. He had always been. He didn't know it was you at first, but he thought you were someone familiar."

"I don't want to hear you talk," I snarl at Nicolas.

"You have to believe that, Sid. Even if you hate him. Hate me. He had been looking for you since he escaped. He'd wanted to find you. To keep you safe—"

"Shut. *Up.*"

"He didn't know who you were. Not when he first... first found you. He didn't know. He told me he didn't know. He told me you didn't fight back—"

"Because I was nearly unconscious!" I scream.

"Nearly," Nicolas repeats. He shakes his head. "And besides, he didn't do it. He didn't. He almost did, Sid, but he didn't."

"You kept this from me." I want to bury all of their bodies. "You kept this from me, and now you're fucking *defending him.*"

Jeremiah groans. "I don't want to be defended. What I did was wrong, Sid. I'm so fucking sorry. It was wrong. It was fucked up. But when I realized you were my own goddamn sister, I stopped, immediately..." He breaks off, and then he sinks to his knees.

My brother.

On his knees.

In a room full of his men, and his enemies.

Everyone is staring at him. Behind me, Lucifer's chest rises and falls against my shoulders, and he keeps both arms around me, gun trained at the floor. He doesn't speak, letting me fight this out with my brother for now. None of the Unsaints speak.

Jeremiah starts to crawl, *on his knees,* to me.

He stops a few inches from my feet and sits back on his heels. He's wearing a suit, unrumpled but caked in blood. I want him to drown in it.

"Please forgive me, Sid. Please. Don't go with him.

You aren't safe with him. You aren't safe with anyone but me. I promise you, Sid. Things will change. I'll be better. I'll do better. He burned down Brooklin's house—"

"She wasn't in it," Mayhem snarls from beside me. "We were sending you a message. And I'll get her back, too. Get the fuck out of here. Your sister is telling you she doesn't want you. Don't come back here. If you do, I'll fucking kill you myself."

It's the most words I've ever heard Mayhem say.

Jeremiah looks like he wants to jump to his feet. Like he wants to retaliate. But he clenches his jaw together and doesn't. He looks to me again, but some of the anger is back in his eyes. This is really what Jeremiah is, at the core of him.

Angry.

He's full of so much anger, he'd burned my entire world down to the ground. In one single night, he had ruined me.

"Sid. I can't lose you again," he tries again. "I can't. Remember, they killed one of our runners—"

"You fucking idiot. We don't bother with petty cash, motherfucker. Fuck would we want with your druggies?" Ezra growls.

"You don't want me. You want to own me, *Jamie*." I snarl his real name. The one he'd been born with. "And I'm not yours to own." I hate that a small piece of my shattered heart wants to go with him. A small piece of me remembers him tending to my foot in the bathroom. Telling me things will be better. That he loves me. I want to fold him into my arms. Because he had fucked me over. But he'd been fucked too. Our pain ran too deep between us, because of our mother. Our absent father.

A father we never knew.

Love we never knew.

His sick, rich foster parents and siblings.

But I can't go back with him. I can never go back with him. I don't even know if I'll ever be able to look at him again after tonight.

I have so many questions. I don't know what Lucifer does. What the Unsaints do. If they work in the same business as my brother, or something different. I don't know what I'm choosing by staying here, on their side, but I cannot go with my brother.

And it hurts.

Because I know, too, that when I black out, it's hard for other people to tell. I act as if I'm awake. As if I'm conscious. Part of me knows Jeremiah is telling the truth when he says I had let him. When I didn't resist, and I seemed awake. I know that's true.

But it doesn't change anything between us. Because whatever stage of consciousness I was in, he knew I was drunk. He wanted to punish the Unsaints. To scare them. To humiliate them by taking me.

I choke back on the bile coming up my throat.

"Sid..."

"If you don't get up and walk out of here, I'll shoot you myself."

Jeremiah shakes his head. "You wouldn't. Not your own brother."

I hold out my hand, palm up. Without hesitating, Lucifer reaches around me and places the gun there, wrapping my fingers around the grip. I aim it at Jeremiah. His men tense and point their guns, however reluctantly, at me. He twists his head around to stare at them. They lower their weapons.

He meets my gaze again. "You wouldn't, Sid. Because you know that I love you. That we're both dark and broken, and I'm the only that *can* love you. You'll always run back to me, because I'm your brother. I'm who you belong to, Sid."

Lucifer tugs me closer to his body, and his breathing grows faster. Shallower. He's going to kill Jeremiah if my brother doesn't get the fuck out of here.

"Get out," I say again. "If you ever loved me, if you still do, get the fuck out of here." I gesture with the gun, my eyes narrowed. "Now."

Jeremiah hangs his head. But slowly, he gets to his feet. Then he looks at Lucifer, at my back.

"I'll come back for her. And she will come with me. She'll never choose you over me. I'm her blood. You are *nothing*."

With a last glance at me, he turns around. Kristof is the first to follow him. Trey and Nicolas both hold my gaze.

"Come with us," Nicolas whispers.

I shake my head. "I never want to see either of you again."

Nicolas bites his tongue. Trey looks like he might try to dash and grab me, haul me out the door. But Nicolas turns first and puts a firm hand on Trey's shoulder. Together, they leave. I watch them walk down the stairs, and then Mayhem moves first, slamming the door closed and locking it behind them.

I step away from Lucifer, and reluctantly, he lets me go.

I spin to face him, the gun still in my hand. Mayhem is at my back. Ezra is still leaned against Atlas, and Cain is watching me carefully with his arms folded. These are the Unsaints. And I am not one of them.

I don't know who I am.

But it isn't this.

"I need to get away from here," I say quietly.

Lucifer frowns. "What? No. Sid. *No.*"

I snatch the keys to the BMW from the table. "I need to get out of here, and if you want to see me again, you won't follow me."

"Sid." That's Ezra. He steps out of Atlas's arm and comes to stand directly in front of me. I see Lucifer tense at his back.

Ezra takes another step toward me, and I don't back down. He pulls me into his arms, and I let him crush me to his chest. He smells like sweat and blood and I don't hug him back. He holds me out at arm's length and presses a kiss to my brow. I'm too stunned to react.

Lucifer looks as if he might pounce on him.

But Ezra says, in that deep voice, "Come back, Lilith. We've got hell to repay."

"No," Mayhem says from behind me. He steps around me, crosses his arms. I see the tattoo of an inverted cross on the side of his face. His baby blue eyes are trained on me. He's tall and lean like Lucifer, but with blonde hair. He looks angry. And a little scared. "No," he says again.

Ezra looks to him. "She'll come back."

No one says a word. Not even Lucifer.

And after giving the Order of Rain a head start, I leave.

CHAPTER TWENTY-FOUR

Present

IT'S BEEN FAR TOO long since I've driven a vehicle. My foster parents hadn't bought me a car, and I'd never bothered with saving enough money to get one myself. The bus worked fine in Alexandria. I don't even have a license.

I had, at one time. One of my foster families had at least given me that much, letting me practice with their SUVs. But still, behind the wheel of Lucifer's BMW, my hands are shaking on the wheel.

Rationally, I know part of that has to do with what just happened.

Irrationally, I don't want to think about what just happened.

I drive down the lonely road, thankful I see no other cars. I look for them, too. In the bushes. The forest. Down gravel drives. Even at the lone gas station that Nicolas and I had passed before we got to Julie's.

Julie.

I wonder if she ever woke up, during that entire encounter. I wonder if Nicolas and Jeremiah will go back and finish the job. I wonder if they would hurt the boy, too.

Jeremiah. *Jamie.*

My brother.

My broken, disgusting, awful brother.

I can't think of him without my skin crawling. I want to tear it all off. I want to throw up. I'm *going to throw up.*

I swerve onto the side of the road, nothing but grassy hills beneath the stars on either side. I jump out of the BMW, leaving it running, and run around to the ditch, heaving. Everything comes up, which isn't much to speak of. My stomach had growled at Julie's house; I can't remember the last time I'd ate.

But now, I'm grateful for that fact. Even after I've puked what was in there up, I still dry heave, and spit hangs from my lips. I'm thankful no one is here. Thankful I'm alone.

Thankful, and scared.

Because who will stop me now? I have no weapons, but I wouldn't be surprised if Lucifer has something in the car. He's as dirty as my brother.

But not quite.

My brother...

I heave again, my hands on my knees as I lean over the ditch.

My fucking brother.

He was so blinded by hatred, by whatever ways the Unsaints didn't make him feel welcome, that he hadn't spared a thought for *who* he was using to fuck them over. And it wasn't just that. It wasn't just the wrongness of what had happened between us. The sin. The disgusting thing we had almost done together.

Because he had stopped.

I have to give him that.

But it's the lies. The bullshit.

Oh God.

I vomit again, bile coming up, my stomach convulsing as my mind refuses to think about what he must have felt when he figured it out.

And then he lied, to cover his tracks He had convinced me Lucifer hadn't given a fuck about me. But I wasn't the only victim that night. Lucifer had been forced to watch. He had the scars to prove he'd tried to help me. Tried to stop it.

But Jeremiah had used me. He had had no intention to save me that night, he just wanted to get to the Unsaints.

What kind of monster was my brother?

I sink to my knees in the ditch, inches away from my own sickness.

I cradle my head in my hands, silent sobs wracking my body. No sounds come from my lips, no tears from my eyes. Just silent grief, engulfing me.

I throw my head back, tilt my chin up, my eyes squeezed closed.

And I scream.

I scream as loud and as long as I can. I don't give a damn that someone might hear. I don't even give a damn that Jeremiah might hear me. That Nicolas might. Kristof. Trey. I hope they do. I hope they think I'm being torn apart by a wild animal. I hope they think I'm dying.

I feel like I am.

The scream echoes in the vast, wild fields around me, and I scream until my throat is sore and all that comes out is another choked sob.

Slowly, I start to come to my senses. If Jeremiah does find me out here, he won't leave without me. We might both die at one another's hands, but he won't leave without me. Not again.

I get to my feet. My legs tremble, but I make it back to the driver's side of the car, crawl into the seat, shut and lock the doors.

I rest. For one minute. I count to sixty, my head back against the seat. My eyes closed. I give myself one more minute to pull my shit together. When I snap my eyes open, do up my seatbelt, and put the BMW in drive, it's done.

The scars Jeremiah left behind, those emotional, gut-wrenching wounds...I know they won't ever leave. But the self-pity has to go. Because Jeremiah needs to learn a fucking lesson.

As much as I hate Nicolas, I was glad we had that little

game between us. 'Yes/No' had been useful, not in learning anything about Lucifer or Julie or the kid. But in learning about my brother. His feelings for Brooklin. Mayhem's sister. He had put his heart on his sleeve in front of Nicolas. He'd done it in front of other people, too, for Lucifer to know that burning down Brooklin's house would get to my brother.

Now I know, too.

Now I'm going to get to my brother.

I'm going to pay him back for what he had done to me and make him feel like I did. Like I wished I'd never fucking been born. Like I wasn't comfortable in my own skin.

He had wanted me to kill Lucifer on Halloween night. He wanted Lucifer and the Unsaints to suffer, and he wanted me to end him so he couldn't tell me the truth about that night. But Lucifer had been looking for me all along.

Now he'd found me.

And now, he was going to help me fuck Jeremiah and the Order of Rain up.

CHAPTER TWENTY-FIVE

Present

THE NEXT MORNING, I wake up feeling as if I have a hangover, even though I hadn't touched a drink the night before. The thought of consuming alcohol again, of getting to where I had been that night Jeremiah found me in Raven Park...it makes me feel sick.

But everything makes me feel sick.

Looking at the ceiling above my head in the old house at the edge of Raven Park makes me feel sick. Rolling over in the twin bed to glance out the window, a crack of light coming from the edge of the curtains, makes me feel sick.

I'll need a drink soon. What does it matter if I feel sick sober or drunk? At least drunk, maybe I can forget. Maybe I won't dream about Jeremiah on top of me. About Lucifer screaming my name while he watched.

For several minutes, I try not to think. About anything

at all. Nothing. Blackness. What I might experience when I'm dead. What I might feel. Weightless. Unburdened. This is exactly why I'd planned to kill myself the night I met Lucifer. Because being in infinite nothingness is much better than feeling.

There's a soft knock on the door to my borrowed room.

I sit up, pulling the pale cream sheets up to my chest. I'm in my bra and shorts, the same clothes I'd worn the night before, minus the hoodie, which is on the floor of this ancient room. The hardwoods are scuffed and rickety, the wallpaper some atrocious floral print. But it feels good being here, hiding in plain sight. My brother knows about this house. He knows Lucifer has been staying here. But he won't come. He wants to give me space right now. He thinks this might be over soon. That I'll come crawling back to him, demand his forgiveness, and then the Rain siblings will move on together.

He always underestimates me.

"Come in," I call out, even as the door is opening without my words.

Lucifer stands in the doorway, shirtless.

My eyes find his sculpted muscles, the veins in his forearms, his impressive six-pack. And the scars around his torso, from the rope my brother had tied around him. His sweatpants hang low on his hips, but I force my gaze up to his, ignoring the deep V cut just above the waistband of his pants.

His eyes are hooded, midnight blue and full of exhaustion. He has circles beneath them, shadows that probably match my own. I didn't sleep well. He probably hasn't slept well. His hands are in his pockets as he watches me, as if he's uncertain how I might behave. As if I'm a wild animal.

I kind of feel like one.

"Do you want to talk?" he asks in that raspy voice that makes my toes curl, even against my will.

I shake my head.

He nods. I watch him swallow, that beautiful vein in his neck drawing my eye. He looks down at the floor, lashes nearly fanning his cheeks. Even when he had skeleton paint on, even when he was masquerading around as Lucifer from hell, I knew he was beautiful. When he had taken my hand the first time we met, at that intersection I had planned to walk through the last time, I had known his beauty.

I'd thought that was what had lured me into him, what had gotten me into that mess I woke up in after Halloween. I had cursed myself for it, for being taken by his charm. Especially when I had seen the warning signs: how his friends spoke about him. How he spoke about his friends. Julie. The pregnancy. The Unsaints, who are all in this house right now. Or at least, they were last night.

But I hadn't been taken in. I'd seen him. As he was, that night. The scars around his torso show me that now. He had been what I needed that night. But I have no time to think that through. After Halloween, I'm leaving. I will never come back to Alexandria. I will never see my brother again. If he doesn't survive Halloween night, even better.

I'll never see Lucifer or the Unsaints again either.

That thought pierces my broken heart a little more. But I can handle it. If I can handle my brother, I can handle this.

"What are you thinking about?" Lucifer asks me quietly, still looking at the floor. He moves his foot, clad in a black sock, back and forth over the wood, as if he can't stand still.

I laugh. It sounds fake even to my own ears. It is fake. Full of spite and anger and pain.

"I'm thinking about what it will be like to get out of here and never come back."

Lucifer's eyes snap up to mine. "Out of where?" he asks, frowning.

I look back out the window, at the sliver of light I can see. I draw my knees to my chest, blankets still pulled up over me. "Out of this city."

I could have sworn I hear him exhale. I turn back to look at him, tilting my head in a silent question.

"I thought you meant..." he runs a hand over his black curls. "I thought you meant you might...like you did when we first met...that you would leave *here*."

Suicide.

He doesn't want to say it.

"How did you know?" I ask him. My voice sounds detached. I try to keep it that way. I clear my throat. "How did you know when you met me?"

He smiles a little, dimple flashing, but the spark doesn't meet his eyes. "I saw the gun," he says, as he had the night before. "I know what a real gun looks like. And you had that air about you..."

"Depressed?" I ask, arching a brow.

He laughs, a sweet raspy sound that makes my chest tighten. "No, no. You weren't depressed. Not then. You were...excited. I knew that was a sign. It always is, at the end."

I frown. "How did you know that?" I *had* been excited. Knowing my next adventure was coming. That this life would be done. That I could start new somewhere else. Or in darkness.

He shrugs. "My stepmom barely tolerated me most of the time, when I lived with her. I got my money and got away from my family when I graduated university a few months ago." He blows out a breath, looking around this room. He forces a laugh. "I swear to God my house is better than this shit."

I frown. "Your stepmom?" I ask him.

He nods. "There's a lot you don't know about me. The Unsaints. Society of 6. But what happened to you, Sid..." He clears his throat, reaches inside his pocket and draws out both a cigarette and a lighter. But he just holds them in his hand, clenching them in his fist. "I can't imagine," he finally says. "But my stepmom...when she wasn't screaming at me...she was...*fond* of me."

The air in my lungs goes out.

I don't want to hear this. I close my eyes, lean my head

back against the headboard. I can't hear this. Can't think of the pain Lucifer had been through before he met me.

"Anyway," he continues, rushing on, "I knew that excitement because I'd felt it before myself. I knew because I'd thought of it before."

I crack open my eyes at that. "What stopped you?"

He holds the cigarette to his lips, lights it and takes a long inhale. He slips the black lighter back in his pocket, exhales a cloud of smoke. When it clears, he finally answers me.

"The gun wasn't loaded." He laughs, shaking his head. Like this is all a joke. It kind of is, our lives. One horrible, awful punchline after another. "I pulled the trigger, not knowing much about guns then, when I was just a kid. It clicked, and I flinched." He takes another drag, blows it out. Taps the ashes right onto the floor. He glances out the window. "When I flinched, I knew. I wasn't really ready to go yet."

I sigh. "You know, Lucifer," I say, drawing out his name. He stares at me, almost as if he's waiting for something. Desperately hoping that whatever I'm going to say next is going to fix this. Fix us. "You were my flinch," I tell him, and I mean it. "When you slipped your hand in mine..." I smile, raking a hand through my short hair. "You were my flinch."

JEREMIAH DOESN'T COME. HE DOESN'T COME THAT day, or the next. Or the week after. I jog every day in Raven Park, buy some clothes, but otherwise, I don't leave. I don't need to. I know all of my brother's hiding spots, or rather, I know enough of them to hit him where it hurts. I know Brooklin. I know her schedule. I know, too, that if I came back to the Rain mansion, they'd let me in.

It's what I'm counting on.

My plan is easy. Deceptively simple.

But it will have to wait.

The Unsaints bring food to the house we're staying in. They even cook. Other people I don't know come too. Men with guns. Men who I know are guards. But they never stay the night. Lucifer dismisses them at sundown every single day.

He told me he owns this house. Not the park, because the city wouldn't sell it to him, but the house. The one he'd taken me to, too. Where I'd learned the truth about Jeremiah. And the one Julie and the kid stay in.

We sit on the back porch of the old home, on the steps, looking out at Raven River a few feet from us. The soft sound of the gurgling stream in the darkness is soothing in its own way. Lucifer is smoking, and I relish in the scent of it. It feels...comfortable somehow.

We haven't touched one another since we've come here. Ezra has been giving me a cold shoulder which is odd, considering he was the first to attack my brother. Atlas has clapped me on the back a few times, and Mayhem is always staring at me. Cain is quiet and stays in his room most days. I wonder what they're missing out on. They don't bring girls here. I wonder if they still keep in touch with Ria, or any of the girls from Unsaints' Night. I wonder what happened to all of the ones that were poisoned.

Lucifer knows what I plan to do. Or rather, he knows I plan to do something. He hasn't pressed me on what, exactly. He hasn't mentioned Jeremiah again at all to me, although I heard him speaking with his guards about him in hushed tones when he thought I couldn't hear.

I've heard Atlas curse my brother even more than I have in my own mind. I can't blame them. They knew him for years. He betrayed them, and me.

But I haven't spoken to Lucifer about it. I haven't wanted to.

"Tell me about Julie," I say, staring out into the night. I'm not sure what I want to hear. I know she's still alive, that my brother hasn't finished that job yet. I hope he isn't so fucked in the head since our last meeting that he screws up so badly someone else kills him before I can get to him.

Lucifer is quiet, blowing out a ring of smoke. I start to think he might just ignore me. I start to think that might be for the best.

"Julie is...she was something like a friend. When I was in high school."

I swallow. Even though Lucifer and I haven't touched one another, I want to. But every night, he had bid me goodnight after silent, moody dinners with the Unsaints. He had more or less tucked me in to bed, without literally doing so. He had a gun on his hip most days, and his room was right beside mine. During the night, I heard him tossing and turning just like I was. I knew he was taking care of me. And giving me space.

I wonder if he thinks I'm tainted now.

I don't want to ask him.

"We hooked up once," he continues.

No shit, I think, but don't say anything.

"She got pregnant." He takes another drag from his cigarette. I want to snap it in half or put it out on my own eyes. "She said it was mine." I see him, out of the corner of my eye, shrug. "It was a mistake, the sex. We were drunk. Young. And stupid." He was twenty-one when we met. Twenty-two now. Not that young.

But this isn't what I care about. I don't want to know any of this. I want to know the outcome. What came next. What happens now.

He snuffs out the cigarette on the porch, grinding it down to nothing, with a little more force than is probably necessary. He leaves it there, between us, and clasps his hands together, hanging his head.

"I believed her, you know?" he asks. He turns his head and looks up at me, hands still clasped. "Hell, she probably believed it, too."

I say nothing. I'm holding my breath.

"I believed it was mine. But after that night, we fought like cats and dogs. She seemed to hate me, for not wanting to be with her. To be a *family.*" He says the last word with a sneer. Knowing what he had been through, with his own family, or what little I knew of it, I can't blame him.

Knowing my own family, I can't blame him. I'm not even sure what that word is supposed to mean any more. *Family.*

"She treated me like shit. I let her. It was my fuck up as much as hers."

My pulse quickens. I need to know. I want to scream at him to tell me, to answer the most important question. But I can't. I won't. He deserves this time. My silence. So he can tell me. I've spent a year hating him for something he hadn't done. Hating him over Julie, too. Thinking that was part of his fucking evil persona.

Now I know better.

So I wait.

"Anyhow," he scrubs a hand over his face. "The baby was born. She named him Finn." He huffs a laugh, shaking his head, as if he doesn't like the name. "Good thing, too. Because his father, *Finley*, wasn't going to have anything to do with him. At least the kid got named after him."

I blink, trying to process what he's saying. Those words mean...that the kid isn't his. Julie's kid isn't his. She hadn't been pregnant with his baby.

But I'm missing something. The story isn't over.

"I don't act like the kid's dad. More like an uncle or a godfather." He meets my gaze again. He looks as if he might be asking me a question, the way his brow is furrowed. But he keeps talking. "I paid for the house they live in. I'm not hiding them there. Julie wanted to live there, away from this place. Away from Finley. I paid for it, and I help her with expenses, too. Because even though it isn't my kid...well, it could have been, right? And Julie and I don't particularly like one another, but it could have been mine just as easily as it was Finley's. Finley doesn't have anything to do with his son, although he does sign child support checks, which I guess is better than nothing. But not much better."

He hangs his head again.

I exhale, letting my eyes trail to the river, the dark water rushing past us, just feet away from where I sit. I feel like I've been swept up in a faster current than that this past year, just waiting to drown. Now, though...I feel like someone has thrown me a life preserver. I'm still in the water, still flowing down the stream, but maybe now I won't drown.

"I knew Jeremiah knew I wasn't sure," he continues quietly. "But I figured he'd come after them. That's why I was there, when you were. I didn't expect to see you there. I wasn't sure why you hated me, but when I met you *here*, after I'd been looking for a sign of you all this time...I knew you didn't know. You couldn't possibly have known."

He rubs his hands together, as if trying to get warm. He's wearing grey basketball shorts and a black tank. I want to move closer to him. But I don't. What's the point?

"I knew Jeremiah recognized you," he continues softly. "That night. But I didn't know what you were. A lost love?" He coughs. "And I knew you were an escort." He flashes me a small smile, white teeth nearly gleaming in the darkness. "I wasn't sure until we met here, in the woods. I wasn't sure you didn't love him or something. But then when I realized you hated me...it clicked. And I knew you wouldn't have been with him if you knew. I don't know much about sex work," he admits. "But I know consent is a big fucking deal. And you didn't seem like the type of girl who would be okay with what happened that night. And your anger toward me, it clicked it all into place." He snaps his fingers, emphasizing the point.

"I had no idea though, that he was your..." He can't say the word. I don't want him to. "Mayhem burned down Brooklin's house, to pay him back for what he did to us and to warn her. And his club, too. But I wanted to find you. I just needed to know you were alive and okay." He sighs. "He never mentioned a sister. I knew what he did to his foster family. I thought it proved his loyalty; that he'd do whatever it took, no matter what." He scrubs a hand over his face. "It did, I guess. But his loyalty is to you."

I breathe a little laugh, feeling my throat tighten. I run my hand along the back of my neck. "It wouldn't have worked before, you know," I say, my voice quiet. But he's staring at me. He looks as if he's hanging onto every word. "I wouldn't have left Jeremiah. He wouldn't have stopped looking for me. He still won't. I'm sure he knows I'm here." I swallow but force myself to keep going. "It never would have been a choice for us. Ties that bind and all that." Even as I say the words, my heart cracks in two.

There's a silence between us a moment.

"These are monstrous ties," Lucifer finally says, his

words heavy. I watch him swallow. And I want to move to him. To fling my arms around his neck. To pull his wiry, lean body into me. To figure out what could happen between us.

But I can't. It will only make it hurt worse. For both of us. No matter that Julie's child isn't his. That isn't the deal breaker. It never had been.

It is, as he said, these monstrous ties. This tainted history. Lucifer had saved my life that Halloween night. But I had broken him. My brother had broken us both. He'd betrayed the Unsaints, and I couldn't deal with being a living reminder of that betrayal to them, even if I was only an estranged sister.

This could never be.

I want to ask him how far it got. I want to ask exactly what he saw, what he watched. But I also don't want to know.

So instead of going to him, instead of touching him, I get up and start to walk inside. And even as he whispers my name like a desperate plea, I don't look back.

Instead, I run right into Atlas, the door closing behind me.

Atlas takes my upper arms in his calloused hands and grins. It's goofy.

"Get that fucking frown off your face," he says lightly. "Tomorrow night we're having a goddamned party."

CHAPTER TWENTY-SIX

Present

I PROTEST. I complain. I bitch. I moan. But it turns out the Unsaints don't give a flying fuck about my feelings, because the next day, when the sun begins to fall behind the river, the little house in the park is fucking packed.

I work up the nerve to ask Mayhem if Ria is coming. He's wearing black, ripped jeans, and his baby blue eyes narrow on me.

"No," he answers, then takes a hit from his blunt as he walks down the stairs of the porch, wandering off.

Well, then.

That officially means I won't know anyone here. But the Unsaints.

I take a drink from Atlas, who shoves a black plastic cup in my hand. All of this reminds me too much of that night, but we're not going to the asylum, Lucifer promised me. He said that's for Unsaint night. And Halloween night is still two days away.

I drink *all* of the vodka soda Atlas gave me, while he watches.

He blinks at me, a girl hanging off his arm, grinning at me with narrowed pupils. I wonder what drug she's on, and if I can have some.

"You just..." Atlas trails off, his dark eyes going from the empty drink in my hand to my face. "You just slammed that down."

I nod. "Didn't you go to university? That's what kids do, right?"

He scoffs. "We're older than you."

Apparently, they are. By a few years, but who's counting? I don't give a fuck.

I hold my cup out to him, shake it a little. "More?" I plead.

He grins and takes the cup. "My kinda girl." He turns, disentangling himself from the girl on his arm. He smacks her ass and winks. "Be right back." He looks to me. "Oh, uh, Sid, this is Natalie, Nat, Sid."

She frowns at him and he smacks her ass again. She releases a giggle, then stumbles toward me on the porch. There are people scattered about the lawn, talking and drinking, and a fire is starting up under Ezra's hands, which is unsurprising. I'm sure he's the one that started it that night. Someone—one of the Unsaints—brought half a dozen kegs here, and there's a goddamn butler wearing white fucking gloves in the middle of the park handing out drinks, too.

Not to mention the men in guns lining it. Because this is still a public park.

But these are the Unsaints. They've funded all of it.

I haven't seen Lucifer since I left him on the porch yesterday, and I haven't looked for him. I hope he has fun. Without me.

"How do you know Atlas?" Natalie asks me, a little breathlessly. I really want to know what she's having, and how I can get some, too. She takes my hand and pulls me to the porch steps. I sink down beside her, feeling dizzy from the vodka.

How do I know Atlas?

I realize then that I don't know what people know in this city. If they know exactly what the Unsaints are. The Society of 6.

I don't ask. I don't wanna be on a hit list for telling everyone. I mean, it's no secret they have Lover's Death and the Death Oath and Unsaint night, but do people think that's some weird college kid prank?

I shrug. "Met him through Lucifer."

Her brown eyes widen. She's got dark hair piled on her head in an elaborate, braided bun. She's wearing a yellow dress, long bell sleeves, and brown boots. She's got a Bohemian vibe going on that seems like it'll suit Atlas. At least, for tonight.

"Lucifer?" she whispers, covering her lipsticked mouth with her hand.

At first, I think she thinks I mean Satan. I start to explain, and she cuts me off, shaking her head.

"Girl, I know what you mean." She laughs. "You didn't go to AU?"

"No." The answer is curt. It reminds me of Ria's question from the year before. It reminds me of how much I don't know.

Natalie sighs, puts a hand on my arm. I let her, even though I kind of want to fling it off.

"Lucifer leads the Unsaints," she whispers to me, in my ear. As if I don't fucking know. "Do you know what that is?"

But what the hell? I know what it is. It's a group of rich ass prick boys that are too brooding for their own good.

"Nope," I lie, ready to hear her version of these kids. Although, as I glance at Mayhem watching us from a small group of people, a drink in his hand and his eyes definitely on me, I have to remind myself they aren't kids. As far as I know, they all graduated university already. They should be doing something with their lives. Leading their daddy's companies or going off to law school. But they're here.

Natalie practically squeals in my ear with the excitement of breaking down to me just what the Unsaints are. She leans in toward me, which means there's exactly zero space between us and I start to feel uncomfortable. I tense, but she doesn't notice.

"They're like Masons, but like, the Masons' kids."

Second time someone compared them to that. I nod,

encouraging her to go on, although I don't think she needs encouraging. In my mind, they're like the Order of Rain. But my brother just made that shit up. There's no elaborate rituals, no Unsaints' Night. No bloodletting except from the people he murders for his "business".

"Kids of the Society of 6."

I breathe a laugh. "And what's that?"

She leans back, but her hand is still on my arm. "They really are Masons. But richer."

"Got it," I say, pulling my arm from her hand. I learned a fuck load of nothing. No surprise.

She stares at me a minute with wide brown eyes, and then she dips her hand into her dress and for a second I think she's going to flash me. Instead, she pulls out two white, oblong pills.

She thrusts them toward me. "Best if you snort 'em," she whispers, winking.

I shake my head, holding my hand up to refuse. But then I hear someone sprinting through the door at our back and she narrows her eyes.

"Take them!" she hisses, and I glance over my shoulder and see Atlas nodding a greeting to a guy who just called his name by the fire. I take the pills and clutch them in my hand. Clearly, Atlas isn't supposed to know she does them. As if these boys are saints or something.

Atlas leans across her and hands me my drink. I take it awkwardly with my left hand, since the pills are in my right and Natalie winks again.

Atlas takes a seat beside her, taking a sip from his own drink.

"You two making fast friends?" Atlas drawls, dark eyes flitting between us.

Natalie laughs and leans into him, taking his cap from his head and putting it on hers. Underneath, his blonde hair is a mess and he scowls for a second but then shrugs and rolls his eyes.

"You didn't tell me this is Lucifer's girl," she mock-whispers, clutching his arm.

He throws his head back and laughs, but before he can say anything, Mayhem interrupts us.

"She isn't." He walked over from the fire and he has his arms crossed over his chest. He's wearing a black tank, and his baby blue eyes are narrowed on me. I make out script on his triceps, and a skeleton with an open mouth, a butterfly in one eye socket. That means his arm is *not* where his Unsaint tattoo is.

I finish half my drink, and I'm very aware the pills in my sweaty hand are going to dissolve if I don't fucking move.

"But you said you were here because of—" Natalie starts to protest. But out of the corner of my eye, I see Atlas capture her mouth with his and she's pulled into a noisy kiss.

My cue to stand to my feet. I do. Mayhem is still staring at me. *Glaring* at me is more like it.

"Gotta pee," I announce, and he scowls. I spin around

and go inside, leaving my drink on the porch. I can feel Mayhem's eyes on me as I walk in.

When I'm inside, I see some girl grinding against Cain on the worn couch in the living room and his eyes flick lazily to mine, but he doesn't speak or otherwise acknowledge me. He's got his shirt off and she's wearing a skirt. I don't stay long to see what else is going on.

I take the stairs two at a time, head to the bathroom at the top. The music is loud outside—*Bow Down,* I Prevail—and I see through a bedroom window across from the stairs that the fire is growing bigger.

I stumble into the bathroom, aware I'm on that verge of tipsy turning into drunk and I close and lock the door behind me. I lean against it, sliding down to the white tiles.

It's shockingly clean, and I wonder if one of the Unsaints has had someone come clean this place. It wouldn't surprise me. I've spent most of my time in my room.

I open my palm and examine the pills. I don't know much about drugs outside of pot and alcohol, but I do know that it's two days until Halloween and I'd love to sink into a peaceful oblivion until then. Or put on a happy face like Natalie has.

I stand up, set the pills on the edge of the porcelain sink. I make my hand into a fist, take a breath, and crush them. I lean down, feeling a little ridiculous, and close one nostril while I snort the small amount of powder into the other. I don't even know if this is a smart thing to do. I have no idea if it'll help or hurt. I just know I don't want to be at this party, but I don't want to fuck it up for all of the Unsaints either. We aren't friends, and I'm pretty sure some of them hate me because Jeremiah is my brother. I know for a fact they're only here for Lucifer, but still...

There's a loud knock on the door, nearly rocking it off its hinges. I jump, startled, but call out, "Just a minute!"

I wipe the back of my hand over my nose and check out my reflection, brushing my bangs out of my silver eyes. They're lined with shadows and after all the vodka I just had, or maybe it's from the lack of sleep, they're also red.

And before I can turn to open the door for whoever is on the other side, it gets jerked open and Mayhem stands there, scowling down at me.

His eyes go to my hand, my nose, and back over my body. I'm wearing a pair of skinny jeans I got on a rare jog out of the park and a loose black t-shirt. In other words, nothing to stare at. I glance down at my shoes.

Combat boots.

But Mayhem doesn't look like he's interested in me. He looks like he hates me.

"All yours," I mutter and make to push past him. But he blocks my way, his chest brushing my shoulder.

I step back, confused. He's still glaring. He's said about zero words to me since I got here. I know next to nothing about him, except he's tattooed his face and he drives a McLaren. I know that because he mentioned going to a drag strip once to the Unsaints before I came into the room and he fell silent.

"Can I help you?" I ask, annoyed. I don't feel anything

from the pills yet but for some reason, I feel like he knows I did them.

He crosses his arms and leans against the doorway. I see no one behind him.

"You saw my sister," he says.

Ah. So this is what this is about. Brooklin.

I throw up my hands. "Yep. I saw her. And to be honest, she was doing a hell of a lot better than me." I frown, as if I'm thinking. I know I shouldn't say it, but I do anyway. "And probably a hell of a lot better than she had been when your father kicked her out of her house when she was just a kid."

He doesn't react for a second. Nothing. Doesn't even blink.

Then he grabs my elbow and pulls me out of the bathroom and down the hall. I'm too stunned to fight back until we're in what I assume is his temporary bedroom at this place and he slams the door closed, locking it.

He throws me inside and I spin around, brain working again.

"I will fucking kill you," I spit at him, fuming. His curtain is closed, his bed made with white sheets like a goddamn hotel.

He doesn't look intimidated by my threat in the least.

"You don't know shit about me. Or her. Or Lucifer. Or *us*."

I roll my eyes and shake my head. "A lot of shit I don't care to know about."

"Your brother betrayed us. We should take you as payment."

"*Payment?* You're not a gang, if you don't know. You're a bunch of spoiled pricks that—" He grabs me by the throat before I have time to finish and throws me on the bed.

I scramble back against the wall, watching him. Waiting.

He walks over to the curtain and pulls it back. "You wanna know how much Lucifer gives a fuck about you?" He points out the window at something I can't make out, but my stomach churns.

And then I feel it. At the worst time, I feel whatever pills I just snorted. They're making me feel...light. Maybe it's my imagination. I don't know fuck about pills but there's no way they could be working this fast, and yet... a smile spreads on my face, but I fight it back.

"He feels sorry for you. That's it," Mayhem is saying, still pointing out the window.

I resist the strange urge to smile and crawl to the end of the bed, sliding off and coming to stand beside him at the window. I can feel his body heat, smell marijuana and cologne and leather.

I follow his finger.

I see a crowd gathered around the bonfire, and I see Atlas picking up Natalie, wrapping her legs around him. I see Ezra, still tending to the fire. I don't see Cain and remember he's downstairs. And for a moment, I don't see Lucifer.

Until I do.

I stop breathing.

He's got his arm around a cute, curvy girl with long blonde hair in a high ponytail. I don't recognize her, but he's leaning against her and she's leaning into him and then he whispers in her ear and she throws her head back and laughs. She's wearing cut off shorts and a jacket is tied around her waist.

"You don't belong here," Mayhem says beside me.

I turn to face him, swallowing down any anger before I can allow myself to really feel it. Instead, I go with the pills. I force a smile. His eyes are slits as he glares at me, but he doesn't move.

"Then make me leave," I whisper, leaning in closer to him.

For a moment, he says nothing. Only stares at me with his arms crossed. I take in his biceps, the tattoos wrapped around them, the inverted cross on his face, his long lashes. And then he pushes me back on the bed.

I laugh. "This isn't the door," I tease him. He pulls his shirt off over his head, undoes his belt. There's more tattoos all over his chest, trailing down to his abs.

But before he comes toward me, he cocks his head and meets my gaze. "You want this?" he asks me.

I bite my lip and his eyes find my mouth. Then I let out a breathless, "Yes", and he takes a step closer.

He yanks down his pants after he unzips his jeans and I see his hard cock beneath his black boxer briefs.

He steps out of his pants and takes another step toward me.

"I know you took pills from Natalie," he says in a low voice. "I saw you do it."

Another step. I back against the wall, bring my knees up to my chest.

"I'm a big girl," I murmur.

The corner of his mouth twitches in a smile but his gaze is anything but playful.

"You sure you want this? Because Lucifer might be rough," he laughs, "but I'm fucking careless."

I take a breath in and glance out the window. But from where I'm sitting on Mayhem's borrowed bed, I can't see anything. I just nod. Fuck Lucifer. Fuck the Unsaints. What does it matter anymore? I'm leaving here when this is all over. I'm leaving and I'm never coming back. I'll never see them again.

"Yes," I answer him.

And then he's on me.

He pulls off my shirt, yanks down my jeans and throws them on the floor. I realize, through the fuzzy haze of alcohol and pills, that I'm wearing drab grey cotton panties, but I also realize it's pretty dark in here and I don't really care.

Mayhem certainly doesn't seem to care. He literally rips them in two and I try to protest, but he shoves my head into the bed, and fuck, I like it. He runs his whole hand over my ass, and underneath me, to my slit.

I moan, and his other hand presses my face further into the bed. He leans over me, abs on my back.

"Keep it quiet, *Angel*," he whispers against my neck.

I laugh, but he wraps his hand around my throat and I'm quiet.

"I told you, I'm careless. Especially with things I want to break."

And then the hand over my pussy moves and he pushes the tip of his thick cock against my entrance.

"Don't scream," he commands, and then he shoves himself inside of me.

His hand on my throat muffles any sound, but I clench around him, gasping.

He pumps once, twice, hard, and then he finds a rhythm, pushing harder and deeper. He lets go of my throat and I gasp, my head hitting the wall on the side of his bed. But fuck I don't care. I don't care because he feels fucking good. I try not to think of what Lucifer might feel like. What he might do, if he saw this.

Mayhem pauses, and then his belt loop comes over my throat and he jerks me upright, my back against him.

"Take off your bra, Angel," he whispers into my ear. I make to turn around and stare at him. His cock is inside me and I can barely breathe with this belt but he wants me to take off my fucking bra?

He pulls the belt tighter around my throat. "Now," he growls.

I reach behind me, my fingers brushing his chest, and I unhook my bra. He pushes the straps down with one hand, and tosses it to the floor. Then he lets go of the belt and palms my breasts, then pinches each nipple, hard. He fucks me like this, us against each other, fingers tugging on my nipples. His teeth find my shoulder and he bites down. I cry out, and his hand goes from my breast to my pussy, pushing his finger inside of me beside his cock.

"You like to be filled up, don't you, Angel?" he purrs.

I nod, and he wraps his other hand in my hair, yanking my head back.

"You're so fucking tight," he groans in my ear. "Say my name, Angel."

He thrusts again, pushing me back to the bed, my head down, ass up as he pumps into me and circles my clit with his thumb.

"Mayhem," I choke out, one of his hands still in my hair. "Mayhem," I gasp it out again.

He groans, leaning over me, his chest against my back, and then he pushes me flat, pulling out. I feel him spill onto my ass, warm and wet. And then we just lay like that for a moment, catching our breath.

He pulls away from me.

"Now if Lucifer doesn't figure out he's gotta find a way to keep you, well, you're shit out of luck."

I freeze.

He licks his hot tongue down my spine. I shiver under him, and roughly, he turns me over, his gaze devouring me from head to toe.

I cross my arms over my chest. I'm not panicking,

because of whatever was in those damn pills from Natalie, but I'm mildly freaked out by his words.

He smirks, pulling on his clothes. I catch a glimpse of the Unsaint's tattoo on his back. It's huge. When he puts his belt through his jeans, he shrugs.

"We don't keep things from each other, Angel."

I sit up, yank my own clothes from the floor after wiping his cum off of myself on his sheets. "You can't tell him."

He walks to the door as I dress. "I can. And I am. Right now." And then he walks out.

I fly down the hall after him, but he turns to me at the stairs and shakes his head.

"Nah, Angel. You don't wanna see this." He jerks his head to the door we just came out of. "That was fun, but you're probably not done for the night."

My face heats with those words and I want to shove him down the stairs. But then I remember that the whole fucking reason I felt justified in having sex with him is because Lucifer has his arm slung around another girl at the fire. Besides that, we aren't anything to each other, Lucifer and I. Just two people who shared one horrible night.

"Fuck it," I say, pushing past Mayhem and taking the stairs down two at a time. "I'll tell him myself."

Mayhem groans behind me and starts running down the stairs as I leap the last two. "You're fucking crazy," he says. He loops his arm through mine. "Fuck it. We'll both tell him." He shakes his head and glances at me as I walk out the front door. "He's going to kill us both."

"He can try."

As Mayhem and I make our way to the fire, I see Lucifer, and he's still got his arm around that girl. But somehow, he has the audacity to narrow his eyes on me and Mayhem as we approach him. The fucking audacity.

I paste a smile on my face that isn't really all that fake, thanks to Natalie and her drugs.

The girl with the blonde ponytail and cut-off shorts offers me a smile, too. A real one. I incline my head to her, but it seems like the crowd around the bonfire has grown quiet as Lucifer silently appraises us.

"Good turnout, huh?" Mayhem asks, and I hear the smirk in his voice. I wonder if he knows what's coming next. Because I sure as hell don't. As I take in Lucifer's midnight blue eyes, his clenched jaw, I kinda don't want to tell him.

I don't regret it, because he sure as hell doesn't look like he regrets his arm around this girl. But I feel something like guilt. I try to tell myself it's stupid. Because it is. Me and Lucifer are not together.

His eyes flick to Mayhem's, who, for his part, seems totally chill.

"I'm Ophelia," the girl pipes up, holding out her hand. "Most people call me O."

I glance at her hand and think about not taking it. But this isn't about her. This is about Lucifer being a shit and me being petty. I shake her hand warmly.

"I'm Sid," I answer. "Most people..." I trail off and shrug, dropping her hand. "Don't call me." I force a laugh, and Mayhem laughs at my side.

Ophelia smiles. Lucifer doesn't. He hasn't said a fucking word.

Mayhem pulls us both closer to Lucifer and nudges him. I glance around at everyone, and see they're still talking amongst themselves but they're also darting glances at us. Even Atlas has Natalie back down on the ground, and while he's wrapped an arm around her waist, he's watching us, his mouth set in a thin line. I can feel the fucking tension in this place, and there's a few dozen people here. Why should Lucifer's mood dictate everything?

"You okay, bro?" Mayhem asks.

I think that might be pushing it. He's clearly not okay. He removes his arm from Ophelia, who, for her part, gets dragged into conversation with a giggling girl that was behind her.

Lucifer stands in front of both me and Mayhem. They're the same height, and while Lucifer is a little leaner, he looks a little meaner, too. Especially right now.

I glance at Mayhem. The fucker is actually smiling.

"Why did you two come out of the house together?" Lucifer asks. The first fucking thing he's said to me at this party. The first fucking thing he's said to me since yesterday.

I laugh out loud and his eyes narrow further. "We both live there," I point out. "For now."

The damn waiter that the Unsaints hired comes to stand by us with a tray in his white-gloved hand, and drinks in black plastic cups atop it. I pluck one from the tray and he flashes me a smile. He's probably in his forties, with a sleek combover. He nods his head in Lucifer's direction, but Lucifer ignores him. Where do these kids find these people?

I start to down my drink as Mayhem takes one, too, and the waiter wanders off.

"You haven't spoken to each other since we've *lived* here," Lucifer says, crossing his arms. His eyes flick to mine and Mayhem's looped arms, and back up to Mayhem's face. "Get the fuck off her."

Mayhem doesn't move. He drinks from his cup and I from mine, and then when he's done, smacking his lips together, he sighs. "If this—" he lifts up our joined arms for a second, "—is what you're worried about, well, bro, you're gonna be really pissed when I tell you where I just—"

He doesn't get to finish his sentence.

Lucifer takes the cup from his hand and throws the rest of it in his face, and then he tackles him to the ground. Mayhem unthreads his arm from mine just in time to stop me from getting pulled down, too.

Lucifer's fists start flying into Mayhem's face and Mayhem lays there, taking it. Atlas runs over, Natalie trailing behind him, her eyes as wide as saucers, and soon there's a giant circle around the boys. People are chanting "Unsaints!" and I'm somehow in the *middle* of the circle, which means people are looking at me *and* them.

Ophelia has the gall to step up beside me. She nudges me. "What the hell?" she asks, in shock. I wonder how often the Unsaints fight. Maybe never?

I shrug. Mayhem has started fighting back. He flips Lucifer over, his hand around his throat. Lucifer reaches for Mayhem's eyes and I cringe.

Mayhem laughs, turns his head.

Then Ezra steps into the circle.

He walks calmly over to Mayhem and pulls him off of Lucifer and to his feet. But Lucifer gets off the ground and grabs Mayhem by the collar. Ezra tries to pry his fingers off, but I think they really need Cain out here, the biggest of them all, to put a stop to this shit. Atlas hasn't joined the fray, but he's still watching.

"Back the fuck up!" Ezra says, his deep voice a growl. His eyes find the crowd gathered around and he waves the hand not holding Mayhem toward them. "And fucking find something else to stare at or you can get the fuck out of here."

People listen.

They scatter, as if he physically pushed them away.

But Ophelia and I stay where we are. Lucifer still has Mayhem's collar in his fist and he's yelling in his face.

"What the fuck did you do? What did you fucking do?"

Mayhem wipes his nose, which is bleeding, and Ezra puts his hand on Lucifer's chest, forcing him away.

Mayhem's eyes find mine and he grins. Lucifer looks

between us as if he's going to throw us both in the fucking fire and watch our bodies disintegrate.

"Ask your girl," Mayhem croons.

Lucifer's fists, covered in blood, clench, but Ezra gives him a warning look, still holding Mayhem by his shirt.

I feel Ophelia's eyes on me. "Are you and Lucifer..." she trails off, letting the question hang between us.

I meet her green eyes, my brow furrowed. "I was going to ask you the same."

At this, she bursts into laughter, shaking her head. I feel my cheeks go warm, but a smile creeps on my face. And now is not the time to be smiling. Damn Natalie.

"No, no," Ophelia says, shaking her head again, her ponytail flying. "No, we grew up on the same street." I see her white teeth, smooth skin, eyelash extensions, spray tan. I mean, she looks like she comes from money, but compared to me, most people here do.

My mouth falls open.

I look to Mayhem. He winks at me.

That bastard knew.

Lucifer walks by me and yanks my arm as he does. "We need to talk," he says through clenched teeth. I gawk at Mayhem as Lucifer pulls me up the porch and into the house, slamming the door behind us.

Cain is fucking the girl I saw him with earlier.

"Don't mind us," he grunts out.

We don't.

Lucifer pulls me up the stairs instead. He pushes me into my room, flicks on the light, and closes the door. Then he starts to pace, his arms crossed. He's looking down at the floor. I sink onto the bed, cross my legs, and run my hand through my hair.

"What happened with Mayhem?" he asks me, his voice low.

"N-nothing," I stutter. I'm not afraid to tell him. I just don't really wanna say it. He's got blood on the corner of his upper lip, and I want to lick it off, but I force my eyes down to the quilted bedspread underneath me. I clasp my hands together, waiting.

"Don't lie to me." He still hasn't looked at me. He's still looking down.

"We're not together," I choke out.

He doesn't stop pacing. "No shit."

"So why does it—"

He stops pacing and sinks down to his knees in front of me, his hands on my legs, squeezing hard. "It doesn't fucking matter, Sid!" He shakes his head and sighs. "It doesn't fucking matter. You're right. It doesn't matter at all." He lets go of one leg and gestures wildly behind him. "It doesn't matter if I fuck every girl here, does it? Doesn't matter at all."

Now it's my turn to get angry. I know I shouldn't. It isn't fair at all. It doesn't make sense. "No," I force myself to say, meeting his gaze.

He chews his lip and stands to his feet, glaring down at me. "There's nothing between us, is there?"

I shake my head. Suddenly, I wish I had more of Natalie's pills.

"There's nothing to stop me from getting my dick sucked by O, is there?"

I clench my fists so hard I know I've drawn blood. "Be my guest."

His blue eyes flash in amusement and my stomach cramps. I wonder, for a second, if he's going to walk out the door and go do just that.

I wonder if I'll feel better if he does.

But he doesn't.

He shifts on his feet, shaking his head, running a hand through his dark curls. "You know, I spent this past year looking for you. Trying to get back to you." He runs a hand absentmindedly over his black shirt, and I think about the scars on his abdomen. "I thought, once I found your pretty ass, this would be done. This bullshit between us." His hand falls to his side as he meets my gaze. "But it's just getting started, isn't it?" He cocks his head. "You never were gonna be mine, were you? That night was just a fantasy."

"Part of your Lover's Death, right?" I prod.

He rolls his eyes. "Lover's Death gives us an illusion of control. We don't usually fall in love with our *lovers*." He huffs out a laugh. "And you were no exception."

He turns on his heel and his hand goes for the door.

"Wait," I call out, my voice trembling.

He rests his hand on the doorknob but doesn't look at me.

"Wait," I say again. I stand to my feet and take a step toward him. He still doesn't look at me.

"I'm sorry," I begin, even though I'm not even sure what I'm sorry for. I see his shoulders tense. "I'm sorry, Lucifer, I...I've thought about you every fucking day since that night. Thinking you'd fucked me over." I take a deep breath, pushing past the fog of the vodka and the pills. "But you didn't. And I don't know what to do now." I tangle my hand in my hair. "I don't fucking know what to do."

For a moment, he still doesn't look at me, and I wonder if he won't. If he'll just walk out that door anyway. Find Ophelia, or someone else.

If he does, there's nothing I can do about it.

But instead, he turns to me, and I don't see rage in his eyes. I see sadness instead.

He closes the space between us and wraps his arms around me, pressing his brow to mine.

"Lilith," he says, and I close my eyes, breathing him in. "I told you before...we'll figure this out. Whatever *this* is... we'll figure it out."

I nod, eyes still closed. "But Mayhem..."

His breath catches. "Fuck Mayhem," he growls. "What's done is done. But for the love of God, please don't do that shit again. I would hate to break his neck."

CHAPTER TWENTY-SEVEN

Present

HALLOWEEN NIGHT COMES SLOWLY. The sky begins to darken slowly. I dress slowly, pulling on black, false-leather pants. A black, long-sleeve shirt, a black zip-up hoodie over it. I do my makeup slowly, white and black skeleton paint, a black nose like a cat's for the fun of it. I exaggerate my skeleton mouth, the teeth inside. I pull my hood over my head, tuck my brown hair behind my ears, splay the bangs from my grey eyes.

When I look in the cracked mirror hanging above the sink in the old house, I smile.

It's beautiful, and terrifying.

I hope Jeremiah is ready for a reunion.

I don't bother to bring a gun. I have a blade in my back pocket instead. Guns are for quick deaths. Knives are for pain. And I need Jeremiah to feel an ounce of the pain I feel at what he's done to us.

When I open the door, see the sun just starting its descent down past the trees of Raven Park through a window, Lucifer stands in the doorway.

And he *is* Lucifer.

He's dressed almost the same as I am, with the same makeup, his haunting blue eyes contrasting against the white and black makeup on his face. He has his arms crossed, and he's watching me carefully.

For a moment, we only stare at each other.

"What are you doing?" I finally ask, trying to calm the butterflies that are swirling like they're swept up in a tornado in my stomach.

Lucifer smiles.

"I'm coming with you, Lilith."

I shake my head, my gut twisting. I put my hands in my pockets. "No," I say forcefully. When I'm done with this, I'm leaving. I had bought a bus ticket to New York. It had taken every penny of the money Jeremiah had let me play with, and I know he'll be able to track it, too. But I don't care. I have to get out of here. And maybe I'll stop somewhere else along the way. Start a new life in a place no one knows my name. My face. My life.

But I can't do that with Lucifer. We talked after the night of the party. We kissed, but nothing more than that. Mayhem went back to ignoring me, Atlas really the only one bothering to speak to me besides Lucifer. Lucifer and

Mayhem kept a cold distance, but I know they'll get over it.

But it didn't change anything. Lucifer said we'd get through anything. But the only way we can do that is without one another. He has a legacy here. I have a life somewhere else. Or I'm going to.

"You can't," I say to him.

He steps closer to me, over the threshold of the bathroom. I think of the scars on our legs, the one that must still be on his. I think of his Unsaint's tattoo. I think of his blood on my tongue. Of tasting him. Of craving him. And then hating him the next morning, believing my brother's lies. Believing Lucifer had forsaken Lilith, after he promised he wouldn't.

I think of how he might have been the devil, but he was my savior, too. For that one night.

My legs feel weak. I want to tell him to stop coming closer to me. To leave me alone. To forget my face. To accept that he'll never see me again. I want to say all of that, but he's staring at me, his chin tilted down, with such hunger in his blue eyes that I can't speak at all.

My body is betraying my mind. Again. I want to stop it. But as I had been that night one year ago, I'm powerless against this beautiful, broken boy.

He takes another step. We're almost touching. We're close enough to. But neither of us reaches for the other. I smell him, still. Cigarettes and pine. A scent I never could have imagined would nearly rip my heart out.

But we're never going to feel what we did then. A year ago. The optimism. The reckless lust. The wild hope.

We're never going to feel it again...and yet...when he closes what little space is between us and reaches out to me, his arms going around my back, I know I still do.

I still feel it.

In all my misery, in all this disgust I feel with my own body, I feel it. When he touches me, I light up. I want to melt into him. I want to burn with him. We can burn the whole world if we want. We can burn up hell if we have to. We can destroy everything we touch, and we can do it together, without burning each other.

A small sound escapes my lips, something somewhere between a moan and a whimper, and his fingers dig into my back, pulling me closer to him. His head is angled down, his eyes on my mouth, but he waits. He waits until I come to him.

And I do.

Our mouths crash together, much like they had that first night a year ago. We're a tangle of anger and despair and brokenness. Our kiss is possessive, urgent, desperate. His teeth drag against my lips and I moan into his mouth. He pulls me even closer, pressing my body against the length of his. And when he bites my lip, I bite back. We draw each other's blood, and I relish in the iron feel of it on my tongue. Iron and tobacco and mint. I want it all. The dirtiness. The rawness.

I want it.

I want this.

I push him, and we stumble out of the bathroom. I shove him against the wall just above the stairs, my hands on his chest. He's nearly panting, I can feel the inhales and exhales under my hands. I don't hear anyone else in this house, although I know the boys are here.

His eyes search mine. Like he's waiting for me to pull back. Like he's waiting for me to not want this.

I want it.

I tug up his hoodie and he pulls it off in one fluid motion. He unzips mine and that hits the floor, too. I run my hands down his biceps, his arms bare. He wears nothing beneath that hoodie. The skeleton paint ends at his throat, and I lean in, licking a line from his chest, up past that vein on his neck, all the way to where the paint starts.

Damn the fucking paint.

We're going to fuck it up anyway.

He tugs on my tank top, and I lift my arms in submission, letting him pull it off of me, scattering my bangs into my eyes. He laughs and brushes them back, and then he reaches around for the clasp of my bra.

But he doesn't unhook it.

Instead, he looks down at me a moment, waiting.

For permission.

My hands are trailing down his sides, to his fitted jogging pants. I nod, and he unhooks my bra, brushing the straps down my shoulders. It hits the floor, and I tug on the waistband of his pants.

His eyes linger on my neck.

For a moment, I forget why.

Then I remember. The bruises. There's probably more from Mayhem, too. His hand goes to my throat, and he gently strokes circles on my neck.

"I'm going to kill him," he whispers, leaning down, putting his brow to mine.

I don't know who exactly he's talking about, but I smile thinly at him, some of the lust leaving my bones. Some of the fight, too. But I don't want to think about that. I don't want to end this. Not right now. Later, maybe, when I'm on that train headed north, I'll regret this. Maybe then I'll curse myself for being so stupid. But not right now. Right now, I want him. I want this moment.

"Don't worry, Lucifer," I say, smiling. "I'm yours tonight."

At that, his hands tighten gently against my throat and he snarls in my ear, that urgency back in his hands, his mouth, his teeth. It's back in mine too.

This is where we thrive.

In the angst. The chaos. The toxicity. These are our own monstrous ties forming. Ties that will have to be broken, have to be severed like a limb. But for now, I don't care. I'm falling fast, and nothing is going to stop me from hitting the ground.

When we're both naked, he picks me up in his arms, cradling me to his chest, and carries me to his bed, lying me down gently. I stare up at him, through the little light that's still left in the sky, streaming in through the open window.

Every inch of him is beautiful. Every inch not covered in paint is smooth and pale and cut, save for the tattoo on his thigh, and the scars there. Even the scars on his torso are beautiful. *Especially* those scars. And the black and white of Lucifer makes his blue eyes all the more devastating.

He's also ready. For me.

I stare at his cock, taking in just how big it is with wide eyes and a small smile.

He grins at me, his eyes raking over my entire body, from my feet to my thighs, to that small scar that he had made, to between my legs, up my abdomen, roaming over my breasts. Finally, he meets my gaze again.

He bites his lip. "Are you ready, Lilith?" he purrs.

Every bone in my body is ready. Every muscle is coiled.

I nod.

"Are you mine?" he asks me, quieter, eyes still locked on mine.

My heart sinks a little at that question.

But still, I say the words he wants to hear. The words he needs to hear. "Yes. I'm yours, *Lucifer.*"

At his name on my lips, he pounces on me, the weight of his body warm and comforting and wild against mine. He strokes my bangs from my face, grinding himself against me.

I gasp, and he bites my bottom lip.

"You're so fucking beautiful," he says against my

mouth, pressing himself against my thigh again. "You're so fucking beautiful, Sid."

I wrap my legs around him, bucking my hips, trying to get him *there*. Where I want him.

"And so eager, too, aren't you?" he teases me, whispering the words against my throat.

"Yes," I whisper. "Yes." My hands go to his muscled back, and I dig my nails into his skin. He groans, then reaches between us, nudging my thighs apart with his hand.

He cups me, slipping one finger in, gently, and then another.

I moan, tightening against him.

"Tell me again," he says against my throat, one hand around the back of my head, the other inside of me. "Tell me who you belong to."

"You," I say into his neck. "Always. It will always be you." *Lies. Beautiful lies.*

"Say it, baby," he urges me. "Say my name."

I don't give a damn that our makeup is smearing, that our plan is delayed, that this will be our last time. I don't have to think about that right now.

"Lucifer," I moan against his ear, and his fingers move deeper inside of me, his cock rock hard against my thigh. "I'm yours, Lucifer."

He pulls back from me, taking his fingers with him, and trailing them up my stomach, over my breast, my nipple, my throat. He brings them to my lips.

"Open your mouth." His voice is hoarse, and it sends a shock of want and *need* through me.

I do as he asks, tasting myself. Earthy and salty and sweet, and he meets my mouth, his fingers between us.

He groans, and bites down on my lip again, fresh blood seeping onto both of our tongues.

He leans back, reluctantly, as if he doesn't want to be apart even for a second. But his fingers trail over my lips and back down my throat, and I move my hips under him, adjust myself, uncrossing my legs from his back, making room for him.

Looking down between us, biting his lip, he guides himself into me. Just a little at a time.

I gasp, my hand around his neck tightening, one around his bicep, my nails digging in. He glances up at me, his brow furrowed.

"Is this okay?" he asks me softly.

I nod, eager for the rest of him.

He pushes his way inside of me, and I relish in the feel of him. The fullness of him. I clench around him and he moans, whispering my name in my ear.

"Fuck, Sid," he groans.

I gasp, wrapping my legs around him again, feeling every inch of him deep within me. This is what I've been waiting for. For a year, I thought I'd missed it. I thought he'd fucked me over, and I didn't even have the memory of the two of us joined together. I thought he had tainted that forever.

But I didn't miss it. It's this.

This is us. We may never be this way again; we might never connect in this way again the rest of our lives. But I know I'll never forget this.

He moves slowly at first, letting me adjust to him. But then his movements come faster and faster. He has one hand against the headboard, the other under my head, cradling me. He gazes down at me as he moves, his eyes searching over every inch of my face.

His own makeup is distorted, warped from my hands on him. There's blood at the corner of his lip and I tilt my head up, pressing my lips against his as he moves. He groans again at the taste of me, the taste of us on our tongues.

He lifts his head up, breaking the kiss off, and he moves faster, slamming into me. I close my eyes tight, drowning in the sensation of *him*.

The headboard creaks against his hand, but he doesn't stop. He slams harder into me, and then his movements become jerky.

"Open your eyes," he commands. "Look at me."

I do.

And I know why he does it. Why he doesn't pull out. Mayhem doesn't give a fuck about anything, but he didn't do *this*.

But Lucifer does. And I know why.

I know why he empties himself into me without asking. I know he wants to keep me here. I know that, even though he hadn't done what I thought he had, he's still toxic. His feelings for me are still so many levels of wrong.

I know that he wants to own me. He wants me to be *his*. I know he thinks that maybe if I have his child, he can keep me.

I know it, and I don't say anything.

Instead I kiss his eyelids as he slows inside of me, as I clench my legs tighter around him. I trail those kisses down his nose, coming over his full lips. He opens his mouth to me, and I take from him, my tongue sweeping in as he stills. We break apart, reluctantly, and he presses his head against my chest, breathing hard.

I kiss his hair, run my hands through his soft black curls.

We're coated in sweat and I'm coated in him.

I don't care.

This will be the last time. I won't have his child. But I don't care. Because I want this too. Slowly, he eases himself out of me.

He gazes down at me, and he's on all fours now over me, his eyes trailing down my breasts. He dips his head and swirls his tongue along one nipple and then the other. I arch my back, pressing into him, even though I'm aware the sun has set. Even though I know it's only darkness outside now.

He runs his tongue down my stomach, letting his teeth scrape against me as he does. I watch his head go lower, until he flicks his tongue on my clit.

I gasp, breathing hard, my hands tangling in his hair.

He moves lower, his entire mouth on me. He doesn't seem to care that he just spilled himself inside of me. He darts his tongue in anyway, then up my slit, flicking my clit again.

He moves that way, back and forth, groaning at the taste of me, until I feel it, that orgasm tightening in my core.

And when I come, moaning his name softly as I do, it feels like the world is finally giving me a piece of everything it's ever owed me.

I say his name again and again, *Lucifer*, like a prayer. Like a confession. Like a secret.

When I'm done, my orgasm echoing through my body still, he lifts his head and gazes at me, smiling.

"I fucking love it when you say my name," he says, and then he kisses my inner thigh, sucking my skin between his teeth. It'll leave a mark. Just like when he came inside of me, he's trying to brand me.

To keep me.

It's like he knows he can't.

He crawls up my body, and his lips find mine again.

We kiss each other until I think our lips will be bruised. When he finally pulls away, he runs a hand down my body, like he had that first night in the woods.

"You're mine," he whispers against my ear.

I smile, letting myself believe that lie. Letting myself savor him saying those words just one more time.

"Let's go burn the world," I murmur against his neck.

CHAPTER TWENTY-EIGHT

Halloween Night, Present

WE DON'T BOTHER FIXING our makeup. It looks more sinister this way, smeared around the edges, our teeth dragged into jagged fangs. The sockets of my eyes are warped, and Lucifer's makeup bleeds down his throat, down into the reaches of the hoodie he shucks back on.

We dress quickly, Ezra calling our name down below.

And then we head down, the knife back in my back pocket.

Mayhem grins at me when we come downstairs, all four of them sitting together on the couch in the living room. I notice they have guns, too.

"Have fun up there?" Mayhem asks, directing his question to Lucifer.

I feel my face heat but head for the door.

"Aw, don't run off, Angel," Mayhem calls after me. "Maybe someone else wants a turn—"

A fucking shot rings out in the living room, the sound of glass shattering. I whip my head around, my heart leaping into my chest. Lucifer is holding his gun, and it's pointed at Mayhem. The window above the Unsaint's heads has a fucking bullet hole in it.

"What the fuck?" I hiss.

Atlas tips his head back and laughs like this is a fucking joke.

Ezra rolls his eyes, Cain says nothing at all, and Mayhem's eyes light like he's just been challenged to a fucking shootout.

"Glad to see you got your balls back," he drawls.

Lucifer puts his gun back on his hip. "Go fuck yourself."

He really shouldn't have said that.

"I didn't have to, bro. Your girl did it for me."

I groan and they look to me, all except Lucifer, who is still staring at Mayhem as if he might actually shoot him this time. "Can we not?" I snap.

"You know what, *bro*," Lucifer says, his lips twitching into a smile. "I'm going to see your sister tonight." I think I know where this is going, and I tense. Mayhem's smile is gone. "And when I do, I'll be sure to pay you back for everything you owe me."

Mayhem's lip curls and he stands to his feet.

"What the fuck?" I hiss. I mean, I know this was really

over before it could even begin, but did he really have to say that right now?

Lucifer looks at me, and his expression is still angry. "If you can have your fun..." he shrugs. "I can have mine, right?"

Atlas snickers. "I mean, he's got a point, Sid..."

I shake my head. "Can we just go?"

All the Unsaints are standing now. I rake my eyes over them and shake my head. "No, you guys cannot come. My brother won't let us in if—"

"This is our payback, too," Ezra says quietly.

I'm quiet a moment, thinking. I can't argue with that. I don't want to argue with it. I just shake my head, throw up my hands, and head for the door.

We walk to an empty parking lot of Raven Park in silence, and I slide into Lucifer's M5. Mayhem gets in his grey McLaren, and Ezra, Atlas, and Cain get in the Range Rover.

We drive to the Rain mansion.

I know my brother will want to kill the Unsaints as soon as he sees them, but he won't if I tell him not to. I also know he'll be at the mansion. He knows what night it is. I hope to God he's drowning in the misery of his own crimes.

There're guards stationed at the gates when the three overpriced cars pull up. We get out, and my brother's guards draw their guns on us, but I step right up to them, glaring.

"Let me see my brother," I spit out, even though that last word tastes wrong on my tongue.

The guard on my side blinks at me, as if he's surprised. He tosses a glare at the Unsaints.

"Not with them."

Atlas laughs and Mayhem whistles.

I step closer to the guard, even though he's got a good half a foot on me. He actually backs up. Atlas laughs again.

"Now."

The guard looks annoyed. But then he nods. I see him speak into the mic on his collar, and the gates open up.

I'm surprised, as we get back in our cars and drive up the paved driveway, that the lawn has been decorated. There're pumpkins among the bushes, white, paper ghosts swaying from the trees. As we pull up to the gargoyle fountain, I see someone has placed a Jason mask over his face.

Tonight, Jeremiah made an effort. It only serves to make me angrier. Because he knows me. God, he knows me, even if I don't want him to. Even if I loathe him for it. Even if he knows far too much. More than a brother should.

Lucifer puts the car in park.

We get out, slamming the doors in unison, and I face the Unsaints, squaring my shoulders. This vengeance is mine. I know they've been betrayed too, but this is mine to take.

Lucifer puts his hand on my shoulder before I have to make that clear. "You get the shot."

The other Unsaints, shocking me, nod, although their jaws are all clenched, and they don't look like they'd hesitate to gut my brother from ass to mouth.

It's the most I can ask for though, this statement from Lucifer. I incline my head and turn around. We stride past the gargoyle fountain, the guards on alert at the automatic doors. But they don't stop us. They don't even search us. They move aside and let us in.

I know those are my brother's orders.

Because I don't need to know his hideouts or his habits to know where he is. I don't need to know any of that. He's waiting for me. And it only just occurs to me as the Unsaints and I stand side-by-side in the foyer that perhaps I'm walking into a trap. That perhaps Jeremiah is sorry for what he did, but not sorry enough to let me get my anger out.

But he isn't in the foyer.

Nicolas is. And Brooklin.

She's behind him.

I hear Mayhem's breath catch, but he doesn't move toward her. Her eyes, however, are locked on her brother's.

And I'm shocked that my brother has left her here, with only Nicolas for protection. Aside from the guards outside, past the automatic doors, there are no others in here that I can see.

Nicolas's gaze goes over the Unsaints, over me, looking

for weapons. I know he knows we have them, even though they're tucked away.

I notice the foyer is decorated for Halloween, too. There's even a fake orange tree nestled in one corner of the vast room, spiders and black cats and white, ghostly garland hanging around it. There are no presents beneath it.

No.

Jeremiah is my present, whether he knows it or not. Whether he expects to be or not.

Brooklin is dressed as a kitten, in a pale pink top and dark grey pants, grey and pink cat ears on her head, a nose with whiskers drawn expertly across her scared face. She's still watching Mayhem, those blue eyes sharp on his.

Nicolas isn't dressed for Halloween. He's wearing black jeans, a white shirt. His arms are crossed, and he doesn't bother hiding the gun at his hip.

"Where's my brother?" I'm the first one to speak. Beside me, I know Mayhem is staring at his sister. Trying to unnerve her. It seems to slowly be working. She begins to shift from one black heeled bootie to the other.

Nicolas uncrosses his arms, clasps his hands behind his back. He looks down at the sparkling floor. "He's waiting for you."

That surprises me.

I expected Nicolas to try to talk me out of whatever he thinks I might do. But my brother always did try to one up me. Try to scare me. I'm not exactly surprised that that's what he's trying to do now.

"Where?" I ask Nicolas, my question cold. I won't show him that surprise.

Nicolas dips his chin and jerks his head in the Unsaints' direction. "They can't come with you."

"Then my brother can't see me."

It's really that simple. I might not have wanted them to come at first, but now that they're here, there's no way I'll leave them alone with Nicolas. I know it's stupid, to think they can't take care of themselves, but I want them with me. Or at least, I want Lucifer with me. Besides, something is up. Brooklin is still shifting foot to foot, and Mayhem hasn't stopped glaring at her. I'm thankful. I need someone else to be uncomfortable in this room.

And despite what he's done, despite lying to me and covering for my brother, Nicolas seems completely unruffled.

He sighs through his nose. "Look Sid, you have to understand that your brother is not in a good place right now—"

Before I even have time to let that anger tighten around me, to let Nicolas's words sink in, Lucifer moves. He draws his gun and fires it, right at Nicolas's feet. Nicolas roars, jumping, covering his head with his hands.

The shot rings in my ears.

But the Unsaints aren't done.

Mayhem shoots this time, another bullet into the floor, and he lunges for Nicolas. He flips the gun in his hand, drops it, and brings his fist across Nicolas's face before Nicolas has time to reach for his own gun. Behind us, I hear the guards from outside the door rushing in, shouting at Mayhem to stand down. But I whirl around, spreading my arms wide, shielding Mayhem with my own body.

Brooklin screams, and I draw the knife from my pocket, flicking the clasp on the blade to unleash it.

"If you don't shut your fucking mouth," I growl to Brooklin without looking at her, "I will slit your goddamn throat."

Mercifully, she stops screaming.

The guards have their guns drawn. They're all dressed in black, with what I know to be bulletproof vests on.

"Drop your weapons," I command them.

They stare at me, unmoving.

Behind me, Mayhem is snarling at Nicolas.

"You fucking piece of shit," he hisses, his voice the only one in the foyer. "You *dare* tell her that Jeremiah is going through a lot? That piece of scum fucked her over and *you*. Did. *Nothing*." With each word, I heard his fist slam against Nicolas's head. Nicolas murmurs something, and I can tell without looking behind me that he's stunned.

Lucifer hasn't said a word. But suddenly, the guards tense, and Brooklin whimpers.

I glance over my shoulder.

Lucifer has a knife held against her face. I didn't even know he had a knife.

I smile at him. He smiles back, but his brilliant blue eyes are cold.

Mayhem glances at his sister held at knifepoint, but

says nothing. He knows Lucifer won't cut her. But no one else does.

I look back at the guards. "Drop your weapons. Leave them here. Go back outside. Or your boss's girl will get her pretty little face carved up."

Slowly, they lower their weapons. But they make to stow them back in the holsters.

I shake my head, the knife still in my hand.

"Nu uh," I command them. "I said *leave them.*"

"Mayhem," Brooklin whimpers.

Mayhem laughs. "Don't call for me now," he growls.

"We can't leave the front doors unprotected," the shorter guard says to me, ignoring the exchange between another fucked up brother and sister.

I don't know what Jeremiah had been thinking, leaving her here. Maybe he meant her as a peace offering. Maybe Nicolas and I had both been wrong. Maybe Brooklin actually didn't mean that much to him.

"Drop them or she dies. That's the last chance I'm giving you. And her."

They stare at me a moment longer, hatred burning in their eyes. They don't want to take orders from Jeremiah's little sister.

"I'd listen to her if I were you," Atlas says cheerfully.

They finally do as they're told, dropping their weapons. And then they back slowly out, never turning their backs on us until they're out the doors. They resume their posts without glancing back.

I grab their guns and turn, nodding to Lucifer. "Take her with us."

Mayhem clicks his tongue. "Leave her here," he says quietly, his eyes on his sister's. "We'll stay down here and watch these fuckers." He jerks his head to the guards at the front door. He's still standing over a cowering Nicolas.

The rest of the Unsaints nod, Lucifer included. He shoves Brooklin forward, and then me and him find our way to the elevator. I punch the number eight, and we go up.

Nicolas is lying motionless on the floor, face down.

I can't find it in me to care.

CHAPTER TWENTY-NINE

Halloween Night: Present

MY BROTHER DOESN'T COME to the door.

It doesn't matter. The damn thing is unlocked. Trey stands guard, but when he sees us, he moves aside without a word.

I walk into my brother's room.

It's the same size as mine. I know he also uses the penthouse too, sometimes, but he liked being above me. Turns out, he had liked being above me in more ways than one, but I'd never before known the sick irony of it until now.

Lucifer slams the door closed, the lock clicking behind us. I scan the entrance hall, looking for any signs of which room my brother might be in.

I can smell liquor and the sharp tang of wine, like bottles have broken somewhere in the room. I set the guns down by the door, keeping only my knife. I don't care if

Jeremiah gets his hands on one of the weapons. I know he'll likely have his own in here anyway.

Lucifer stands at my side.

"Jeremiah!" I scream, letting my knife scrape down the hall, along the walls. "Come out and play with your sister!" I taunt, my voice loud, my throat raw.

Nothing.

Silence answers me.

I pass room after room, making my way to the back of the unit, and then I see the last door is ajar. His bedroom door.

I hadn't been in here much during my year at the Rain mansion, but I know it's his. The smell of alcohol is sharper here, and I kick the door all the way open.

"Jeremiah?" I call out. "Are you ready to play?"

I step inside without waiting for an answer. I glance at Lucifer over my shoulder, and he nods, correctly reading my look.

I don't want him to come in until Jeremiah knows I'm in here.

I flip on the light inside my brother's room and let my eyes adjust. Immediately, I see the balcony door is open. His bed is made, all white and red sheets and comforters. There are, indeed, liquor bottles smashed on the floor, rivers of pink champagne and brown liquid forming a disgusting puddle by the balcony door. I'm thankful I'm wearing my combat boots.

"Sid," Lucifer calls softly to me. He leans against the doorway.

I raise a brow, impatient. Ready to get to my brother.

"Be careful. I won't wait long."

I smile at him. "I know," I whisper.

And then I carefully step over the spilled liquor and broken glass, and shove my way onto the balcony, nudging the door open wider as I do.

Jeremiah is sitting in a leather chair, ankle over knee.

He has a glass dangling from his fingertips, full of something clear. Vodka, probably.

He glances up at me, his pale green eyes widening, just a fraction of a second. He has a mask on, a masquerade-type thing, all black and only covering around his eyes and the bridge of his nose. He looks almost like Batman.

If Batman was into his sister and fucking up her world.

"You came," he whispers, almost as if he doesn't believe I'm here. As if he thinks I'm a ghost.

I grip the knife tighter in my hand but don't raise it.

I underestimated how much it would hurt to see him again. How it would feel like getting stabbed in the chest all over again after two weeks apart. And that sick feeling is back. I think I might vomit again.

I stumble to the railing of the balcony, the knife falling from my hand onto the cement floor, my fingers curling along the edge of the balcony, my head hanging off the side.

In an instant, Jeremiah is up out of his seat and his hand is gentle on my back.

And for an instant, I don't shove him off. For a second, I pretend he's my big brother again. I pretend he's the same guy who cleaned my foot. Who told me he loved me. Who had been looking for me for fourteen years. Who saved me from the devil.

But the second passes.

And so does the moment.

Because that's all a lie.

I spin around, knocking his hand away from me. He still holds his glass of vodka, and I rip it from his hand and throw it against the wall of the balcony, where it shatters behind him. I see, beyond him, Lucifer stepping into my brother's room, his blue eyes wide and frantic until they find me.

I regret throwing the glass.

I'm not ready to share my brother's suffering yet.

But Jeremiah just stands there, staring at me. Blinking. I notice, in the dim light from the balcony, that the whites of his eyes are red.

"What have you done to us?" I scream at him, the knife still on the concrete. I kick it aside. I don't want to use a blade. I want to use my bare hands.

I lunge for him, slamming him against the wall, glass beneath our shoes.

"What have you fucking done?" I scream again, hitting him, my hands flying over his chest, over his suit, my nails digging into his neck, his face. I slap him, again and again and again, and he takes it, unmoving, all while his eyes stay glued to mine. It's a different kind of torture. I want him to fight back. I want him to hit me, too. I want him to resist. To argue with me, cut me down, like he used to.

I know he's drunk.

I can smell the vodka on his breath. It's like he's drowned in it. And his eyes are bleary. He's barely standing upright as I attack him, over and over and over. And he could have seen Lucifer. I know he could have. He could have glanced at him, right then. But he didn't. I don't know if he truly hasn't seen him, or if he just doesn't care anymore.

I slap him one more time, the sound ringing in the night, his head twisting sideways.

I put my hands down, breathless.

"Fucking say something!" I scream at him. The words come out on a sob. I take a step back, the glass crunching under my boot.

Someone clears their throat. All three of us whirl around at the same time.

Monica.

The bartender. Of course she would have a key. She has two bottles of vodka in her hands, and she looks around at all of us, at Jeremiah's red face, at the scratches down his neck. His skewed mask, nearly knocked off of his face from my attack. At Lucifer.

"I, um…" she gestures with the bottles, her eyes finding mine.

"It's okay, Monica," I say, the first words I've spoken since I've arrived that aren't angry. "Just…" I shrug. "Just leave them on the bed."

She opens her mouth, closes it again, then nods. Her

eyes find Lucifer again, and her gaze lingers on him a second too long. Jealousy lights up my gut.

"On the bed, *Monica*," I hiss, harsher than I mean to.

She nods again, tearing her eyes away from Lucifer, and steps back into the room. I wait until I hear the front door to Jeremiah's unit click behind her.

I look back at my brother.

But it seems he catches sight of Lucifer for the first time. His eyes narrow. He shoves the mask off of his face and makes to step toward him.

I shove his chest, pushing him back against the wall.

"I'm going to kill him," he says to me, pointing in his direction. "I'm going to kill Lucifer." His words stumble, slur.

I laugh. "Lucifer is the least of your concern," I mock him. "Brooklin is downstairs with the rest of the Unsaints. She'll be safe if you listen to me."

He lowers his hand and looks down at me, his eyes shining. "I don't care about *Brooklin*," he spits.

And in that moment, I know he's telling the truth. This isn't a bluff. He was just using her.

"I care about *you*, Sid." He shakes his head and presses the palm of his hand to his eyes. "He's going to take you from me, isn't he?" he asks quietly. "He's always been good at getting what he wants."

I laugh out loud. "You fucking idiot," I hiss. "*You* took me away from you. You fucked me up, Jeremiah!" I punch his chest again, beating on it with the heel of my hand.

"You fucked me up!" I hang my head, and he presses his hands against my back.

"Don't fucking touch her," Lucifer growls. But I wave him off.

I rest my head against Jeremiah's chest. Nothing will save us. Nothing will fix this. But the sobs rip through me, and I can't move. Tears blind my vision, burning with the makeup near my eyes and I still can't move.

Can't think.

"Oh my God," Jeremiah says against my hair. "What the fuck have I done?" He pulls me closer, and at the feel of him, of my body pressed against his, I stiffen.

Lucifer notices.

He's between us in a second, pulling me off of my brother, pointing the gun at his chest. He wraps a possessive arm around me.

"I'm not sorry," he says to me. "I won't let you do this."

I try to squirm out of his arms. I don't know what was wrong with me. I know what Jeremiah has done. That he's lied to me. That he's nearly done the worst thing a brother could do to their little sister. I know it, and yet I still want to get to him. To hold him one last time. Because it will be the last time.

I beat against Lucifer's chest, but he's like a rock, unmoving, the gun in his hand unwavering.

Jeremiah's face is equal parts rage and grief. He hates Lucifer, that much is clear, but he wants to get to me, and Lucifer has me.

"I am so sorry, Sid," he says, swallowing, tears lining his cheeks, clinging to his lashes. "I'm so fucking sorry."

I try to reach for him again and Lucifer holds me back, his fingers digging into my upper arm.

"Let her go," my brother pleads, shaking his head. "Let her go, man."

Lucifer laughs. "Fuck no," he growls. He cocks the gun. "I never fucking trusted you. None of us trusted you. You were never one of us." He lets that dig in deep. "Get out of here. Leave this place to her. Leave all of it to her."

"I don't want it—" I start to say, stiffening in Lucifer's arms. I don't want this place. It was horror. Trauma.

I expect Jeremiah to laugh. To tell Lucifer to go to hell, where he belongs. Where all of us belong.

Instead, he smiles.

"I already did."

Silence.

I stop moving. It feels like Lucifer has stopped breathing. The tears stop falling from my brother's green eyes.

"It's yours, Sis."

The word makes me feel sick all over again. I don't want to get to him again, to touch him again. I don't know why I did before.

"It's yours. All of it. Order of Rain is yours. The men are yours. The staff is yours. And there's plenty of money in the bank account to pay for it for decades to come. You don't have to do anymore dirty work. The cops won't come for you because it's all halted now, unless you want to continue it." He sighs, his chest heaving. "It's yours, Sid."

"What the fuck are you talking about?" Lucifer asks him. I'm glad someone does. I can't get the words out.

Jeremiah's eyes narrow on Lucifer. "Fuck you and the Unsaints. This is all hers. I changed the title, the money, the accounts. All of this," he gestures vaguely with one hand, "it belongs to Sid Rain. She'll have more than all of you. She won't need you. And don't you dare think of taking any of it for yourself or I will fucking cut you into tiny pieces—"

Lucifer laughs, cutting off my brother's words. "Go fuck yourself."

I swipe a hand over my face. "Why?"

Jeremiah offers me a small, pained smile. "You deserve it. I don't want to hurt you anymore. I need to leave, Sid. I have to get away from here. From...from you. Because he —" he darts a glance at Lucifer, "—is going to take you from me. The Unsaints will own you. They own everyone they catch. And I can't watch that happen."

I want to scream at him some more. I want to tell him that he took himself away from me. That all this, all this hell, he had set it ablaze.

But I don't say anything at all.

Jeremiah just stares at me.

"Let me hold you. One last time, Sid?"

Lucifer's grip on me tightens. He's no longer pointing the gun at my brother, but it's by his side.

"No," Lucifer answers for me.

I look up at Lucifer, pleading with him. I see his indecision. His confusion. I feel it, too. Why I want this

monster's hands on me again, I don't know. But this is a
night of lasts. For me, for Jeremiah. For Lucifer.

Lucifer's lip curls. "Why, Sid?"

"Please," I breathe.

He sighs.

"Okay," he forces himself to say, wincing as if the word
physically hurts him. He takes his arm out from around
me. "Okay," he whispers again.

I touch my fingers to his lips, his skeleton paint
smeared, and then I turn to my brother.

But before we can cross the balcony floor to one
another, glass and a small river of vodka from what Jeremiah had been drinking beneath us, Lucifer shoves me
aside and lunges for my brother, balling Jeremiah's shirt in
his fist.

"She might not know better. She might be wrecked.
But I'm not. I've seen you for what you are. You are a piece
of fucking filth. You do not deserve to live." And he aims
the gun in my brother's gut. "This isn't just her vengeance,
you know. You betrayed us. No one gets to do that and
live."

I freeze.

Lucifer glances back at me, Jeremiah is crumpled over,
getting ready for Lucifer to pull the trigger.

"No," I manage to say, shaking my head. "No...please,
Lucifer." I swallow, my throat dry. My mouth dry. "No."

Lucifer's eyes close, as if he's wrestling with himself.
Wrestling with Lucifer. Wrestling with Lilith. With me.
With Jeremiah.

He wants to kill him. I know he does. I understand why. Jeremiah fucked with the Unsaints. He was one of them, and he betrayed them.

But I can't let him do this.

If I do, I'll never forgive myself.

Never forgive *him*.

Lucifer drops the gun. I breathe a sigh of relief.

But then he cocks his fist back, and I hear it connect with Jeremiah's nose. Jeremiah stumbles backward, against the wall of the balcony.

I call Lucifer's name, but he either doesn't hear me or doesn't care. He rains down blows all over Jeremiah's body, most of his focus on his head. Jeremiah doesn't even cover himself. He takes it. He slumps against the wall, sliding down into the broken glass and he lets Lucifer beat the shit out of him.

His head snaps one way and then the other underneath Lucifer's fists, and then Lucifer drags my brother back to his feet and hits him again. For a moment, they stand there, Jeremiah's face oozing blood again, both of them heaving.

I'm frozen. I want to run to my brother. I want to run to Lucifer.

I stay where I am.

And then Lucifer drags Jeremiah over to the balcony railing. Fear spills over me like ice water. Lucifer squats down, lifts my brother by his waist, and holds him over the balcony.

Eight floors up.

He might survive the fall. But it won't be pretty.

My hands are over my mouth, but I need to get a grip on myself. Lucifer is going to kill my brother. My brother, horrible and broken and twisted as he is, is about to die.

His hand tightens on Lucifer's arm, and there is fear in his bloodied eyes. But he doesn't say a word. He only looks to me.

"Lucifer," I whisper, unable to move. I'm worried if I get closer, Lucifer will toss him over before he loses his nerve. I wonder if the Unsaints planned this all along.

Lucifer is glaring down at my brother, hatred in his eyes. His jaw is clenched, and he's still breathing hard. Blood coats his knuckles. Jeremiah's blood.

"Lucifer," I say again, bringing my hands to my side. I try to swallow. "Lucifer, please don't."

He still doesn't look at me. But Jeremiah does. His eyes seem to be pleading, but not for mercy. Maybe forgiveness. His bloodied face is full of sorrow. A grief I feel, too, deep in my bones. We will never go back to what we were. And what we were hadn't been good in the first place. We were broken beyond repair.

"Lucifer."

I hold my breath, waiting. Hoping I can still reach him.

Slowly, mercifully, he turns to me. His blue eyes are so cold.

"Don't," I say softly, shaking my head. "Please don't."

At those words, something in his gaze softens. I see his

grip loosen on my brother, and I worry he'll drop him without meaning to.

But he doesn't.

He hauls him back over the side, onto his feet. And then he lets go of him, backing away.

Jeremiah puts his hands on his knees and looks up at me, fear in his gaze.

"Leave," Lucifer orders him. "And never fucking come back."

For a moment, time stands still. I don't know what will happen next. I feel sure that if Jeremiah doesn't leave, Lucifer will kill him. I feel sure I won't be able to stop him again.

But slowly, my brother straightens. His mouth twists, as if he's fighting with himself on saying something to me one last time.

"Find out everything you can," he says softly. "Find Ria."

And then he limps through the balcony door and walks away, without looking back.

I watch him go.

CHAPTER THIRTY

Present

HE LEAVES. Jeremiah leaves, and the Unsaints that were waiting in the foyer on the main floor let him. He didn't take anything or anyone with him except his black Mercedes. He left without telling anyone goodbye, even as his men watched him walk away. They already knew. They had known everything was now mine.

That they now serve me.

They'd known, and like before, when they knew Jeremiah's darkest secret, they hadn't told me.

Brooklin left too. Mayhem and her exchanged words, but she left. He let her walk out of here. I have no idea where she went. I have no idea if she told her brother where she went. She took a cab from the other side of the gate, and she left.

And I'm leaving, too.

My brother is gone. Whatever he intended me to do in handing the keys to Order of Rain to me, I have no intention of doing it. The Rain mansion can burn for all I care.

I'm packing my bag the next morning, after sleeping in my brother's room the night before, the liquor and glass still on the floor, when Lucifer comes in.

He had slept next door, in an empty room.

He had tried to hold me, after my brother left. But I wanted to be alone. I needed to be alone. Because what comes next will probably hurt more than anything else has. But I can't stay. I can't be with Lucifer. Or the Unsaints, who are still at the hotel.

Lilith and Lucifer are only good at burning things down, not building them anew.

He stands in the doorway, watching me. He's wearing his fitted black jogging pants, but he doesn't have a shirt on. I hold his gaze, refusing to look at the scars on his abs, marring his perfect skin. Scars for me. I'd spent so much time hating him, so much time loathing my brother but trusting in him all the same, that I feel shame when I see those scars.

They remind me, too, of what had happened to me.

That I was wrong. Sick. Unlovable.

The year I had worked as an escort, I'd never felt that way. Sex was a transaction. My time was valuable. I was paid for my work. But what my brother did, even if he stopped himself, the lies afterward...that was a transaction of hate, revenge, disgust. It was a transaction that he could never repay me for. Never make up for. And I didn't want to be with someone who knew that. Someone who knew the darkness in me. The filth.

I zip up my black bag and toss it over my shoulder. I tuck my hands in my hoodie's pockets and straighten, facing Lucifer.

There's a lump in my throat. I have no idea what to say, but I know I have to say something. If I don't get this goodbye right, it will haunt me for the rest of my life. It probably will no matter what I do or don't say, but I need to say *something*.

"All this time I wanted to find you..." Lucifer whispers. He leans against the door, as if he can't stand on his own two feet. "To see if you had survived that night..."

I nod, biting my lip, looking down at the dirty floor between us. "I'm so sorry you had to see that." I am sorry. Even if it was me that had to go through it, I have no memory of it. I wouldn't forget what Jeremiah had done to me, but at least I didn't have to relive it over and over. I felt certain Lucifer didn't get that luxury.

He laughs, a hollow sound. "Don't apologize to me. Don't ever apologize to me for that."

I still can't meet his gaze, but I feel his eyes on me. I close my own for a moment. When I open them, I try to steel myself. To straighten my spine, to take back the control I haven't had in so long over my own life.

"I'm leaving."

His eyes flicker. "Where?"

I don't know. The train ticket is to New York. I don't know if I'll stop there. Although I have no intention of staying in this hotel and running my brother's company, I'm going to use his money. It's the least of what he owes me. I can go anywhere I want with that kind of money. I can *do* anything I want. The world is mine. And I can find out what he meant, about Ria. I'm free.

But it doesn't feel like it. I don't feel freedom. I don't feel the excitement I should, leaving this place behind. I feel nothing but emptiness. Brokenness. I wonder if that feeling will ever leave, or if, eventually, I'll finish what I started that night Lucifer and Lilith met.

"I don't know," I answer him honestly. I adjust the strap of my bag on my shoulders. "I haven't figured that out yet."

"Let me come with you," he says at once, stepping further in the room. His hands are in his pockets, but I see the muscles in his forearms tense, like he wants to reach for me, but he's clenching his fists to keep himself from doing it. "We'll go together. Between us, we have so much fucking money, we don't need to work or to worry or—"

"No." I cut him off, even though it hurts. I have to cut him off. "No," I say again, my voice stronger. "I can't go with you. You can't come with me. I need..." I close my eyes, biting back on the tears that threaten to fall.

But I have to get away.

"I'm going alone. Get back to your life, Lucifer. Back to the Unsaints. Now that my brother isn't competing with you," I force a smile on my face, "you can expand your empire."

He doesn't smile. "That's not what the Unsaints do. And really, Sid, we can't let you leave."

I tense, cross my arms over my chest. "I didn't ask for your permission."

Something seems to change in the air between us.

His hands are still in his pockets, and he doesn't move closer, but something in his demeanor changes. It's like he's morphing from broken boy into whatever it is that an Unsaint actually is.

"Lover's Death is only the least of what we do," he says, and there is no longer any emotion in his words. "It's an illusion. It's a rite. But it really, truly, means nothing. But you...you know things. Jeremiah knew things. And I let him walk out of here, alive, for you." His eyes narrow.

"I don't know shit about you and your cult friends," I say, growing angrier. I shake my head and stuff my hands into my pockets. "What happens next to Jeremiah isn't my concern." I make to walk past him.

He grabs my arm. "If you have my kid, you might live." He scoffs, shaking his head. "I gave you that chance, at least."

I yank my arm out of his grip. "You're just as bad as my brother," I spit at him.

"You have no idea what you're doing." He shrugs. "You have *no idea* how much more the Unsaints can hurt you."

I step closer to him, rage making my hands shake. "Are you threatening me? After what we went through? You really want to do that right now?"

He smiles. It's empty. He slips his hands back into his pockets and shakes his head. "It's like I told you, Lilith. You can run, but you can't hide."

I roll my eyes and step around him, heading out of my brother's room.

"Stay here one night," he says at my back. "One more night. Just give *him* enough time to get far away from you. Because if I see him again, Sid, I'll kill him. You won't be able to stop me." His voice hardens. This is Lucifer. An Unsaint.

I brush my bangs out of my eyes, turning his words over. His threats.

I let out a breath. "Okay," I finally say, without looking at him. "But if you try to stop me when I leave, it won't end well for you, either." I turn to glance at him.

His full lips curve into a small half smile, but it doesn't meet his eyes.

Despite what I'd said, despite agreeing with him, his eyes are still cold.

CHAPTER THIRTY-ONE

Present

NICOLAS TRIES to talk to me. Trey tries to talk to me.

I want nothing to do with them. I don't fire them or send them away, because I'll be leaving the next day. But I have nothing to say to them. After I left Lucifer on the eighth floor, I went down to my own rooms. They're clean, and they don't smell like Jeremiah. They don't feel like Jeremiah. But the bathroom...I don't want to go in there.

He had cleaned my foot in there. He had told me he loved me in there.

All the while, he knew.

Kristof has made himself scarce. I don't know where he is, and I don't care. If he was smart, he'd leave. But then again, he'd never been very smart.

I force myself to take a shower. I dress in black yoga

pants, black tank top, and pull on my black tennis shoes. I put a gun on the holster on my hip, taken from my own closet, and then I make my way down to the gym.

I need to move, but I don't want to go outside yet. I don't want to see anyone else in this Godforsaken place.

The gym is empty. I plan on making sure it stays that way, too. If anyone comes in, I'll threaten to blow their fucking heads off. And if they don't leave, well...I'm not so sure I won't actually pull the trigger.

I start on the treadmill, enjoying the sound of my own breathing. I hadn't brought my phone down, or anything to play music. I just want to drown in myself. My own grief in my head. I need it to consume me, so maybe it will burn through me.

I glance at my reflection in the mirror. I'm pale, shadows beneath grey eyes. My hair is still wet from my shower, my bangs cover my brows. I realize I've done this whole workout and shower thing in the wrong order. Fuck it. Everything in my life has gone in the wrong order.

Jeremiah crosses my mind.

I hope he dies from it, the guilt. I hope it eats him alive. I hope it's his guilt that kills him.

I'm so focused on those thoughts of vengeance, and the flashes of my own guilt that threaten to sneak in under my hate, that I don't notice two people have come in until they're right behind me, staring at me in the mirror.

I finish my sprint, locking eyes with Mayhem as I do, glancing once at Atlas. Only after I'm done do I slowly come to a stop. I wipe my wrist over my brow. I'm breathing hard and sweating worse. I turn to glare at them, waiting for them to speak. To tell me why the fuck they're here. I know they have their own mansions to go to. They can fuck right off. But maybe Lucifer told them my plans.

Hell, maybe they've come to kill me.

Atlas has on a backwards cap, dark jeans, a red shirt that stops at his elbows, showing off his muscular forearms. Mayhem is wearing a tight black shirt and black jeans. His arms are crossed as he stares at me.

I'm thankful I'm still on the treadmill. It doesn't make me taller than them, but at least I don't have to look up to meet their eyes.

"You're leaving." Mayhem doesn't phrase it as a question, which is a good sign. But why he gives a fuck is beyond me. Maybe he's come to threaten me, too.

I don't bother to say anything. I just keep staring at him, waiting for one of them to get to the point.

He sighs, turns from me and sits on one of the weight benches, facing me again. He has his elbows on his knees, palms rubbing together. He's looking at the floor, dark brows furrowed.

I glance at Atlas in question. Atlas laughs.

"Hey, this is Mayhem's mayhem. I'm just here for shits and giggles." He leans in toward me, lowers his voice conspiratorially. "And to make sure he doesn't fuck you again."

Mayhem flicks him off. I roll my eyes.

No one else speaks.

I wait.

"Did you know that Lucifer talked about you every fucking day for a year straight?" Mayhem finally asks. His voice is low, but he doesn't wait for me to respond. "Every goddamn day. I felt the guilt, of course, because he'd never wanted your brother in the Unsaints. I'd convinced him to let it happen. Convinced him a rich fuck who shot his abusive foster parents *needed* to be with us." He meets my gaze again, but his baby blue eyes are hooded. His expression is unreadable. "Your brother was never good at taking 'no' for an answer anyway." He sighs. "He never got the tattoo. At least I can say it didn't get that far."

My gut churns. I grip the edge of the treadmill at my side, thinking I might be sick if Mayhem keeps talking. But I still don't say anything. Atlas wanders off, picking up and setting down various sized weights.

"Me and Lucifer," he continues, "we've known each other since we were kids. We grew up in the same neighborhood, but his life was a little different than mine." He threads his fingers together, moving his fists up and down. He looks like he's reflecting on their life together. I know Lucifer probably sent him here. I know I should be angry and tell him to get the fuck away from me. To stop trying to guilt-trip me, or scare me. But I also find myself imagining Lucifer, as a child. I imagine his stepmother's cruelties. What he must have went through to become what he is. What they all must have gone through, even if they were rich and spoiled.

"My dad is a dick, but Lucifer's...he was absent. And

his stepmother..." He shakes his head, and I watch him swallow. "Well, she wasn't any better than your brother." He meets my gaze again.

I feel that wave of nausea all over again.

"His father is in legitimate business. But he didn't mind throwing Lucifer to the wolves, letting him into the darker side of business. Letting him take the Unsaints from rich kid secret society to corporate crimes for hire. Before that, his father didn't say a damn thing when Lucifer tried to tell him what his stepmom was doing. No," Mayhem snorts with disgust. "He told him he was a liar and no wife of his would want to fuck his son, so he could stop trying to get her to." He licks his lips, glares at me. "And believe me, Sid. The Society of 6 has more power than the Unsaints. His father could have made his stepmom disappear if he'd wanted to."

I close my eyes for a second, try to fight back against the images Mayhem's words conjure in my head.

"His mom died when he was little. She's the one that named him Lucifer." I blink but say nothing. He laughs. "She was weird, I've heard. A good weird. He'd also been close to her, as a kid. She had worshiped him, my own mom said. But she was killed in a car accident, and Lucifer lost the only woman who ever loved him, for good."

Mayhem is smiling now.

"Obviously, women threw themselves at the dude. I mean...those eyes." He lifts his brows, laughing. "But he used them, just like they used him. For money. Sex. Status.

And then he met you." His eyes narrow on me, and I feel a flurry in my gut. But it doesn't feel like sickness anymore. "He met you, and Jeremiah's true colors came out. He wrecked both of your worlds."

I finally speak, the words raw in my throat. "I know what happened. I don't need to hear it again."

"I think you do," Mayhem argues. "I think you don't get it." I tense, but say nothing. "You think Jeremiah only wronged *you?*" His voice is cold. "Nah, Angel. This isn't just your revenge. This is all of ours. He knows too much." He stands to his feet and walks toward me. He stops, looking down for a second, then he brushes his thumb over his lip and meets my gaze again. "This all might be yours," he huffs a laugh, shaking his head, "but the secrets your brother has..." His eyes narrow. "They're ours." He yanks my arm, pulling me off the treadmill so he's looking down at me. "Lucifer has always been too soft. But me? I'm not even close. So you might think Jeremiah got away with this, but he didn't. He's a liability. And since you've spent the past year living with him, well," he shrugs, "so are you."

Atlas whistles, amused, somewhere beyond Mayhem.

Mayhem flashes a cold smile. "Say your goodbyes to your brother's idiot guards before you leave, Angel. You won't see them again. And when you get on that train, do some digging. Lucifer's last name, it's Malikov." He leans down until he's close enough for our breath to mingle. "You see, we needed you to lead us to Jeremiah. Jeremiah to lead us to you. But we don't really need either of you anymore. So I hope that wherever you go, you're always looking over your shoulder. Because we'll always know where you are, *Lilith*."

CHAPTER THIRTY-TWO

Present

I LEAVE THAT NIGHT.

But I don't get on the train. Instead, I look for Ria. I leave in one of my brother's black SUVs, and the guards say nothing as I pass through the gates of the hotel. I don't look for Lucifer, even though a part of me wants to. I don't say a word to any of the Unsaints about my leaving.

I had tried to leave before, when I'd turned from Lucifer that night a year ago. When I had said *fuck this,* and left. I'd unwittingly walked right into Jeremiah's arms then. But I won't again. I don't know what happened to Ria that night, hell, I don't even know what happened to *me,* but I'm going to find her.

And she's going to make me understand what the hell is going on in this city.

THAT NIGHT, AS I TOSS AND TURN IN A HOTEL ROOM across town, after fruitlessly searching for all the Rias that live in this city (there's hundreds), I see smoke beyond my window. For a second, I wonder if the Unsaints found me that fast. If they followed me here. Or if it's Jeremiah or one of his men.

I throw off my blankets, snatching up my knife from the nightstand. But I breathe a sigh of relief when I realize the fire is far off. It's past the city, up on the highest hill in Alexandria.

It's the Rain mansion, coming down in flames.

But it's something else, too.

It's a warning.

EPILOGUE

Jeremiah

Present

THERE'S SO much blood in the bathtub, I don't understand how I'm still alive. It's turned the water a bright red, and even though I can't sit up, even though my head leans against the cool tiles at my back, I'm still here.

I'm still breathing.

I shouldn't be.

I should have died that night I found her.

When I tried to stand a few minutes ago, the world spun around me. The hotel room shifted, what little blood I had draining too fast from my head.

I had had to sit back down, but I can't reach for the razor. I'd thrown it over the side after carving up my arms.

My phone is somewhere in the Raven River, and no one will come to me, even if I call them.

My heart breaks for her. Even now, as I take in what I wish are my last breaths, I think of her. I want to hold her. To beg for her forgiveness. I would have crawled through glass for it. I would have swallowed glass for it. I would do anything for her to forgive me. To look at me with that little bit of love that had been growing since I found her that night.

That night that I should have died.

That night that vengeance made me into a monster.

But who the fuck am I kidding?

Jeremiah Rain has always been a monster.

I was five when my mom took her in. She was a toddler, long brown hair, strange grey eyes. I'd adored her, even then. How my mother was able to foster children when she couldn't even take care of *me*, her own, was beyond me. I knew even then I'd be the one to raise Sid.

And I did.

For three years, I watched out for her. Until the authorities finally came to their senses, and then, since we weren't blood related, we were ripped apart. I would have burned through the world to find her.

I did.

I just didn't know I'd burned through her, too.

It never mattered to me that she wasn't *really* my sister. Because she was. She still is, even after what I've put her through. Even after she chose him over me. *Them* over me. A holier-than-thou fucked up cult that I never really belonged to. I'd never been close to the Unsaints. They'd barely tolerated my presence. They'd only been intrigued by my story.

But she's still my little sister.

And if I'm not going to die in this tub—and I'm not so sure the exhaustion weighing on my eyelids isn't death knocking—then I'm going to protect her, whether she likes it or not. Whether she knows it or not.

The Unsaints are vile. Dangerous. Dark. She has no fucking idea. She thinks the bodies I forced her to see were the worst of her nightmares?

The Unsaints will scar her.

I close my eyes, content to slide into oblivion.

In the morning, I'll be in hell.

Or I'll find her again.

Lucifer isn't the only one who knows how to burn for her.

AFTERWORD

Unsainted continues with Pray for Scars.

Sign up for my newsletter so you don't miss any news on the next release: **authorkvrose.com/newsletter**

Turn the page for a sneak peek at *Pray for Scars*.

PRAY FOR SCARS SNEAK PEEK

They say that Lucifer was a fallen angel, cast out from a heaven too pure for his brand of evil.

But they were wrong.

Lucifer was a god, biding his time until he found his own kingdom in hell.

When Sid Rain gets on the wrong side of the Unsaints, she finds out just how deep their ties run, and just how dark their sins are.

She finds out, too, that Lucifer is not at all who she thought he was.

He's worse.

While she searches through the history of Alexandria and the twisted connection to her brother, she discovers not all secrets are meant to be shared, and sometimes, running away is far less brutal than fighting back.

PRAY FOR SCARS

Sid

I find Ria, and it's not at all where I expect to find her. It's not even while I'm looking for her. Which I've been doing in the two weeks since Halloween. My schedule has looked something like this:

1. Class at AU (well, technically, today is the first day that's happened...)
2. Change hotels
3. Look over my shoulder
4. Stalk Ria leads on social media
5. Check out obituaries (spoiler alert: Kristof is dead. He was ran over. No charges were filed because multiple witnesses saw him dart in front of a black Mercedes)

I had come to the conclusion Ria just doesn't do social media by the time I sink down into my non-degree local history class. I can't get into a degree program because I don't have a diploma. But I paid for non-degree programs because with the amount of cash I took out of Jeremiah's —*my*—bank account, I can do that.

The supply is dwindling already. There was only so much I could withdraw in a day, and I know either my brother or Lucifer and his gang of pricks will track my withdrawals.

But I'm not hiding. Not really.

Still, I don't want to be completely stupid.

I pull out my notebook and a pen, and lean back in my seat on the last row. There's a bunch of senior citizens in here and a few kids my age, probably two dozen of us in total. The professor walks in, clad in tweed and a damn bow tie, and then *Ria* trails in after him.

I sit up straighter, heart slamming in my chest. What the hell is she doing here? I mean, I get why she's actually at Alexandria University because she was a university student when I met her a year ago. A junior, I think she said. But it looks like now she's about to teach this class. She has a folder in hand, she's wearing black dress pants and a white collared shirt and she fiddles with a lock of her long, curly hair. Her and Professor Tweed exchange a few murmured words and then she turns to face the class. There's a few dozen of us in here, but immediately, her eyes lock on me.

For a second, I think maybe she doesn't recognize me.

But then her deep brown skin flushes pink and she clears her throat. I feel a wave of secondhand embarrassment for her and also a little elated because obviously I'm going to corner her after class.

I never did get on that train.

I haven't been sleeping well since Halloween—hell, I've never slept well, but it's only gotten worse—and my brother's words keep haunting me: Find Ria. Find out everything you can.

Part of me thinks Jeremiah might be dead. Part of me doesn't care. But a small part of me...well, a small part of me does. It's hard to go anywhere in Alexandria without hearing about the private hotel that burned to the ground, and I can't help wondering what my brother thinks about that.

I tear my eyes away from Ria, and Professor Tweed prods her with a harsh, wet cough. Gross.

As this is a non-degree course, when I decided to enroll, I'd only missed the first day, on Monday. Today is Wednesday and no one seems too comfortable with each other yet so it's safe to say I haven't missed much.

Another wet cough from Tweed and I *know* I haven't missed much, and I'm already regretting this decision, although I'm glad I've got Ria in sight.

"Today," she begins, her voice sounding crackly. She clears her throat, and Professor Tweed furrows his brow but sinks into a seat on the front row, watching her. How stressful. "Today," she begins again, peeling her eyes away from me and staring at the back wall of the classroom, "we're going to..." She trails off and Tweed leans over the desk. I can't see his face anymore, but I'm sure he's annoyed.

I blow my bangs out of my face and Ria catches the movement. I smile at her. She doesn't return it, but she nods, as if to give herself strength, and starts one more time. She walks around the podium, tapping the folders she set there, looking thoughtful as she chews on her lip.

"I had planned a lesson on the early settlers here, and the Native American tribes they displaced, but," she shrugs, "instead, we'll fast forward a little." She glances at Tweed as if waiting for permission, but the class seems eager, so she plows ahead. "Today, we'll talk about the famous families of Alexandria that are still around *now*." She stares at me as she says those last words.

I had signed up for this course specifically to get information on Alexandria. A college town in the piedmont region of North Carolina, there are clearly secrets here I don't get. Things at work involving the Unsaints and the Society of 6 that could very well concern me, and, you know, staying alive.

But I didn't expect Ria and *this* lecture to just fall into my lap like this. Is she doing this for me? I pick up my pen, ready for her next words.

She clasps her hands behind her back and slowly starts to pace at the front of the room, surveying all of us.

"How many of you know of the Malikov family?" she asks, nothing but mild curiosity in her voice.

I, however, tense, gripping the pen in my hand a little tighter.

Hands all over the room shoot up. An elderly woman shakes her head and chuckles before saying, "I think the better question is who *hasn't* heard of them?" she asks good-naturedly.

Ria eyes me. I don't raise my own hand. I have, technically, heard of them. Two weeks ago, actually, when one of the Unsaints, Mayhem, informed me it was Lucifer's last name.

Lucifer Malikov.

A perfect name for a boy who, right underneath my brother, is the cause of most of my more frequent nightmares.

Ria nods at the woman who spoke up and everyone puts their hands down. She continues pacing, slowly, confidently. I assume she's in here teaching this class because she wants to be a teacher. I realize I never asked her much about herself on Unsaints Night one year ago.

But I cut myself some slack. That was the night I was going to kill myself. The nights afterward didn't get too much better and I didn't get any nicer or less self-absorbed, but still. I get a free pass for that night.

Ria stops pacing and stands just off to the side of the podium, hands still clasped behind her back. Professor Tweed is now drumming his hands on the table in front of him. Loudly. Maybe he's not too into the Malikovs. If a fraction of what I know about them is true, I'm not either.

But I need to know.

"The Malikovs are one of the oldest families in Alexandria. They immigrated from Russia, taking their wealth with them. Their wealth," Ria pauses and glances at me, as if she wants to be sure I'm listening, "and their organized crime. *Bratva*," she says, surveying the class again. She smiles. "Now, they turned away from their life of crime and found success in legitimate businesses." She holds up her hand, ticking some of these so-called businesses off on her fingers. "Banking, security, vodka," the class laughs at this, "and weapons manufacturing for the private sector."

No surprises there. Tweed has stopped drumming his fingers.

"Our very own science building," she gestures vaguely to the windows on the side of the room, "is named after the Malikovs, thanks to a generous donation from Lazar Malikov." She smiles again, looking toward me. "Father of one of our alumni, Lucifer Malikov."

Professor Tweed clears his throat. Ria doesn't look away from me. A few people whisper among themselves at Lucifer's name, but I don't catch what they're saying.

"Lucifer graduated summa cum laude from Alexandria's business school, and now..." she shrugs, still pinning me with a stare. "He's generously offered to rebuild the beautiful, private hotel that recently burned down atop Alexandria's highest peak."

Someone raises their hand. A girl probably not much older than me, with pink-framed glasses. Ria nods at her.

The girl puts her hand down and adjusts her glasses. "Who owned that hotel?"

I swear I couldn't have asked for a better day to actually go to a class.

Ria arches a brow, as if thinking. "I believe it was a man with the last name of Rain." Another glare toward me. Which means she knows. Somehow, she knows I'm Jeremiah's sister, even though that night, she didn't know.

A guy across the row from me snorts. "Shouldn't this Rain dude have enough money to rebuild his hotel, if he owned the damn thing?" He slouches down in his seat. "I tried to sneak in there once. Dude had *armed guards* outside of the gate."

My gaze snaps back to Ria. Professor Tweed is shifting in his chair.

Ria nods. "You would think. As it is, this *dude* hasn't been found."

The guy rolls his eyes. "Maybe he set it on fire himself. Taxes or something." He laughs to himself.

The hotel is no longer in my name. I made sure Nicolas at least did that one thing for me, even though he screwed up everything else. It's listed back under Jeremiah's name. But apparently, Jeremiah has gone MIA. Which is fine with me.

"Maybe," Ria says unconvincingly. "Back to the Malikovs," she starts pacing again, looking down at her heels. "Whose heard the rumors?" She glances up. Hands raise. She grins. "Throw 'em at me."

I look around, waiting.

"Devil worshipers," someone calls out. A few people laugh.

"I mean, dude named his son *Lucifer* after all," the guy in the back of the class says, voice full of practicality.

Ria nods. "Anything else?" she asks.

"Billionaires."

"Probably true," Ria confirms.

"Unsaints!" someone calls out, loud and clear.

I freeze.

It was the same older woman who had asked who hadn't heard of the Malikovs.

Ria stops in her tracks and nods toward the woman. "That's what I was looking for," she says with a small smile.

Tweed is getting really uncomfortable. He's back to drumming his hands on the desk, rapidly. But Ria keeps talking, ignoring his body language.

"The Unsaints have become a bit of a local legend around Alexandria." Her eyes meet mine for a second. "The sons of some of the oldest families in town, Lucifer Malikov being one of them. They have a reputation for being handsome, lewd, and, of course, filthy rich."

A few chuckles, and then someone says, "Yeah, and don't forget, murderers."

Ria's eyes narrow on the guy who called that out. "Oh?" she asks, as if she doesn't know.

I realize I'm holding my breath. Tweed has stopped his drumming again, and I wonder if he's holding his, too.

"I mean, we all know about Unsaints Night. Their

little orgies in the woods." The guy talking clasps his hands together on the desk and leans forward, almost conspiratorially. "And," he says, pitching his voice lower, "my sister said they skipped it this year because last year, someone fucking poisoned them. And then they killed who did it!"

My heart clenches.

"Language!" Tweed shouts, twisting in his seat. I can see his face. It's blotchy and red. He narrows his eyes at the guy who holds up his hands as if in surrender. He turns back to Ria. "Miss Cuevas, I think that's more than enough. We aren't here to discuss wild rumors and base-less speculations. This is a *history* course, not theatre." He stands to his feet.

"Well," the older woman who has been answering Ria's questions says gently, looking down at her nails, "it's not all rumors, Professor Moore." Moore, still standing, frowns at her, but doesn't say anything. "I don't know about *all* of them, but the Society of 6, their parents, are well known in the community." She meets Moore's eyes and shrugs. "That Rain boy, he's the one that killed his foster parents. They were in the 6. The Malikov boy didn't offer to rebuild the hotel out of the goodness of his heart. It's because Rain is an Unsaint, too."

Moore shakes his head. "Those murders were self-defense." He walks to the podium, glaring at Ria. "Thank you, Miss Cuevas, for this colorful contribution to my classroom today." He nods to the seat he just vacated, indi-cating she should sit. She shakes her head.

"Actually, Professor, I'm not feeling great," she whispers, but there's not that many people in here. We can hear her. She clutches her stomach. "I'm just going to..."

Moore basically shoos her out. I snap my notebook shut and shove it, along with my pen, in my bag, and then I race down the steps that divide the lecture room and hurry after her, yanking open the door just as she closes it. I don't offer an explanation, even as Moore is saying, "Excuse me!" after me.

I slam the door shut and look down the hallway. Ria is easy to spot. She's the only one out here besides me. I race after her and grab her arm, whirling her around.

She looks pissed. I drop her arm.

"What was that about?" I ask her. "I've been looking everywhere for you—"

She throws up her hands. "Yeah? Well I didn't really want you to find me. Especially not after what *your brother* did to us."

"Us?" I ask, rearing back, surprised.

She rolls her eyes, crosses her arms. "The girls," she grits out. "We...all of us...he spiked everyone's drink."

"I know," I snap back, shaking my head. Is she actually accusing me of having something to do with this? "And how do you know he's my brother?"

She chews her bottom lip. "I talk to Mayhem."

I instantly feel guilty about hooking up with him at the party two weeks ago, even though I don't know why. But then I see a dark bruise on her neck, barely visible over the collar of her shirt, and wonder if they've already *kissed* and made up.

She rubs her hand over it, catching my eye. She looks down. "I shouldn't be talking to you."

"What? Why?" I cross my arms, adjusting my backpack. "I didn't have anything to do with those drinks that night! Surely Mayhem told you *that*."

She frowns, her golden eyes downcast. "I actually *can't* talk to you." She meets my gaze and her eyes narrow. "I had to sign a fucking NDA after that night, Sid. Mayhem's family came to my dorm early the next morning, with fucking *guns!*"

I gesture behind me. "That kid in class knew what happened. Why the hell would you have to sign an NDA?"

She drops her gaze again. "Not about the drinks," she says quietly. She sighs, shaking her head. "I really shouldn't be telling you this. Any of it. Mayhem will literally kill me." She looks up.

I laugh, bitterly. "If you think he'll kill you," I point to her neck, "maybe stop fucking him then?"

She looks like she might slap me. Maybe I'll deserve it. Instead, she just shakes her head, biting her lip.

"The NDA wasn't about the drinks. Or the Unsaints. Or...Lover's Death." She takes a breath. "It was about *you*." She turns to walk away and I'm too stunned to move. She glances back over her shoulder. "Get out of here, Sid. Unless you still have a death wish."

Pray for Scars is available now.

ACKNOWLEDGMENTS

Thank you first of all to you, the reader. I'm grateful for you and always will be. It's you who I write to.

Thank you, too, for my husband for not divorcing me after all the shit this series has put us through.

Thanks to my mom who has always supported my dream of being a writer. Love you, Mom.

As always, I'm eternally grateful for music, because without it, I wouldn't be able to get what's in my brain on the page.

ABOUT THE AUTHOR

K.V. Rose is an author of dark romance and lover of the profane. You can find her on social media nearly everywhere at AuthorKVRose.

▼

pinterest.com/authorkvrose
instagram.com/authorkvrose
facebook.com/authorkvrose
goodreads.com/authorkvrose
authorkvrose.com

▼

ALSO BY K V ROSE

Unsainted

Pray for Scars

The Cruelest Chaos

Boy of Ruin

Like Grim Death: Part One

Like Grim Death: Part Two

Ecstasy Series

Ecstasy

Ominous Book One

Ominous Book Two

Sick Love Duet

Unorthodox